The Search for Roots

PRIMO LEVI

The Search for Roots

A PERSONAL ANTHOLOGY

Translated and with an Introduction by Peter Forbes

ALLEN LANE
THE PENGUIN PRESS

ALLEN LANE
THE PENGUIN PRESS

Published by the Penguin Group
Penguin Books Ltd, 80 Strand, London WC2R 0RL, England
Penguin Putnam Inc., 375 Hudson Street, New York, New York 10014, USA
Penguin Books Australia Ltd, Ringwood, Victoria, Australia
Penguin Books Canada Ltd, 10 Alcorn Avenue, Toronto, Ontario, Canada M4V 3B2
Penguin Books India (P) Ltd, 11 Community Centre,
Panchsheel Park, New Delhi – 110 017, India
Penguin Books (NZ) Ltd, Cnr Rosedale and Airborne Roads,
Albany, Auckland, New Zealand
Penguin Books (South Africa) (Pty) Ltd, 24 Sturdee Avenue,
Rosebank 2196 South Africa

Penguin Books Ltd, Registered Offices: 80 Strand, London WC2R 0RL, England

www.penguin.com

Originally published in Italian as *La ricerca delle radici* by Giulio Einaudi Editore 1981
This translation first published in Great Britain by Allen Lane The Penguin Press 2001
  3 5 7 9 10 8 6 4

Original text copyright © Giulio Einaudi Editore s.p.a., Torino, 1981, 1997
Translation, Introduction and Notes copyright © Peter Forbes, 2001
Afterword copyright © Italo Calvino, 1981
All rights reserved

Typeset in 9.5 /12.75 pt PostScript Linotype Electra
Typeset by Rowland Phototypesetting Ltd, Bury St Edmunds, Suffolk

Printed and bound in Great Britain by Clays Ltd, St Ives plc

Cover repro and printing by Concise Cover Printers

A CIP catalogue record for this book is available from the British Library

ISBN 0–713–99–4878

Contents

Introduction

Primo Levi was a man for whom the Two Cultures debate initiated by C. P. Snow was redundant. He had a lifelong innocent and equal love of both science and literature, a love uncorrupted by academic training in the case of literature or great ambitions in the case of science. He was a workaday industrial chemist, a specialist in electrical resins, a field in which science has to be tempered by utility and economic considerations.

The Search for Roots is the last complete book published during Levi's lifetime to be translated (his stories and essays were mostly published in English editions that did not correspond to the Italian compilations). It consists of thirty extracts from works of prose and poetry, ranging from the Bible and Homer to an article from *Scientific American* on Black Holes, with succinct introductions by Levi.

Levi is unusual in being a writer revered for his accounts of his own experiences who was none the less far more interested in things around him than in his own inner workings ('the ecosystem that lodges unsuspected in my depths, saprophytes, birds of day and night, creepers, butterflies, crickets and fungi'). In his books he celebrated work and made a passionate plea for it as a fit subject for writers. He had no time for the notion that working life in a scientific, industrial society was automatically alienating, instead believing that an involvement in practical science and engineering could enhance the old rapport between man and nature traditionally found in gardening or farming, pastoral poetry or landscape painting.

In his work, Levi repeatedly created metaphors for himself as a humble creature, hidden in the depths like a woodworm (the analogy he uses in the Preface here). When I asked him, at our only meeting, in 1986, which chemical element he would choose as a personal emblem, he said: 'It would have to be something like an obscure rare earth, or gallium.' 'It has been my fate to be ambiguous,' he used to say, but it is this ambiguity, this ability to slip into many alien worlds and report back from them, that is Levi's distinctive quality in modern literature. In a world saturated with knowledge and theory vendors, he quietly found his way to places no one else had discovered.

In *Other People's Trades*, the book this collection most nearly resembles, Levi has essays on chewing gum, beetles, Ukrainian hop-scotch, chess and many other topics. The Preface to this book explains his wide-ranging curiosity in terms of his family tradition of indiscriminate reading. In selecting passages from science fiction, from his practical chemistry manual, from Bertrand Russell's *The Conquest of Happiness*, Levi demonstrates the virtues of the disorderly serendipitous approach to reading that he favoured.

Levi was an autodidact, and despite confessing in his Preface to areas he had not explored 'through laziness, through prejudice or a lack of time', in fact, he read widely. Although he was a scientist who experienced the crucial nightmare of the mid-twentieth century – Auschwitz – there is much of the seventeenth, eighteenth and nineteenth centuries in him. Of the five pieces from Italian literature, three (Carlo Porta, Giuseppe Parini and Giuseppe Belli) are pre-twentieth century. Like Orwell, the only twentieth-century writer with whom I would compare him, he loved Swift. Levi lived all his life, except for his two years of forced exile in Auschwitz and the protracted return, in the same house, and compensated for this with a great love of the literature of travel and adventure.

Levi's Jewishness is strongly expressed in the texts he chose (Job, Paul Celan, Sholem Aleichem, Thomas Mann), but he was a very secular Jew in whom the ancient Talmudic probing had been channelled into a love of interrogating profane texts and the world of nature. Science for Levi wasn't a substitute religion, but in his writing he demonstrated – and this is rare among modern scientific writers – that a scientific worldview *does* have moral implications: 'Matter is also a judge, and the most impartial one. It never forgives your errors, and most often punishes them severely. When you transgress it strikes back, like Conrad's sea' (*The Periodic*

Table). Levi was a wary, sceptical individual, an adherent of no pre-formulated creed, but if you had to characterize his philosophy, it would be closest to the atomic meliorism of the Latin poet Lucretius, one of his choices in this book, and an influence on several others.

Beyond the four routes through the book given in Levi's introductory graphic, Lucretius provides an overriding key. It is Lucretius who provides the link between Levi's scientific, moral and aesthetic worldviews. Lucretius was the Roman poet (*c*. 100–55 BC) who transmitted the atomic theory of the pre-Socratic philosophers Democritus and Leucippus (and the later Epicurus) to us. These thinkers are remarkable among the philosophers of antiquity for having anticipated a large part of modern science. Lucretius's poem teems with passages that cry out to be under-lined when you read them because in places the argument is very close to the modern conception of matter, and this theory of the material world was arrived at by pure thought, without the benefit of any of the experimentation that over 1,500 years later led to the steady development of the reliable knowledge we call science. In its pursuit of a logical train of thought it is exhilarating.

Chemists have an especial affection for Lucretius because the atomic theory is the absolute hub of their discipline. There was no real chemistry before the atomic theory was taken up again in the seventeenth century. Levi became a chemist after reading the book by Sir William Bragg *Concerning the Nature of Things* (included here, of course), which pays homage to Lucretius and presents for the twentieth century the fruits of Lucretius's science. In his headnote to Bragg, Levi affirms his moral as well as his scientific commitment to Lucretian atomism: 'I would become a chemist: I would share Bragg's faith (which today seems very ingenu-ous). I would be bound up with him, and with the legendary atomists of antiquity, against the discouraging and lazy herd of those who see matter as infinitely, fruitlessly, tediously divisible.'

Levi says of Lucretius that he is not widely read at school in Italy because 'there has always been a whiff of impiety' about his work. This is a delicious understatement. To Catholics, Lucretius's philosophy must seem a very dangerous counter creed. Galileo was explicitly a Lucretian, borrowing whole sections of his arguments, especially in *The Assayer*.

The Lucretian philosophy has been quietly influential down the centuries but almost always as a side-show, despite, or because of, its appeal to scientists. Lucretius's great achievement was to make a connection between the physical and the moral worlds; with superstition and irrational fears banished by scientific knowledge, men and women could lead a balanced life, enduring hardship without tormenting themselves even further with demented phantoms of the imagination, and in good times enjoying the delights that nature has provided. In Lucretius the world of sensation is a joy: it sings with the sights and sounds and feel of the world, with the spirit of healthy animals enjoying their animality. There is a wonderful Italian tradition of science writing that derives from Lucretius. Galileo is its greatest figure as a scientist, and Italo Calvino, Levi's contemporary and friend, is another exponent. In Levi's case, his philosophy was put to the starkest test in Auschwitz. The result is as if Lucretius had endured Dante's hell and emerged, a survivor, tempered by the experience.

When Ronald Latham's prose translation of Lucretius was published in 1951, the jacket copy said: '[it] can be read today as it was intended two thousand years ago: as an appeal to a disillusioned age to take comfort from the sanity of science'. Levi takes comfort from the sanity of science throughout his work, and in this book it is one of his routes to salvation. Levi's headnotes to his choices are shot through with modulations from Lucretius. Introducing Kip Thorne on Black Holes, he says, 'Not only are we not the centre of the universe, but the universe is not made for human beings; it is hostile, violent, alien. In the sky there are no Elysian Fields, only matter and light, distorted, compressed, dilated, and rarefied to a degree that eludes our senses and our language.' It is in Lucretius that we find the first expression of this sombre mood:

> . . . nowhere in the universe can be
> A final edge, and no escape be found
> From the endless possibilities of flight.

(ll. 983–5)

Levi's last words in the book make explicit the connection between the universe of science and the moral order: '[I]f the human mind has conceived Black Holes, and dares to speculate on what happened in the first moments of creation, why should it not know how to conquer fear, poverty and grief?'

An anthology could be compiled of Lucretian literature down the ages. It would certainly include Bertrand Russell. The philosophy became generally known to its critics as 'atoms and the void', and that phrase was intended to convey the chill of being alone in the universe. Russell paraphrased the supposedly bleak aspect of Lucretius beautifully:

That Man is the product of causes which had no prevision of the end they were achieving; that his origin, worth, his hopes and fears, his loves and beliefs, are but the outcome of accidental collocations of atoms; [. . .] that the whole temple of man's achievements must inevitably be buried beneath the debris of a universe in ruins – all these things, if not quite beyond dispute, are yet so nearly certain, that no philosophy which rejects them can hope to stand.

(*A Free Man's Worship*)

It is thus not surprising to find Russell in Levi's anthology but Russell, like Levi, was also one of the most eloquent exponents of the positive side of Lucretius; the extract that Levi chose, from *The Conquest of Happiness*, does for the moral component of Lucretius what Bragg did for the science.

Levi is famous for his advocacy of clarity and simplicity in writing, and his chosen extracts certainly exemplify these virtues. He sets out his rules for good writing in the headnote to Stefano D'Arrigo's *Horcynus Orca*: 'Your writing shall be concise, clear, composed; you will avoid whatever is willed and over-elaborated; you will know how to use each of your words, because you have used this and not another; you will love and imitate those that follow the same path.' But the D'Arrigo passage shows that he had a good ear for writing that breaks his rules: contorted, moving at a snail's pace, baroque – it nevertheless finds a style completely adequate to its brutal theme.

Another surprising aspect of Levi's attitude towards language is revealed by the extract from Thomas Mann's *The Tales of Jacob*. He calls the piece 'A Different Way of Saying "I"' and stresses that the protagonists in Mann's story have a dual role: they are who they are while at the same time *acting* who they are. The unreliable narrator is a pillar of postmodernism, but Levi had nothing of the postmodernist about him. He often praises authors such as Mario Rigoni Stern and Parini who take absolute responsibility as men for the words they have written. Many readers, of course, see Primo Levi himself as an exceptional case of the reliable narrator – what Levi says of Rigoni Stern applies equally well to himself: 'It is rare to find such an accord between the man who lives and the man who writes.'

The clue to Levi's interest in other ways of saying 'I' is his exceptional modesty and the great store he set by this quality in others. Many authors and characters who appear in this book are commended for their modesty, including Parini, Porta and Stern, but for Levi, Joseph Conrad has a place of honour. Levi speaks of him choosing not to write in the first person '[to avoid] the anguish of having to say "I"'. Levi's whole stance stresses a man going out into the world, learning from experience, speaking, like his chemistry mentor Gattermann, with 'the authority of one who teaches things because he knows them, and knows them through having lived them'. So pronounced was this tendency in him that 'A Different Way of Saying "I"' was Levi's preferred title for the book.

The need not to reveal too much of himself was a feature of all his writing. Hence, in *The Periodic Table*, actually an autobiography, the focus is shifted towards the chemical elements: in its opening chapter his admittedly remote and not especially striking forebears are metamorphosed into Inert Gases – elements, like argon and neon, that exist proudly alone and can be induced to pair with other elements only under the most extreme conditions. Similarly, when, in *The Wrench*, he wanted to write about work and the industrial world he knew, he made the protagonist a rigger rather than a laboratory chemist. The Preface to the present book confirms this tendency when he says: 'I felt more exposed to the public, more unbosomed, in making the choices than in writing my own books.'

In his Preface, Primo Levi talks mainly of his reasons for choosing the authors he has, rather than the rationale behind the specific texts. He admits the existence of unconscious forces at work and expresses surprise at the number of examples of the world turned upside down that appear in his selections. This is indeed striking: Job is transformed from a happy and prosperous *paterfamilias* into a scabby wreck of a man; humankind becomes an alien species in Fredric Brown's 'Sentry', as it also does in the extract from Swift; Ulysses,* a 'man of no account', turns the tables on the giant Polyphemus; in Belli's poem 'Dead', man is a beast and an ass 'dies the death of a martyr'; and above all, in *Horcynus Orca*, a German soldier in World War II is kept helpless for ten pages while every aspect of his impending death is discussed. Levi also refers in his headnote to Thomas Mann to another reversal: 'the victory of the weak and shrewd over the strong and stupid, a theme dear to the fairy tales of all times'. This is a powerful thread throughout the book. Levi was a slight man who admitted to never having been in a fight in his life. He joined the partisans but was captured before he saw any action. Everyone who met him commented on his exceptional alertness of expression: like the little girl in *Horcynus Orca*, Levi's face was 'the face of one who, ever anxious at heart, is always fleeing in [his] soul', and with some luck, his shrewdness, a strong core of self-belief, and the resilience of the lean and wiry man, he did prevail against the brutal but sluggish Germans. Famously level and unjudgemental in most of his writing about Germans and the Holocaust, it is hard not to see the choice of the passage from *Horcynus Orca* as Levi's revenge.

That Levi is drawn to situations of role reversal has its roots in Auschwitz, which was a total inversion of civil society: the motto over its entrance gate read *Arbeit Macht Frei* ('Work Makes Free'), which being translated back into the world most of its inmates would never see again signifies 'Slave Labour Kills'. In Auschwitz all the normal rules of human society were inverted. As a survivor, Levi experienced a double inversion of all values, on entering and leaving the camp. That he is sympathetic to accounts by those such as Swift and Fredric Brown, in which humanity is seen from the outside as a perhaps repellent species, is not surprising. Levi comments that there is little directly about Auschwitz in the book (although the piece by Hermann Langbein is a substantial one, and there is also Paul Celan's 'Death Fugue', which Levi said he wore inside him 'like a graft'). But, just as in *The Periodic Table*, where he tended to project himself on to the chemical elements to divert attention from the 'I', the Auschwitz experience is transmuted into many of the passages in this book. The first two selections, from the Book of Job and the *Odyssey*, correspond to his time in Auschwitz and his return, respectively, and to the two books he wrote about those experiences, *If This is a Man* and *The Truce*. His headnote to the *Odyssey* makes this explicit: 'its poetry grows from a reasonable hope: the end of the war and exile, the world rebuilt on the foundation of a peace gained through justice'. The wounded giant Cyclops or Polyphemus is Nazism and many of the details run parallel: in Cyclops's cave, many of the band are lost, but in his triumph the small, insignificant, astute man 'wants to make known to the tower of flesh just who is the mortal that has defeated him'.

Besides these two *leitmotif* pieces that open the book, the travails and endurance of his experience of Auschwitz emerge in several stories of ordeal and physical challenge: Conrad's story of a crew trying to save a ship at sea; Rosny's tale of prehistoric men who have lost the art of fire and are wandering in search of it; Vercel's sea-rescue missions; Melville's whale-hunt; Saint-Exupéry's plane crash in the desert.

Primo Levi disagreed with Adorno's famous statement: 'To write a poem after Auschwitz is barbarous.' But the notion finds an echo in the piece Levi chose from Eliot's *Murder in the Cathedral*. Some acts, such as the murder of Thomas Becket or the Holocaust, are such a violation of the moral order, it would be necessary to 'clean the sky! wash the wind!' to efface the blot. Another way of saying that it can't be done, and, obviously, silence is not far behind. But Primo Levi was not silenced, and his response to the privations inflicted on him was to give more generously than anyone had a right to expect.

Apart from the light it sheds on Levi, the fascination of this book lies in the introduction it makes to writers most of us will not know, including Roger Vercel, Stefano D'Arrigo, Mario Rigoni Stern, Joseph-Henri Rosny, Carlo Porta, Giuseppe Parini and Fredric Brown. Levi's choices obviously have a somewhat different flavour for English readers than for the Italian audience he originally had in mind. In interviews that he gave on publication of the Italian edition of the book in 1981 he commented on his omissions: 'I have deliberately excluded names that are (or should be) part of the patrimony of all such as Dante, Leopardi, Manzoni, Flaubert, etc.; to have included them would be like writing on an ID card under "identifying marks", "two eyes".' Besides the antipathies revealed in his Preface for Dostoevsky and Balzac, in interviews he also confessed to negative feelings about Proust and Borges, and ambivalence about Kafka (whom he nevertheless translated). Of writers such as Rigoni Stern and D'Arrigo, Levi's contemporaries, he admits to feeling proprietorial, as if their writing were almost his own, and to an intense desire to share them with others.

Levi's selections from scientific writing display his unusual balance between the rational and the fantastical. He saw science as mostly a supporter of the good sense he valued so highly, exemplified here by his extracts from Darwin, Lucretius, Gattermann and Sir William Bragg, but, as a good Lucretian, he didn't flinch when science threw up disconcerting or counter-rational conclusions, such as Black Holes. Indeed, he wrote science fiction himself and had a penchant for futurological speculation. It is characteristic that he was an admirer of Arthur C. Clarke, because Clarke, famous for his successful predictions of future technologies such as communications satellites, also has a strong vein of common sense and, as in the piece Levi selected, an ability to debunk the wilder kind of scientific futurism. Levi was proud of his profession of chemist but aware that, like everything else, science was vulnerable to corruption and misuse. The strangest piece in the book, the specification for testing adhesive films for their susceptibility to attack by cockroaches, is Levi's dryly witty way of ridiculing, in a Swiftian manner, the footling pedantry that sometimes dogs the lower reaches of industrial science – the equivalent in science of the otiose Ph.D. thesis in the humanities.

In the context of the twenty-first century, all of Levi's choices are striking, whether they are reaffirmations of what are now unfashionable texts – the Bible, Swift, Conrad – or unfamiliar but lucid passages from science, or stark examinations of the human condition (Eliot, Celan, Langbein). Levi is an excellent guide and the terrain he has mapped in his thirty passages has a beguiling flavour of serious but unacademic reading, of a kind of chastened curiosity rare in our time, and of an undiminished sense of wonder and horror at a universe that has such things in it. To appropriate a passage from his Preface, in this book you will find new friends, add provinces to your territory, 'marvellous by definition, because every unexplored territory is marvellous'.

Peter Forbes

I should like to thank Diana Reich, Barbara Haynes, A. S. Byatt, Emmanuela Tandello, Gillian Stellman and Luca Guerneri for help with the translations and textual matters. I am particularly grateful to P. D. Royce, who read and commented in depth on all the translations from Italian and prepared the initial translation of Hermann Langbein's *Menschen in Auschwitz*.

P.F.

The Search for Roots

A PERSONAL ANTHOLOGY

Preface

At a certain point in the journey it is natural to draw up one's accounts. Everything should be included: what you have received and what you have given; receipts, remittances, and the balance sheet. It is a need, and it can be pleasant to satisfy it, but to attempt it is a fateful step. It means that many more things may yet happen, branches will fall and new shoots break through, but the roots have been consolidated.

How many of our roots come from the books we have read? All, many, a little, or none, depending on the environment in which we are born, our temperament, and the labyrinth that fate has assigned to us. There are no rules: Christopher Columbus's logbooks make for pithy reading but they contain no trace of a literary input; they are redolent of the man of adventure, the merchant and the politician, no more. At the other extreme, Anatole France remains a master of life and an amiable companion of the road, and yet his many books seem to derive from other books which are themselves bookish.

Always inclined to a hybrid input, I accepted willingly and with curiosity the proposal to compile a 'personal anthology', not in the Borgesian sense of an auto-anthology but in that of a harvesting, retrospectively and in good faith, which would bring to light the possible traces of what has been read on what has been written. I accepted it as a bloodless experiment, rather as one submits to a battery of tests because it is agreeable to experiment and to observe the effects.

Willingly, then, but not without some reservations and some sadness. The principal reservation arises precisely from my hybrid nature: I have read quite widely, but I don't believe I am anchored in the things that I have read; probably my writing shows more the effects of having for thirty years followed a technical career than of the books I have ingested; therefore the experiment is a little unsound, and its results should be viewed with caution. Anyhow, I have read a great deal, above all in my apprentice years, which in memory seem strangely extended; as if time, then, could be stretched like an elastic band, doubled, tripled. Perhaps the same thing happens to those animals of short life and rapid reproduction like the sparrows and squirrels, and, generally, in anyone who manages, in the same span of time, to do and perceive more things than the average middle-aged man: subjective time becomes longer.

I have read a great deal because I came from a family for whom reading was an innocent and traditional vice, a gratifying habit, a mental exercise, an obligatory and compulsive way of killing time, and a sort of fairy wand bestowing wisdom. My father was always reading three books simultaneously; he read 'when he sat at home, when he walked by the way, when he lay down and when he got up' (Deut. 6.7); he ordered from his tailor jackets with large and deep pockets each one of which could hold a book. He had two brothers just as interested in indiscriminate reading; the three (an engineer, a physician and a stockbroker) were very fond of each other but stole books from each other's respective bookcases on every possible occasion. The thefts provoked complaints for form's sake but were actually accepted with good grace, as if there were an unwritten rule by which he who truly desired a book should *ipso facto* be allowed to carry it away and possess it. And so I spent my childhood in an ambience saturated with printed paper, and in which scholastic texts were rare; because of this I read confusedly, without any plan, according to the custom of the house, and from it I must have extracted a certain (excessive) faith in the nobility and necessity of the printed word, and, as a byproduct, a certain ear and a certain flair. Perhaps, reading, I was unknowingly prepared for writing, just as the eight-month-old foetus remains in the water but is all the while preparing to breathe; perhaps things read here and there came to light again in the pages that I then came to write, but the kernel of my writing does not derive from what I have read. It seems only honest to me to say this clearly in these 'instructions for use' of the present volume.

Above all, and fully recognizing that a choice such as this cannot be exhaustive, and that it cannot give to the reader (who would like them) the keys to the author, in compiling this volume I became aware that the enterprise was not all that facile. It was not empty, nor superficial, nor gratuitous: it wasn't a parlour game. Strangely, I felt more exposed to the public, more unbosomed, in making the choices than in writing my own books. Halfway through the journey I felt naked – and not in the manner of the exhibitionist who thinks that it is good to be naked, or of the patient in bed waiting for the surgeon to open his belly – on the contrary, I felt I was opening myself, like Mohammed in the ninth pit and in the illustration by Doré, in which moreover the masochistic satisfaction of the damned is enormous.

I would not have foreseen, setting out on the work, that among my selected authors I should not find a rogue, nor a woman, nor anyone from a non-European culture; that my experiences in the concentration camp should weigh so little; that the magicians should prevail over the moralists, and the latter over the logicians. Never mind, it is not my job to explain why: which means that the reader who wishes can enter the passage and cast an eye on the ecosystem that lodges unsuspected in my depths, sapro-phytes, birds of day and night, creepers, butterflies, crickets and fungi.

Which is exactly how Alcofribas explores the mouth and throat of Pantagruel in the piece I have cited here: nevertheless, I swear, in choosing it I was not aware that it might be of any such significance. It shows that, however much I want to deny it, there is a trace of the *id* in me too. In short, while writing in the first person is for me, at least in intention, the work of day and conscious lucidity, I am aware that the choice of one's roots is more nocturnal work, visceral and for the most part unconscious. But in reality we should distinguish between two moments: the first, distant in time and spread out over the decades, in which you really choose the books that will accompany you throughout the years, and the second (that is to say, this moment) in which these choices come to be ratified, catalogued, declared and justified to an extreme degree. The first moment is genuine and beyond suspicion; the second risks being tendentious and polluted by the taste of the day. I realize that some of the justifications that precede each piece may carry little conviction: they have a flavour of a posteriori and of rationalization.

It could not be otherwise: I did not espouse those writers *because* they had these specific virtues or congeniality; I met them through the workings of chance and their virtues emerged. Such occasional and erratic reading, reading out of curiosity, impulse or vice, and not by profession, is always going to produce this kind of happy and inexplicable serendipity. With due respect to the psychosociologists, in human relations there are no rules: I don't mean only in the case of the rapport between author and reader, but in all relations. I am a chemist, expert in the affinities between elements, but I find myself a novice faced with the affinity between individuals; here truly all is possible, it is enough to think of certain improbable and lasting marriages, of certain one-sided and fruitful friendships. I only have to cite Rabelais again (to whom I have been faithful for forty years without in the least resembling him or knowing exactly why): his Pantagruel, this generous giant, rich, noble, wise and courageous, meets by chance Panurge, skinny, poor, thieving, cowardly, deceitful, laden with all the vices; he will be Pantagruel's companion through his every adventure and will love him all his life. We are evidently dealing here with 'the reasons of the heart' of which Pascal spoke: whom I respect and admire, who surprises me, but around whom I have circled endlessly in vain like trying to get around certain inaccessible pinnacles of the Grigne.*

I ought rather to make it clear that my own deeper and more lasting loves are the hardest to explain: Belli, Porta, Conrad. In other cases the deciphering is easier. Professional affinity enters into the game (Bragg, Gattermann, Clarke, Lucretius, the sinister unknown author of the ASTM specification concerning cockroaches), a shared love of travel and adventure (Homer, Rosny, Marco Polo and others), a remote Jewish kinship (Job, Mann, Babel, Sholem Aleichem), a closer relationship in Celan and Eliot, the personal friendship that I have with Rigoni Stern, D'Arrigo and Langbein, which makes me feel (presumptuously) that their writing is almost in some way my own, and it gives me pleasure to bring their work to those who have not read them. The novel of Roger Vercel is a case apart: I believe it has its own intrinsic value, but it is important to me for my private reasons, symbolic and charged, because I read it on a day (18 January 1945) when I expected to die.

Thirty authors extracted from thirty centuries of written messages, literary or not, are a drop in the ocean. Many omissions are due to limitations of space, to excessive specialization, to an acute knowledge that my bias is pathological, a fancy, an obsession, maybe permanent and justifiable who knows how, but not transmissible. Other omissions are more serious, and stem from my deafness, or insensibility, or emotional block, of which I am aware and about which I am not proud. The antipathies are as inexplicable as the loves: I confess to having read Balzac and Dostoevsky out of duty, late, wearily, and with little profit. I have omitted other categories, especially some kinds of poetry, for the opposite reason: I did not feel it right to propose foreign authors dear to me, and who write in languages I know (Villon, Heine, Lewis Carroll), because the existing translations seem to me reductive and I don't have the ability to improve them; or if I don't know their language (many Russians, the Greek poets), because I know the deceptions that lurk in translations.

In yet other cases, a threshold effect, a barrier, certainly entered into the process: one is dealing here with an impasse (of language, style, character, ideology), beyond which I would have found firm ground again. I have not made that decisive step, through laziness, through prejudice or a lack of time. If I had done so I would perhaps have found a new friend, would have added a province to my territory, marvellous by definition, because every unexplored territory is marvellous. I am guilty: I must confess, I prefer to play safe, to make a hole and then gnaw away inside for a long time, maybe for all one's life, like the woodworm when he has found a piece of wood to his liking. And finally, of course, there are even bigger gaps, bottomless voids, my own voids – those of a culture of autogestion, unbalanced, factious, Sunday-amateurish and even forced: nothing of music, nothing of painting, little or nothing of the world of sentiment. Be that as it may, I cannot pretend to be what I am not.

As regards the individual texts and authors, or the passages within the work of each author, the choice was sincere, and almost automatic. I have a habit of placing my favourite books on the same shelf, independently of their theme and their age, and all are profusely underlined in the places that I love to reread: so I have not had to work very hard. Now, in the ultimate compilation, I notice a pattern that was not in the programme, the more so because I didn't have a programme. More or less all the choices contain or imply a tension. More or less all show the effects of the fundamental dichotomies customary in the destiny of every conscious person: falsehood/truth, laughter/tears, judgement/folly, hope/despair, triumph/disaster.

The lapidary-funereal quality of a work like this does not escape me, and it gives me a mild pang; I should like to undermine it: in spite of his perverse habit, a woodworm can find other timbers, or new sap in old wood. Only the dead can no longer change and no longer put out other roots, and for this reason only the dead are entitled to criticism, as it has been wisely said: 'It is a recognized maxim of literary ethics that only dead writers should be commented on, seeing that they are no longer in a position to explain themselves, nor to dispute the explanations of those who are dedicated to the pleasant, and sometimes not altogether useless task of making clear that which was at first dark, and profound that which was formerly only clear' (F. C. S. Schiller, in his commentary on Lewis Carroll's *The Hunting of the Snark*).

The authors are not arranged in the chronological order traditional in anthologies, and are not even grouped according to similarity of argument. I have followed approximately the succession in which I happened to discover and read them, but I have often succumbed to the temptation to contrive contrasts, as if I were staging a dialogue across the centuries: as if to see in this way how two neighbours can react to each other, what could come (for instance) of an interaction between Homer and Darwin, between Lucretius and Babel, between Conrad the sailor and Gattermann the careful chemist. To Job I have instinctively reserved the right of primogeniture, although I then find myself struggling a little to find good reasons for this choice.

The diagram that opens the anthology suggests four possible routes through some of the authors in view.

P.L.

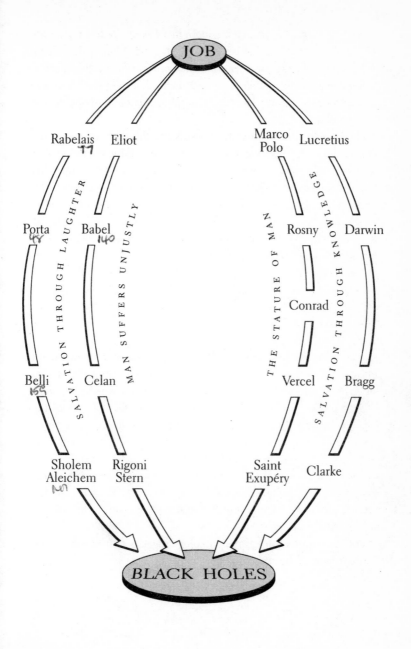

1

The Just Man Oppressed by Injustice

The Book of Job, Bible, Authorized Edition, Chapters 3, 7, 14, 38, 40, 41

Why start with Job? Because this magnificent and harrowing story encapsulates the questions of all the ages, those for which man has never to this day found an answer, nor will he ever find one, but he will always search for it because he needs it in order to live, to understand himself and the world. Job is the just man oppressed by injustice. He is the victim of a cruel wager between Satan and God: what will Job – pious, healthy, rich and happy – do if he is deprived of his wealth, deprived of family love, and finally assailed under his own skin? Well then, Job the Just, degraded to an animal for an experiment, comports himself as any of us would, at first he lowers his head and praises God ('Shall we receive good at the hand of God, and shall we not receive evil?'), then his defences collapse. Poor, bereft of his children, covered in boils, he sits among the ashes, scraping himself with a potsherd, and contends with God. It is an unequal contest: God the Creator of marvels and monsters crushes him beneath his omnipotence.

3 After this opened Job his mouth, and cursed his day.
²And Job spake, and said,

> ³'Let the day perish wherein I was born,
>   and the night in which it was said,
>   "There is a man child conceived."
> ⁴Let that day be darkness;
>   let not God regard it from above,
>   neither let the light shine upon it.

11

⁵ Let darkness and the shadow of death stain it;
>>   let a cloud dwell upon it;
>>>   let the blackness of the day terrify it.
⁶ As for that night, let darkness seize upon it;
>>   let it not be joined unto the days of the year;
>>>   let it not come into the number of the months.
⁷ Lo, let that night be solitary,
>>   let no joyful voice come therein.
⁸ Let them curse it that curse the day,
>>   who are ready to raise up their mourning.
⁹ Let the stars of the twilight thereof be dark;
>>   let it look for light, but have none;
>>>   neither let it see the dawning of the day:
¹⁰ because it shut not up the doors of my mother's
>>   womb, nor hid sorrow from mine eyes.
¹¹ Why died I not from the womb?
>>   why did I not give up the ghost
>>>   when I came out of the belly?
¹² Why did the knees prevent me?
>>   Or why the breasts that I should suck?
¹³ For now should I have lain still and been quiet,
>>   I should have slept: then had I been at rest,
¹⁴ with kings and counsellors of the earth,
>>   which built desolate places for themselves;
¹⁵ or with princes that had gold,
>>   who filled their houses with silver:
¹⁶ or as an hidden untimely birth I had not been;
>>   as infants which never saw light.
¹⁷ There the wicked cease from troubling;
>>   and there the weary be at rest.
¹⁸ There the prisoners rest together;
>>   they hear not the voice of the oppressor.
¹⁹ The small and great are there;
>>   and the servant is free from his master.

²⁰Wherefore is light given to him that is in misery,
and life unto the bitter in soul;
²¹which long for death, but it cometh not,
and dig for it more than for hid treasures;
²²which rejoice exceedingly, and are glad,
when they can find the grave?
²³Why is light given to a man whose way is hid,
and whom God hath hedged in?
²⁴For my sighing cometh before I eat,
and my roarings are poured out like the waters.
²⁵For the thing which I greatly feared
is come upon me, and that
which I was afraid of is come unto me.
²⁶I was not in safety, neither had I rest,
neither was I quiet; yet trouble came.'

7 'Is there not an appointed time to man upon earth?
Are not his days also like the days of an hireling?
²As a servant earnestly desireth the shadow, and as
an hireling looketh for the reward of his work,
³so am I made to possess months of vanity,
and wearisome nights are appointed to me.
⁴When I lie down, I say,
"When shall I arise, and the night be gone?"
and I am full of tossings to and fro
unto the dawning of the day.
⁵My flesh is clothed with worms and clods of dust;
my skin is broken, and become loathsome.
⁶My days are swifter than a weaver's shuttle,
and are spent without hope.
⁷O remember that my life is wind:
mine eye shall no more see good.
⁸The eye of him that hath seen me
shall see me no more:
thine eyes are upon me, and I am not.

⁹As the cloud is consumed and vanisheth away,
    so he that goeth down to the grave
        shall come up no more.
¹⁰He shall return no more to his house,
    neither shall his place know him any more.
¹¹Therefore I will not refrain my mouth;
    I will speak in the anguish of my spirit;
        I will complain in the bitterness of my soul.
¹²Am I a sea, or a whale,
    that thou settest a watch over me?
¹³When I say, "My bed shall comfort me,
    my couch shall ease my complaint";
¹⁴then thou scarest me with dreams,
    and terrifiest me through visions;
¹⁵so that my soul chooseth strangling,
    and death rather than my life.
¹⁶I loathe it; I would not live alway.
    Let me alone; for my days are vanity.
¹⁷What is man, that thou shouldest magnify him?
    And that thou shouldest
        set thine heart upon him?
¹⁸And that thou shouldest visit him every morning,
    and try him every moment?
¹⁹How long wilt thou not depart from me,
    nor let me alone till I swallow down my spittle?
²⁰I have sinned; what shall I do unto thee,
    O thou preserver of men?
        Why hast thou set me as a mark against thee,
    so that I am a burden to myself?
²¹And why dost thou not pardon my transgression,
    and take away mine iniquity?
        For now shall I sleep in the dust;
    and thou shalt seek me in the morning,
        but I shall not be.'

14 'Man that is born of a woman is of few days,
　　and full of trouble.
[2] He cometh forth like a flower, and is cut down;
　　he fleeth also as a shadow, and continueth not.
[3] And dost thou open thine eyes upon such an one,
　　and bringest me into judgment with thee?
[4] Who can bring a clean thing out of an unclean?
　　Not one.
[5] Seeing his days are determined,
　　the number of his months are with thee,
　　　and thou hast appointed his bounds
　　that he cannot pass,
[6] turn from him, that he may rest,
　　till he shall accomplish, as an hireling, his day.
[7] For there is hope of a tree, if it be cut down,
　　that it will sprout again, and
　　　that the tender branch thereof will not cease.
[8] Though the root thereof wax old in the earth,
　　and the stock thereof die in the ground,
[9] yet through the scent of water it will bud,
　　and bring forth boughs like a plant.
[10] But man dieth, and wasteth away;
　　yea, man giveth up the ghost, and where is he?
[11] As the waters fail from the sea,
　　and the flood decayeth and drieth up,
[12] so man lieth down, and riseth not;
　　till the heavens be no more, they shall not awake,
　　　nor be raised out of their sleep.
[13] O that thou wouldest hide me in the grave,
　　that thou wouldest keep me secret,
　　　until thy wrath be past, that thou wouldest
　　appoint me a set time, and remember me!
[14] If a man die, shall he live again?

all the days of my appointed time will I wait,
    till my change come.
[15] Thou shalt call, and I will answer thee:
    thou wilt have a desire to the work of thine hands.
[16] For now thou numberest my steps;
    dost thou not watch over my sin?
[17] My transgression is sealed up in a bag,
    and thou sewest up mine iniquity.
[18] And surely the mountain falling cometh to nought,
    and the rock is removed out of his place.
[19] The waters wear the stones;
    thou washest away the things
        which grow out of the dust of the earth;
    and thou destroyest the hope of man.
[20] Thou prevailest for ever against him,
    and he passeth; thou changest his countenance,
        and sendest him away.
[21] His sons come to honour, and he knoweth it not;
    and they are brought low,
        but he perceiveth it not of them.
[22] But his flesh upon him shall have pain,
    and his soul within him shall mourn.'

38 Then the Lord answered Job out of the whirlwind,
and said,

[2] 'Who is this that darkeneth counsel by words
    without knowledge?
[3] Gird up now thy loins like a man;
    for I will demand of thee, and answer thou me.
[4] Where wast thou when I laid
    the foundations of the earth?
        Declare, if thou hast understanding.
[5] Who hath laid the measures thereof,
    if thou knowest?

Or who hath stretched the line upon it?
⁶Whereupon are the foundations thereof fastened?
Or who laid the corner stone thereof,
⁷when the morning stars sang together,
and all the sons of God shouted for joy?
⁸Or who shut up the sea with doors,
when it brake forth,
as if it had issued out of the womb,
⁹when I made the cloud the garment thereof,
and thick darkness a swaddling-band for it,
¹⁰and brake up for it my decreed place,
and set bars and doors,
¹¹and said, "Hitherto shalt thou come, but no further:
and here shall thy proud waves be stayed"?
¹²Hast thou commanded the morning since thy days,
and caused the dayspring to know his place;
¹³that it might take hold of the ends of the earth,
that the wicked might be shaken out of it?
¹⁴It is turned as clay to the seal;
and they stand as a garment.
¹⁵And from the wicked their light is withholden,
and the high arm shall be broken.
¹⁶Hast thou entered into the springs of the sea?
Or hast thou walked in the search of the depth?
¹⁷Have the gates of death been opened unto thee?
Or hast thou seen the doors of
the shadow of death?
¹⁸Hast thou perceived the breadth of the earth?
Declare if thou knowest it all.
¹⁹Where is the way where light dwelleth?
And as for darkness, where is the place thereof,
²⁰that thou shouldest take it to the bound thereof,
and that thou shouldest know the paths
to the house thereof?

[21] Knowest thou it, because thou wast then born?
Or because the number of thy days is great?
[22] Hast thou entered into the treasures of the snow?
Or hast thou seen the treasures of the hail,
[23] which I have reserved against the time of trouble,
against the day of battle and war?
[24] By what way is the light parted,
which scattereth the east wind upon the earth?
[25] Who hath divided a watercourse
for the overflowing of waters,
or a way for the lightning of thunder;
[26] to cause it to rain on the earth, where no man is;
on the wilderness, wherein there is no man;
[27] to satisfy the desolate and waste ground;
and to cause the bud of the tender herb
to spring forth?
[28] Hath the rain a father?
Or who hath begotten the drops of dew?
[29] Out of whose womb came the ice?
And the hoary frost of heaven,
who hath gendered it?
[30] The waters are hid as with a stone,
and the face of the deep is frozen.
[31] Canst thou bind the sweet influences of Pleiades,
or loose the bands of Orion?
[32] Canst thou bring forth Mazzaroth in his season?
Or canst thou guide Arcturus with his sons?
[33] Knowest thou the ordinances of heaven?
Canst thou set the dominion thereof in the earth?
[34] Canst thou lift up thy voice to the clouds,
that abundance of waters may cover thee?
[35] Canst thou send lightnings, that they may go,
and say unto thee, "Here we are"?
[36] Who hath put wisdom in the inward parts?
Or who hath given understanding to the heart?

³⁷Who can number the clouds in wisdom?
Or who can stay the bottles of heaven,
³⁸when the dust groweth into hardness,
and the clods cleave fast together?
³⁹Wilt thou hunt the prey for the lion,
or fill the appetite of the young lions,
⁴⁰when they couch in their dens,
and abide in the covert to lie in wait?
⁴¹Who provideth for the raven his food
when his young ones cry unto God,
they wander for lack of meat.'

40 [. . .]

¹⁵'Behold now behemoth, which I made with thee;
he eateth grass as an ox.
¹⁶Lo now, his strength is in his loins,
and his force is in the navel of his belly.
¹⁷He moveth his tail like a cedar:
the sinews of his stones are wrapped together.
¹⁸His bones are as strong pieces of brass;
his bones are like bars of iron.
¹⁹He is the chief of the ways of God;
he that made him can make his sword
to approach unto him.
²⁰Surely the mountains bring him forth food,
where all the beasts of the field play.
²¹He lieth under the shady trees,
in the covert of the reed, and fens.
²²The shady trees cover him with their shadow;
the willows of the brook compass him about.
²³Behold, he drinketh up a river, and hasteth not;
he trusteth that he can draw up Jordan
into his mouth.
²⁴He taketh it with his eyes;
his nose pierceth through snares.'

41 'Canst thou draw out leviathan with an hook?
   Or his tongue with a cord which thou lettest down?
   [2] Canst thou put an hook into his nose?
   Or bore his jaw through with a thorn?
   [3] Will he make many supplications unto thee?
   Will he speak soft words unto thee?
   [4] Will he make a covenant with thee?
   Wilt thou take him for a servant for ever?
   [5] Wilt thou play with him as with a bird?
   Or wilt thou bind him for thy maidens?
   [6] Shall the companions make a banquet of him?
   Shall they part him among the merchants?
   [7] Canst thou fill his skin with barbed irons
   or his head with fish spears?
   [8] Lay thine hand upon him,
   remember the battle, do no more.
   [9] Behold, the hope of him is in vain; shall not one
   be cast down even at the sight of him?
   [10] None is so fierce that dare stir him up;
   who then is able to stand before me?
   [11] Who hath prevented me, that I should repay him?
   Whatsoever is under the whole heaven is mine.
   [12] I will not conceal his parts, nor his power,
   nor his comely proportion.
   [13] Who can discover the face of his garment?
   Or who can come to him with his double bridle?
   [14] Who can open the doors of his face?
   His teeth are terrible round about.
   [15] His scales are his pride, shut up together
   as with a close seal.
   [16] One is so near to another,
   that no air can come between them.
   [17] They are joined one to another, they stick together,
   that they cannot be sundered.

¹⁸By his neesings* a light doth shine,
and his eyes are like the eyelids of the morning.
¹⁹Out of his mouth go burning lamps,
and sparks of fire leap out.
²⁰Out of his nostrils goeth smoke,
as out of a seething pot or caldron.
²¹His breath kindleth coals,
and a flame goeth out of his mouth.
²²In his neck remaineth strength,
and sorrow is turned into joy before him.
²³The flakes of his flesh are joined together;
they are firm in themselves;
they cannot be moved.
²⁴His heart is as firm as a stone;
yea, as hard as a piece of the nether millstone.
²⁵When he raiseth up himself, the mighty are afraid;
by reason of breakings they purify themselves.
²⁶The sword of him that layeth at him cannot hold
the spear, the dart, nor the habergeon.*
²⁷He esteemeth iron as straw,
and brass as rotten wood.
²⁸The arrow cannot make him flee;
slingstones are turned with him into stubble.
²⁹Darts are counted as stubble;
he laugheth at the shaking of a spear.
³⁰Sharp stones are under him;
he spreadeth sharp pointed things upon the mire.
³¹He maketh the deep to boil like a pot;
he maketh the sea like a pot of ointment.
³²He maketh a path to shine after him;
one would think the deep to be hoary.
³³Upon earth there is not his like,
who is made without fear.
³⁴He beholdeth all high things;
he is a king over all the children of pride.'

2

A Man of No Account

Homer, 'New Coasts and Poseidon's Son', *The Odyssey*,
translated by Robert Fitzgerald
(London: Panther, 1965), pp. 155–7

I find reading the Iliad *almost intolerable: that orgy of battles, wounds and
death, that stupid and endless war, the puerile anger of Achilles. The* Odyssey,
*however, has a human dimension, its poetry grows from a reasonable hope: the
end of the war and exile, the world rebuilt on the foundation of a peace gained
through justice.*

*We are in Canto 9. Ulysses has escaped from imprisonment in the Cyclops's
cave. He has lost many companions, but thanks to his shrewdness he has got the
better of Polyphemus's coarse violence; Ulysses has made him drunk, blinded
him, has eluded the surveillance of the monster thanks to the trick of the sheep.
He could have escaped in silence, but prefers to take his revenge to the limit: he
is proud of his name, which up till now he has kept quiet about, and proud of his
courage and ingenuity. He is a 'man of no account', but he wants to make known
to the tower of flesh just who is the mortal that has defeated him.*

We saw, as we came near, our fellows' faces
shining; then we saw them turn to grief
tallying those who had not fled from death.
I hushed them, jerking head and eyebrows up,
and in a low voice told them: 'Load this herd;
move fast, and put the ship's head towards the breakers.'
They all pitched in at loading, then embarked
and struck their oars into the sea. Far out,

as far off shore as shouted words would carry,
I sent a few back to the adversary:

'O Kyklops! Would you feast on my companions?
Puny, am I, in a Caveman's hands?
How do you like the beating that we gave you,
you damned cannibal? Eater of guests
under your roof! Zeus and the gods have paid you!'

The blind thing in his doubled fury broke
a hilltop in his hands and heaved it after us.
Ahead of our black prow it struck and sank
whelmed in a spuming geyser, a giant wave
that washed the ship stern foremost back to shore.
I got the longest boat-hook out and stood
fending us off, with furious nods to all
to put their backs into a racing stroke –
row, row, or perish. So the long oars bent
kicking the foam sternward, making head
until we drew away, and twice as far.
Now when I cupped my hands I heard the crew
in low voices protesting:

                                        'Godsake, Captain!
Why bait the beast again? Let him alone!'
'That tidal wave he made on the first throw
all but beached us.'

                                        'All but stove us in!'
'Give him our bearing with your trumpeting,
he'll get the range and lob a boulder.'

                                                        'Aye

He'll smash our timbers and our heads together!'

I would not heed them in my glorying spirit,
but let my anger flare and yelled:

                                        'Kyklops,

if ever mortal man inquire
how you were put to shame and blinded, tell him
Odysseus, raider of cities, took your eye:
Laërtês' son, whose home's on Ithaka!'

At this he gave a mighty sob and rumbled:

'Now comes the weird upon me, spoken of old.
A wizard, grand and wondrous, lived here – Télemos,
a son of Eurymos; great length of days
he had in wizardy among the Kyklopés,
and these things he foretold for time to come:
my great eye lost, and at Odysseus' hands.
Always I had in mind some giant, armed
in giant force, would come against me here.
But this, but you – small, pitiful and twiggy –
you put me down with wine, you blinded me.
Come back, Odysseus, and I'll treat you well,
praying the god of earthquake to befriend you –
his son I am, for he by his avowal
fathered me, and, if he will, he may
heal me of this black wound – he and no other
of all the happy gods or mortal men.'

Few words I shouted in reply to him:

'If I could take your life I would and take
your time away, and hurl you down to hell!
The god of earthquake could not heal you there!'

3
Why are Animals Beautiful?

Charles Darwin, 'Utilitarian Doctrine, how far true:
Beauty, how acquired', *The Origin of Species*,
6th edition (Oxford: Oxford University Press, 1951), pp. 208–14

Darwin had many enemies: he has some still. They were the upholders of religion, and they attacked him because they saw in him a destroyer of dogmas. Their myopia is incredible: in Darwin's work, as in his life, a deep and serious religious spirit breathes, the sober joy of a man who extracts order from chaos, who rejoices in the mysterious parallel between his own reasoning and the universe, and who sees in the universe a grand design. In these pages, in sharp and almost amusing polemic, directed against the absurd thesis that animals and plants are created beautiful to be admired by human beings, Darwin attains the harmonious beauty of strenuous and rigorous reasoning. Denying man a privileged place in creation, he reaffirms with his own intellectual courage the dignity of man.

But how is it that what is beautiful for us is equally so for the insects and the birds? It is typical of the great answers that they give rise to big new questions.

UTILITARIAN DOCTRINE, HOW FAR TRUE: BEAUTY, HOW ACQUIRED

The foregoing remarks lead me to say a few words on the protest lately made by some naturalists, against the utilitarian doctrine that every detail of structure has been produced for the good of its possessor. They believe that many structures have been created for the sake of beauty, to delight man or the Creator (but this latter point is beyond the scope of scientific discussion), or for the sake of mere variety, a view already discussed. Such doctrines, if true, would be absolutely fatal to my theory. I fully admit that many structures are now of no direct use to their possessors, and may never have been of any use to their progenitors; but this does not prove that they were formed solely for beauty or variety. No doubt the definite action of changed conditions, and the various causes of modifications, lately specified, have all produced an effect, probably a great effect, independently of any advantage thus gained. But a still more important consideration is that the chief part of the organisation of every living creature is due to inheritance; and consequently, though each being assuredly is well fitted for its place in nature, many structures have now no very close and direct relation to present habits of life. Thus, we can hardly believe that the webbed feet of the upland goose or of the frigate-bird are of special use to these birds; we cannot believe that the similar bones in the arm of the monkey, in the fore-leg of the horse, in the wing of the bat, and in the flipper of the seal, are of special use to these animals. We may safely attribute these structures to inheritance. But webbed feet no doubt were as useful to the progenitor of the upland goose and of the frigate-bird, as they now are to the most aquatic of living birds. So we may believe that the progenitor of the seal did not possess a flipper, but a foot with five toes fitted for walking or grasping; and we may further venture to believe that the several bones in the limbs of the monkey, horse, and bat, were originally developed, on the principle of utility, probably through the reduction of more numerous bones in the fin of some ancient fish-like progenitor of the whole class. It is scarcely possible to decide how much allowance ought to be made for such causes of change, as the definite action of external conditions, so-called spontaneous variations, and the complex laws of growth; but with these important exceptions, we may conclude that the structure of every living creature either now is, or was formerly, of some direct or indirect use to its possessor.

With respect to the belief that organic beings have been created beautiful for the delight of man, – a belief which it has been pronounced is subversive of my whole theory, – I may first remark that the sense of beauty obviously depends on the nature of the mind, irrespective of any real quality in the admired object; and that the idea of what is beautiful is not innate or unalterable. We see this, for instance, in the men of different races admiring an entirely different standard of beauty in their women. If beautiful objects had been created solely for man's gratification, it ought to be shown that before man appeared, there was less beauty on the face of the earth than since he came on the stage. Were the beautiful volute and cone shells of the Eocene epoch, and the gracefully sculptured ammonites of the Secondary period, created that man might ages afterwards admire them in his cabinet? Few objects are more beautiful than the minute siliceous cases of the diatomaceæ: were these created that they might be examined and admired under the higher powers of the microscope? The beauty in this latter case, and in many others, is apparently wholly due to symmetry of growth. Flowers rank amongst the most beautiful productions of nature; but they have been rendered conspicuous in contrast with the green leaves, and in consequence at the same time beautiful, so that they may be easily observed by insects. I have come to this conclusion from finding it an invariable rule that when a flower is fertilised by the wind it never has a gaily-coloured corolla. Several plants habitually produce two kinds of flowers: one kind open and coloured so as to attract insects; the other closed, not coloured, destitute of nectar, and never visited by insects. Hence we may conclude that, if insects had not been developed on the face of the earth, our plants would not have been decked with beautiful flowers, but would have produced only such poor flowers as we see on our fir, oak, nut and ash trees, on grasses, spinach, docks, and nettles, which are all fertilized through the agency of the wind. A similar line of argument holds good with fruits; that a ripe strawberry or cherry is as pleasing to the eye as to the palate, – that the gaily-coloured fruit of the spindlewood tree and the scarlet berries of the holly are beautiful objects, – will be admitted by every one. But this beauty serves merely as a guide to birds and beasts, in order that the fruit may be devoured and the manured seeds disseminated: I infer that this is the case from having as yet found no exception to the rule that seeds are always thus disseminated when embedded within a fruit of any kind (that is within a fleshy or pulpy envelope), if it be coloured of any brilliant tint, or rendered conspicuous by being white or black.

On the other hand, I willingly admit that a great number of male animals, as all our most gorgeous birds, some fishes, reptiles, and mammals, and a host of magnificently coloured butterflies, have been rendered beautiful for beauty's sake; but this has been effected through sexual selection, that is, by the more beautiful males having been continually preferred by the females, and not for the delight of man. So it is with the music of birds. We may infer from all this that a nearly similar taste for beautiful colours and for musical sounds runs through a large part of the animal kingdom. When the female is as beautifully coloured as the male, which is not rarely the case with birds and butterflies, the cause apparently lies in the colours acquired through sexual selection having been transmitted to both sexes, instead of to the males alone. How the sense of beauty in its simplest form – that is, the reception of a peculiar kind of pleasure from certain colours, forms, and sounds – was first developed in the mind of man and of the lower animals, is a very obscure subject. The same sort of difficulty is presented, if we enquire how it is that certain flavours and odours give pleasure, and others displeasure. Habit in all these cases appears to have come to a certain extent into play; but there must be some fundamental cause in the constitution of the nervous system in each species.

Natural selection cannot possibly produce any modification in a species exclusively for the good of another species; though throughout nature one species incessantly takes advantage of, and profits by, the structures of others. But natural selection can and does often produce structures for the direct injury of other animals, as we see in the fang of the adder, and in the ovipositor of the ichneumon, by which its eggs are deposited in the living bodies of other insects. If it could be proved that any part of the structure of any one species had been formed for the exclusive good of another species, it would annihilate my theory, for such could not have been produced through natural selection. Although many statements may be found in works on natural history to this effect, I cannot find even one which seems to me of any weight. It is admitted that the rattlesnake has a poison-fang for its own defence, and for the destruction of its prey; but some authors suppose that at the same time it is furnished with a rattle for its own injury, namely, to warn its prey. I would almost as soon believe that the cat curls the end of its tail when preparing to spring, in order to warn the doomed mouse. It is a much more probable view that the rattlesnake uses its rattle, the cobra expands its frill, and the puff-adder swells whilst hissing so loudly and harshly, in order to alarm the many birds and beasts which are known to attack even the most venomous species. Snakes act on the same principle which makes the hen ruffle her feathers and expand her wings when a dog approaches her chickens; but I have not space here to enlarge on the many ways by which animals endeavour to frighten away their enemies.

Natural selection will never produce in a being any structure more injurious than beneficial to that being, for natural selection acts solely by and for the good of each. No organ will be formed, as Paley has remarked, for the purpose of causing pain or for doing an injury to its possessor. If a fair balance be struck between the good and evil caused by each part, each will be found on the whole advantageous. After the lapse of time, under changing conditions of life, if any part comes to be injurious, it will be modified; or if it be not so, the being will become extinct as myriads have become extinct.

Natural selection tends only to make each organic being as perfect as, or slightly more perfect than, the other inhabitants of the same country with which it comes into competition. And we see that this is the standard of perfection attained under nature. The endemic productions of New Zealand, for instance, are perfect one compared with another; but they are now rapidly yielding before the advancing legions of plants and animals introduced from Europe. Natural selection will not produce absolute perfection, nor do we always meet, as far as we can judge, with this high standard under nature. The correction for the aberration of light is said by Müller not to be perfect even in that most perfect organ, the human eye. Helmholtz, whose judgment no one will dispute, after describing in the strongest terms the wonderful powers of the human eye, adds these remarkable words: 'That which we have discovered in the way of inexactness and imperfection in the optical machine and in the image on the retina, is as nothing in comparison with the incongruities which we have just come across in the domain of the sensations. One might say that nature has taken delight in accumulating contradictions in order to remove all foundation from the theory of a pre-existing harmony between the external and internal worlds.' If our reason leads us to admire with enthusiasm a multitude of inimitable contrivances in nature, this same reason tells us, though we may easily err on both sides, that some other contrivances are less perfect. Can we consider the sting of the bee as perfect, which, when used against many kinds of enemies, cannot be withdrawn, owing to the backward serratures, and thus inevitably causes the death of the insect by tearing out its viscera?

If we look at the sting of the bee, as having existed in a remote progenitor, as a boring and serrated instrument, like that in so many members of the same great order, and that it has since been modified but not perfected for its present purpose, with the poison originally adapted for some other object, such as to produce galls, since intensified, we can perhaps understand how it is that the use of the sting should so often cause the insect's own death: for if on the whole the power of stinging be useful to the social community, it will fulfil all the requirements of natural selection, though it may cause the death of some few members. If we admire the truly wonderful power of scent by which the males of many insects find their females, can we admire the production for this single purpose of thousands of drones, which are utterly useless to the community for any other purpose, and which are ultimately slaughtered by their industrious and sterile sisters? It may be difficult, but we ought to admire the savage instinctive hatred of the queen-bee, which urges her to destroy the young queens, her daughters, as soon as they are born, or to perish herself in the combat; for undoubtedly this is for the good of the community; and maternal love or maternal hatred, though the latter fortunately is most rare, is all the same to the inexorable principle of natural selection. If we admire the several ingenious contrivances, by which orchids and many other plants are fertilised through insect agency, can we consider as equally perfect the elaboration of dense clouds of pollen by our fir-trees, so that a few granules may be wafted by chance on to the ovules?

4
To See Atoms

Sir William Bragg,* *Concerning the Nature of Things:*
Six Lectures Delivered at the Royal Institution
(London: G. Bell & Sons, 1925), pp. 1–4, 12–16, 17

Sir William Bragg, Nobel Prize winner for Physics in 1915, belonged to an epoch in which a pioneering genius could still do brilliant work in isolation. With his son, he constructed the first X-ray spectrometer, a valuable but conceptually simple instrument: it exploited the fact (already known) that the wavelength of X-rays is of the same order of magnitude as the interatomic distances, and therefore allowed us to 'see' the spatial arrangement of the atoms in crystals.

I owe a great deal to this book. I read it by chance at the age of sixteen; I was captivated by the clear and simple things that it said, and I decided I would become a chemist. Between the lines I divined a great hope: the models on a human scale, the concepts of structures and measurement, reach very far, towards the minute world of atoms, and towards the immense world of the stars; perhaps infinitely far? If so, we live in a comprehensible universe, one accessible to our imagination, and the anguish of the dark recedes before the rapid spread of research.

I would become a chemist: I would share Bragg's faith (which today seems very ingenuous). I would be bound up with him, and with the legendary atomists of antiquity, against the discouraging and lazy herd of those who see matter as infinitely, fruitlessly, tediously divisible.

Nearly two thousand years ago, Lucretius, the famous Latin poet, wrote his treatise *De rerum natura* – concerning the nature of things. He maintained the view that air and earth and water and everything else were composed of innumerable small bodies or corpuscles, individually too small to be seen, and all in rapid motion. He tried to show that these suppositions were enough to explain the properties of material things. He was not himself the originator of all the ideas which he set forth in his poem; he was the writer who would explain the views which were held by a certain school, and which he himself believed to be true. There was a rival set of views, according to which, however closely things were looked into, there would be no evidence of structure: however the water in a bowl, let us say, was subdivided into drops and then again into smaller drops and so on and on, the minutest portion would still be like the original bowl of water in all its properties. On the view of Lucretius, if subdivision were carried out sufficiently, one would come at last to the individual corpuscles or *atoms*: the word atom being taken in its original sense, something which *cannot be cut*.

There is a mighty difference between the two views. On the one, there is nothing to be gained by looking into the structure of substances more closely, for however far we go we come to nothing new. On the other view, the nature of things as we know them will depend on the properties of these atoms of which they are composed, and it will be very interesting and important to find out, if we can, what the atoms are like. The latter view turns out to be far nearer the truth than the former; and for that all may be grateful who love to enquire into the ways of Nature.

Lucretius had no conception, however, of atomic theories as they stand now. He did not realise that the atoms can be divided into so many different kinds, and that all the atoms of one kind are alike. That idea is comparatively new: it was explained with great clearness by John Dalton at the beginning of the nineteenth century. It has rendered possible the great advances that chemistry has made in modern times and all the other sciences which depend on chemistry in any degree. It is easy to see why the newer idea has made everything so much simpler. It is because we have to deal with a limited number of sorts only, not with a vast number of different individuals. We should be in despair if we were compelled to study a multitude of different atoms in the composition of a piece of copper, let us say; but when we discover that there is only one kind of atom in a piece of pure copper, and in the whole world not many different kinds, we may feel full of enthusiasm and hope in pressing forward to the study of their properties, and of the laws of their combinations. For, of course, it is in their combinations that their importance lies. The atoms may be compared to the letters of the alphabet, which can be put together into innumerable ways to form words. So the atoms are combined in equal variety to form what are called molecules. We may even push the analogy a little further and say that the association of words into sentences and passages conveying meanings of every kind is like the combination of molecules of all kinds and in all proportions to form structures and materials that have an infinite variety of appearances and properties and can carry what we speak of as life.

Let us now ask ourselves what binds the atoms together into the various combinations and structures. Like our builder, we have got in our materials – the bricks, slates, beams and so on; we have our various kinds of atoms. If we look round for mortar and nails we find we have none. Nature does not allow the use of any new material as a cement. The atoms cling together of themselves. The chemist tells us that they must be presented to one another under proper conditions, some of which are very odd; but the combination does take place, and there is something in the atoms themselves which maintains it when the conditions are satisfied. The whole of chemistry is concerned with the nature of these conditions and their results.

The atoms seem to cling to one another in some such way as two magnets do when opposite poles are presented to each other; or two charges of electricity of opposite nature. In fact, there is no doubt that both magnetic and electric attractions are at work. We are not entirely ignorant of their mode of action, but we know much more about the rules of combination – that is to say, about the facts of chemistry – than we do about the details of the attractions. However, we need not trouble ourselves about these matters for the present; we have merely to realise that there are forces drawing atoms together.

We may now ask why, if there are such forces, the atoms do not all join together into one solid mass? Why are there any gases or even liquids? How is it that there are any atoms at all which do not link up with their neighbours? What prevents the earth from falling into the sun and the final solidification of the entire universe?

The earth does not fall into the sun because it is in motion round the sun, or, to be more correct, because the two bodies are moving round one another. It is motion that keeps them apart; and when we look closely into the matter we find that motion plays a part of first importance in all that we see, because it sets itself against the binding forces that would join atoms together in one lump. In the gas, motion has the upper hand; the atoms are moving so fast that they have no time to enter into any sort of combination with each other: occasionally atom must meet atom and, so to speak, each hold out vain hands to the other, but the pace is too great and, in a moment, they are far away from each other again. Even in a liquid where there is more combination and atoms are in contact with each other all the time, the motion is so great that no junction is permanent.

In a solid the relative importance of the attractive forces and the motion undergoes another change: the former now holds sway, so that the atoms and the molecules are locked in their places. Even in the solid, however, the atoms are never perfectly still; at the least they vibrate and quiver about average positions, just as the parts of an iron bridge quiver when a train goes over it. It is difficult to realise that the atoms and molecules of substances which appear to be perfectly at rest, the table, a piece of paper, the water in a glass, are all in motion. Yet many of the older philosophers grasped the fact. For example, Hooke, an English physicist of the seventeenth century, explains by a clear analogy the difference which he supposed to exist between the solid and the liquid form: ascribing it to a movement of the atoms which was greater in the liquid than in the solid state. 'First,' he says, 'what is the cause of fluidness? This I conceive to be nothing else but a very brisk and vehement agitation of the parts of a body (as I have elsewhere made probable); the parts of a body are thereby made so loose from one another that they easily move any way, and become fluid. That I may explain this a little by a gross similitude, let us suppose a dish of sand set upon some body that is very much agitated, and shaken with some quick and strong vibrating motion, as on a millstone turn'd round upon the under stone very violently whilst it is empty; or on a very stiff drum-head, which is vehemently or very nimbly beaten with the drumsticks. By this means the sand in the dish, which before lay like a dull and unactive body, becomes a perfect fluid; and ye can no sooner make a hole in it with your finger, but it is immediately filled up again, and the upper surface of it levelled. Nor can ye bury a light body, as a piece of cork under it, but it presently emerges or swims as 'twere on the top; nor can ye lay a heavier on the top of it, as a piece of lead, but it is immediately buried in sand, and (as 'twere) sinks to the bottom. Nor can ye make a hole in the side of the dish, but the sand shall run out of it to a level. Not an obvious property of a fluid body, as such, but this does imitate; and all this merely caused by the vehement agitation of the conteining vessel; for by this means, each sand becomes to have a vibrative or dancing motion, so as no other heavier body can rest on it, unless sustein'd by some other on either side: nor will it suffer any body to be beneath it, unless it be one heavier than itself.'

[. . .]

We know now that the motion of the atoms of the body is really its heat: that the faster they move or vibrate the hotter the body becomes. Whenever we warm our hands by the fire, we allow the energy radiated by the fire to quicken up the movements of the atoms of which the hands are composed. When we cool any substance we check those movements. If we could still them altogether we should lower the temperature to a point beyond which it would be impossible to go, the absolute zero, as it is usually called, 273 degrees centigrade below zero.

*   *   *

A drop of fluid which tries to draw itself together into a sphere looks as if it were being held in an elastic bag. The atoms of mercury in the surface are not quite in the same circumstances as those in the interior, because they are exposed on one side, but it is only in this sense that there is a surface film. We use the idea of a surface film, nevertheless, finding it a convenient term; and we speak of its tendency to contract and of its tension. Sometimes, however, there is a real film on the surface which is different in composition from the liquid of the interior, and then we find many strange and beautiful consequences. The example most familiar to us is, no doubt, that of the soap bubble. We put into the water a little soap, and at once we find it easy to churn the soapy water into a pile of froth or blow it out into bubbles. What has the soap to do with this effect? The answer is to be found in the properties of the soap molecule. It is of very curious shape, many times as long as it is broad; and it is made up of a chain of carbon atoms fringed along its length with hydrogens, and ending, at one end, in a little bunch of three hydrogen atoms, at the other in a little group consisting of oxygen and sodium. The former of these bunches (that with the CH_3 group on the left of the diagram) is very self-contained: its attractions for other atoms and molecules are small.

But the latter (the CO_2Na group on the right) is by no means so unsociable: it is an active group tending to enter into association with others, and especially it has a strong desire to join up with molecules of water, for which reason the soap dissolves in the water. Because, however, it is only one end of the chain which is very active in this respect – the other end and the sides of the chain behave differently – the soap molecules are apt to stay on the outer fringe of the water if they come there in the course of their wanderings. In this way a real film forms on the surface of the water, consisting of soap molecules standing on end, so to speak, one end rooted in the water, and the other exposed to the air. They are packed together side by side like the corn in a field, or the pile on a piece of velvet. They are not as free, however, as the hairs of the pile: they are tied together side by side, because there is some force of attraction between them when so laid alongside. We find that effect displayed under other circumstances, as we shall see later. Thus they form a sort of chain mail over the surface of the water: a real envelope.

The sheet can be stretched in the sense that if it has to be extended other long molecules will come out of the body of the liquid and take their place with the rest.

5

The Pact with the Mammoths

Joseph-Henri Rosny aîné*, *La Guerre du Feu*
(Paris: Plon, 1911), pp. 88–91, translated by Peter Forbes

The elder of the brothers Rosny was celebrated as a novelist in the naturalistic tradition, and then forgotten. This novel of his 'from the savage age', written around 1910, is the last product of an era in which our civilization had not yet begun to doubt itself, and in which many European nations were going in search of a noble origin that would make them the equal of the Romans and Greeks: these are the years in which Germany rediscovered Arminius, France Vercingetorix,* and even Swiss painters painted decorous villages built on stilts that had never existed.*

This is perhaps the first book that I read in French, one that piled exoticism on exoticism and adventure on adventure. The protagonist Naoh is a Victorian gentleman, modest and strong, unimpeachable and unafraid. I don't exclude the possibility that my sympathy for him is connected with his name, which happens to be the chemical formula of caustic soda. Naoh and his companions Nam and Gaw belong to a tribe that knows fire, and how to maintain it, but not how to light it. The fireplace of the Ulhamrs has been extinguished by a hostile tribe, and the three have been sent on a mission to seize the fire of other tribes.

The Ulhamrs slept in turns until the Dawn. Then they resumed the descent of the gorge of the Great River. The mammoths blocked their path. The herd was a thousand cubits wide and three times as long; they browsed, they tore up the tender plants, they unearthed roots, and they appeared to the three humans to be happy, confident and majestic. Sometimes, delighting in their strength, they chased each other on the soft earth, or entwined each other gently with their hairy trunks. Beneath their giant feet the Great Lion would be no more than clay; their tusks stripped the oaks, their granite heads shattered them. And marvelling at the suppleness of their trunks, Naoh couldn't help but exclaim:

'The Mammoth is the master of everything that lives on the earth.'

He wasn't really afraid of them: he knew that they never attacked another creature unless disturbed. He spoke again:

'Aoum, son of the Crow, once made friends with the mammoths.'

'Why shouldn't we do as Aoum did?' asked Gaw.

'Aoum understood the mammoths,' Naoh objected; 'we don't.'

Nevertheless, this question had struck him; he pondered it while circling the enormous herd from a distance. And putting his thought into words, he went on:

'Mammoths don't have a language like humans. They have an understanding among themselves. They know the call of the chiefs; Goûn says that they take, when ordered, the place allotted to them, and that they consult before leaving for new territory . . . If we could interpret their signals we could make friends with them.'

He saw an enormous mammoth who was watching them go by. He was grazing on the tender shoots by himself, lower down the river, among the poplars. Naoh had never encountered anything so formidable. It spanned twelve cubits in height. A thick mane like a lion's hung from his neck; his hairy trunk seemed like a being in its own right, with a hint of vegetation or serpent.

The sight of the three humans seemed to interest him, because one couldn't suppose they alarmed him. And Naoh cried out:

'The mammoths are strong! The Great Mammoth is greater than all the others: he crushes the Tiger and Lion as if they were worms, he topples ten aurochs with a flick of his chest . . . Naoh, Nam and Gaw are the Great Mammoth's friends.'

The mammoth pricked up his membranous ears; he heard the sounds that the standing creature made, gently shook his trunk and bellowed.

'The mammoth has understood!' shouted Naoh with joy. 'He knows that the Ulhamrs recognize his power.'

He cried again:

'If the sons of the Leopard, the Saiga, and the Poplar recover Fire again, they will cook chestnuts and acorns as a gift to the Great Mammoth!' As he spoke, he noticed a pond where water lilies were growing. Naoh knew that the mammoths loved their underground stems. He signalled to his companions and they set out to gather the long browning plants. When they had a good bunch they washed them carefully and carried them towards the colossal beast. At fifty cubits, Naoh spoke again:

'Here! We have gathered these plants for you to eat. So that you will know that the Ulhamrs are the friends of the mammoths.'

And he retreated.

Curious, the giant approached the roots. He knew them well; they were to his taste. While he ate, slowly, with long pauses, he watched the three men. Sometimes he withdrew his trunk to sniff, then he held it aloft in a friendly gesture.

Then Naoh approached stealthily: he found himself in front of the huge feet, under the trunk that shredded the shrubs, under the tusks as long as the body of an aurochs; he was like a fieldmouse in front of a panther. With a single blow, the beast could reduce him to shreds. But, imbued with the confidence he had acquired, he radiated hope and inspiration. The mammoth's trunk brushed against him, passing swiftly over his body; Naoh, without a whisper, replied by touching the hairy trunk. Then he picked up the leaves and young shoots that he offered as a token of friendship: he knew that he was doing something profound and extraordinary, and his heart swelled with pride.

But Nam and Gaw had seen the mammoth come after their chief: they were better placed to see how tiny the man was; then, when the enormous trunk touched Naoh, they murmured:

'Look! Naoh is going to be crushed, Nam and Gaw are alone in front of the Kzamms, the beasts and the waters.'

Then, they saw Naoh's hand stroke the beast; their hearts swelled with joy and pride.

'Naoh has made friends with the Mammoth!' murmured Nam. 'Naoh is the most powerful of men.'

Meanwhile the son of the Leopard shouted:

'Nam and Gaw should come now in the same manner as Naoh . . . Pick up the leaves and shoots and give them to the mammoth!'

They listened, gladly, full of confidence; they advanced with the same ease that Naoh had demonstrated, picking up plenty of herbage and young roots as they went.

When they were near, they offered their harvest. As before with Naoh the mammoth came to eat.

So was born the alliance between the Ulhamrs and the mammoths.

6

The Hobbies

Giuseppe Parini,* *The Day*, translated by
Herbert Morris Bower (London: Routledge, 1927), pp. 171–9

Parini is a dear man and a poet of restrained flights, honest, witty and precise, responsible for every word he has written. He did not believe that the trade of writing should elevate the writer above the masses, instead he believed in poetry as a means to make the world a little better, but I do not think he entertained grand illusions. He was one of those men who, across the centuries, you would like to have met, to have spent some time with: perhaps at table, in the evening, beside a lake, drinking vintage wine in moderation.

This, his survey of imbecilic softies, represents a class that is lost, but a human type that survives.

> What crush of heroes! Thou who'rt born to be
> In ev'ry noble virtue and high deed
> A pattern to thy peers, for thee it is
> Thy peers to know, and gather to thyself
> All the good gifts of beauty, glory, greatness,
> Among a hundred of them. Some but now
> Tread the first footsteps in the path of fame,
> Some a good stage have run, others already
> The half have cover'd. In rash phrase the vulgar
> Call the first children, and the next adults;
> The last they even dare to call old men.
> 'Tis vain: they're all alike. Ev'ryone jests

And frolics, ponders and adjudicates;
Their very pettings and embracings too
They give in mutual equality;
They differ only in the sev'ral cares
Where each prefers most brilliantly to shine.

    Here's one straight from the three-lane-ends resorts
That minister to thirst for bev'rages,
And news, and idleness. He went this morning,
Left but for dinner, and return'd till night.
Full thirty years have run since he a lad
Began to seek life's fair significance.
Oh who can sit there dreaming sweeter dreams
Than his? Yawn longer yawns? Or oft'ner tickle
The nose with black rappee?* More eagerly
Lend ear and faith to all the common talk?
Louder declaim it? There's the gracious youth
Whose agile arm, with masterly address,
Swings splendidly the whistling lash, and thrills
The air with shocks that glorify the hours
In the vast halls hung round with ancestors
And trophies old. That other is the hero
Who from puff'd cheeks through twisted brass proclaims
To street and square his own immortal skill
As, perch'd on famous palaces aloft,
He emulates th' impetuous messenger
Sounding arrival. Oh how fine he looks,
When girt within his trimly fitting jacket,
His legs engulf'd in the capacious leather,
He rides the plain, whirling the coach away
And lady, husband, maid, son, dog, within it!
Wouldst thou some solemn day in chariot bright
Make the triumphal circuit of the Corso?*
Lo! there's the one who'll see the work accomplish'd.
Wood, hide, silk, iron, in their sev'ral kinds,
Smiths, carpenters beside to him are known,

As he is known throughout Ausonia.
To him Calabrians of proud estate
And dignity, the dukes and princes too
Who pasture the broad slopes of Mongibello,*
Nay, the exalted children of old Rome,
Such care shall oft confide. Away he hurries,
One after one the workshops visiting,
That under his auspicious eye may grow
The lucky edifice; and when 'tis ready,
Enswath'd in cloth, securely fortified
'Gainst harm of rain or sun, himself he'll go
T' escort it a full mile beyond the walls;
Then fondly gaze, and watch it vanishing
As the road sinks. That other sure thou know'st?
Most famous pupil he of Maia's* son,
To whose wise counsels all the others yield
In grave perplexities where dice are thrown,
Where pieces stand or lie upon a board,
Where cards, or long or short, in battle join.
He'll spend the morning soothing with his play
The stupifying headaches and sharp coughs
Of agèd dames. When dinner's done 'tis he
Who teaches to the waning fair the games
Newborn that very hour. At night he draws
A hero troop about him, all afire
With lofty zeal, the subtle art to learn
Of conquering and mastering the fortune
Of someone else, and how a noble slice
O' the fields of one dear friend yield to the other.
  Seest thou arriving the invincible
Breaker of horses who divides the day
Between them and his lady? Her warm hand
One moment he'll be pressing, and the next
Stroking their hairy backs or, prone on earth,
With finger trying shoes and hoofs. Alas!

How pitiful her case when from afar
A crowded fair's announc'd! Forsaking her,
Untrodden peaks he'll cross and frightful glens,
To swap or buy in some remote resort.
But happy she when mud-splash'd he returns
With a new string of fretting steeds superb;
And then for many moons to her alone
Tells o'er their country, pedigree and manners!
Now mark another: never maid was seen
More constant and more diligent to work
A knotted web, or yet to separate
The warp of golden cloths. His pockets both
Still bulge with hidden stuffs that once display'd
In precious tapestry, prick'd out with gold
And gorgeous wools, the chances that befell
Unhappy Troy. E'en now the cavalier
Was sitting in the lady's cabinet,
With tireless hand was picking out the throng
Of Argos and of Phrygia,* into threads
The tiniest. One side alone remains
Of her who from her Grecian home was torn;
And, when the hero's ten years' task's achiev'd,
He'll step as proudly as the two Atrides.*
See! There is he who knows the mode precise
On paper to convey the happy news
Of marriage, or the dolorous announcement
Of fate extreme. New-made inheritors,
Dishevell'd and perturb'd at their great grief,
Rush for his counsel. In the olden time,
Near the Cumæan cave* were never seen
So many leaves with mark oracular,
As all the notices he's brought together,
Some day to be conserv'd for the great public.
　　But when the rooms are cramm'd with cavaliers
And ladies, who could tell the varied tale

Of all their talents and accomplishments?
Come, throw thyself into the circling scene;
And bravely daring turn, sit, stand or push,
Yield, pardon beg, ask here and answer there,
Give one the slip and beckon to another,
Chatter thy way among the troops divine,
And, blending with them, at the selfsame moment
Fill all things with thyself, and look, and learn.
  See there those charming fellows, Cupid's freshmen,
Who in each other's ears confide aloud
Their budding fortunes, skip and clap their hands
And laugh outright – whether he lead them on
To enterprises gay with unknown mortals,
Or gather them within the radiancy
Of dames who share their own divinity.
Here his fam'd champions of an earlier day,
With thin voice hardly squeez'd from panting breast,
Recall to memory their proud adventures
In by-gone love. Yonder the beardless heroes
Whose fathers gave them their first pair of horses
But yesterday, see them already joking
With manly spirit by th' old beauty's side,
Who as they laugh explodes in laughter too,
And spreads nude charms scarce veil'd, to seek the glances
That once were seekers. There grown men behold,
Upon whose brow the wig-maker has fix'd
The first deceptive lock; jesting they hover
Near the new bride, and lay for her a snare
Of pretty epigrams, wherein to tangle
Her simple soul, her timid modesty.
Fools for their pains! She meets their ev'ry sally
As bravely as a mother of ten heroes.
Apart sits he who promises the ladies
Amusement rare of merry anecdotes
And stories no one's heard; he laughs, he tells,

He laughs again, though on the lovely arch
O' the ladies' lips hang hovering the while
Involuntary yawns. Away from him
Another changes words by lucky study
To meanings new, and plays a game divine
With sounds alike that hit. His genius wins
Applause from the stout matrons' rattling fans,
Whose voices echo still a homely accent;
But the young mothers, us'd to drink the milk
Of graver doctrine, wrinkle in disgust
Their delicate noses, seeming by their looks
To implore the pity of those clever souls
Who sit beside them and whose minds absorb
Volatile knowledge from great store distill'd
Of learned journals. Yonder mark the challenge
Of him that's bravely backing 'gainst all comers
The pony that he rides, or else the poet
Or singer whom his hospitality
Rejoices. Over there's another vaunting
The bright and beauteous sword-hilt that, at last,
Unheard-of luck supplied to him alone
From England's cunningest artificer.
With solemn countenance one tells to one
The order due wherein the meats appear'd
At a great banquet, while another counts
On lifted fingers, and with mien amaz'd
At the vast thought, how many playing boards
Gave proud distinction to some rare assembly.
With first and second fingers slily bent,
One softly laughing gives his neighbour's cheek
A furtive pinch; behind another's back,
One whips the pendent hat from's arm away,
And prides himself upon the lucky stroke.

7

A Deadly Nip

Primo Levi, from *Vizio di Forma* (Turin: Einaudi, 1971), pp. 17–68;
Carlo Porta,* *Olter Desgrazzi de Giovannin Bongee*, from *Le Poesie*
(Milan: Feltrinelli, 1964), pp. 146–54, translated by Peter Forbes

*I am bound to Carlo Porta by an intense and lasting rapport that I cannot
fully account for. Perhaps it is because his characters, such as Giovannin,
Ninetta, Marchion, are Jobs in miniature, good human material that, for other
people's pleasure, is worn down, torn, and finally ripped to shreds. Perhaps it
is because Porta has succeeded, like Belli, in the miraculous enterprise of
constraining, in a strict metre, a fluid dialect, natural and mimetic, which
coincides with the portrait he is delineating. Perhaps it is for his magical
capacity to suggest an atmosphere by subliminal means, by a gesture, a rapid
brushstroke (like that of his lamplighter, who after the deadly nip gazes aloft
and 'pretends to count the beams').*

*I allow myself to quote here, as a mark of renewed homage, a page of my
story 'The Park' from* Vizio di Forma. *The writer Antonio is exploring the
National Park of Characters, a limbo in which the celebrated characters of all
books live on.*

A little further on, the street widened to form a little cobbled piazza,
surrounded by bleak sooty buildings; at the gates they caught a glimpse
of steep stairs, damp and gloomy, and little courtyards full of rubbish,
surrounded by rusty balconies. There was an odour of cabbage boiled
too long, of lye and of mist. Antonio immediately recognized a quarter
of old Milan, or rather, more precisely, the Carrobbio, frozen for ever in
the aspect it must have had two hundred years ago; in the uncertain light

he was just trying to decipher the faded signs of the shops, when, at the entrance to number 808, Giovannino Bongeri himself leaped out, lean, brisk, pale like one who never sees the sun, cheerful, rowdy, and avid for affection like an ill-treated puppy: he was wearing a tight and threadbare suit, with some patches, but punctiliously clean and even ironed. He immediately addressed the two men as if he had known them for a long time, nevertheless calling them 'Most Honourable Sirs': he treated them to a long discourse, in dialect, full of digressions, which Antonio half understood and James not at all; as far as one could make out, he had received some wrong, and he was wounded by it, but not to the point of seriously losing his dignity as a citizen and a craftsman; he was angry about it but not to the point of seriously losing his head. In his speech, which was witty and verbose, one sensed, under the bruises of daily toil, poverty and misfortunes, an intact candour, a good human heart and an age-old hope: Antonio, in a moment's intuition, saw something truly perfect and eternal that lived in the ghosts of this quarter, and that the little and irascible Giovannino, secondhand-dealer's errand-boy, frequently beaten, jeered at and betrayed, son of the little and irascible Milanese Carletto Porta, was more splendid and rich than Solomon in all his glory.

While Giovannino was speaking, Barberina came to his side, as white and pink as a flower, with a lace bonnet, filigree hatpins and eyes a little bit more lively than modesty demanded. Her husband took her under his arm, and they moved off towards La Scala: after a few steps, his wife turned and cast at the two strangers a keen and curious glance.

*   *   *

Let us turn to the Porta. Giovannino Bongeri, 'indefatigable worker', and his young wife Barberina, are in the gods at La Scala; crushed by the throng, they are dazzled by the spectacle of the ballet Prometheus, *but amusements always turn sour for Giovannino: it is his destiny.*

> In fact, after this laugh, amazingly loud,
> and with the ballet in full flight,
> I felt myself floating among the clouds

49

and saw, strolling in the realm of delight,
the saints all wrapped up in their shrouds
with candles lit around their bodies,
when all of a sudden Barberina gave a shriek
so piercing and loud I have never heard the like.

Believe it or not, it was some dreadful type
who'd let his hand stray out of bounds
and given her bare arse a nasty nip.
My blood just leapt. I wheeled around
and let my fiery temper rip,
said to the fireman and the lamplighter:
by Christ, I'd like to know what sort
of wretched booby does a thing like that.

The lamplighter and gang were keeping schtum
but the soldier in an instant went berserk,
threw me a punch and said, 'shut up, chum,
or I'll drop you in the Stalls, by the Turk!'
I who light up whenever there's a rum
do in the offing, like a match catching fire,
replied loud and brash to his cowardly slur:
'You can take that back, you mangy cur!'

'Step outside,' he replied, 'dimwit,
I'm going to give you one, Egyptian mummy.'
'If I step outside,' I says to the twit,
'I'll teach you to speak more plummy.'
Meanwhile the gallery rises in reproach:
Everywhere it's *Silence! Quiet! Shush!*
And he, all the while pushing me about
– What a type – adds his *Shush!* to the shout.

Most distinguished Sir, I was an inch away
from finding myself in next day's paper,

and if it wasn't for my guardian angels along the way
who deflected me away from the impending caper
or, it would be more true to say,
made an inspector topple on me like an arrow,
there'd have been the kind of slaughter
you'd be hearing about for ever after.

Enough: the matter ended there,
at least as far as the fracas and the rumours,
but as for what you might care
to call good will and good humour,
well, the night was lost beyond repair;
the ballet itself might have been a stunner
(Tell Viganò* he needn't spike it)
But Barberina and me, we didn't like it.

With respect, I had some grounds
for being on edge, and as sharp as vinegar:
this pest of a soldier hanging around,
whose mockery ran from alpha to omega
while his eyes raked me from head to ground;
besides, I noticed, glancing in the mirror,
he had his gang of accomplices in tow;
I hope to God Christ never meets him on the way.

I who know precisely my temperament,
how far you can push me before I explode,
seeing in the mirror that this malcontent
was shaping up as if to goad
me still further, to escape more harassment
I signalled to Barberina, made for the stairs . . .
at the right moment, down! down! let's go for it . . .
He who knows prudence should make good use of it.

And now I'd swapped him for the corner of the street,
while regretting the pleasures I'd sacrificed,
you'll no doubt be thinking the rest would be neat,
that things would fall out like rolling a dice;
that after scoffing some tidbits of meat
and quaffing good drink,
poor Giovannin, far from danger,
would be safe in bed, snug in his manger.

My dear Sir, you'd be a real seer
if this were a tale of some other bright spark,
but seeing as it's Bongee we've got here,
pardon me, you're wide of the mark.
Now for the prize: you're going to hear
not about comfort, a bed and a woman,
but prison, cops, handcuffs, cold and anger:
this is my dream of bedroom languor.

Ah, my dear bed! It's true you're too firm
and it's true your bumps don't make for bliss.
But, chez Bongee, this is the first time
you've been empty for a scuffle like this.
Speak, tables, mattresses, bedheads, eiderdown,
pillows, covers, say if in three hundred years
you've seen anything able to kindle
warmer gleams than my bedside candle.

But tell me, dear Sir, that you'll lend an ear
to what's still to come, the rest of my tale;
I'll not abuse your patience, never fear,
I shall tell it all before it goes stale.
So, nipping out of the gallery by the rear,
I found the quickest route, made good speed,
and without meeting any further grief
I and my woman arrived home, safe.

Softly softly, through the door, higher,
quiet on the stairs, not to disturb anyone,
open my fine door calmly, light the fire
with matches and put the light on.
'Barberina, where are you?' I inquire.
I see her there, head on the pillows,
sprawled across the bed, hand on her hind zone,
all the while racked by sniffles and groans.

What is it, Barberina? . . . *It hurts* . . . Where?
Here like this . . . Your bum? You're joking! . . . *It's right
here* . . . It was perhaps . . . ? *Yes, that bear!*
Let me see . . . *I don't want to* . . . It's a husband's right . . .
I'm ashamed . . . Are you mad? . . . *That's nice* . . . There,
don't move . . . *Go gently* . . . Don't fight . . .
Enough: at last with all my mollifications
she gave up her naked body to my inspection.

Heavens, your Honour, if you had been aware
of that scarlet weal, livid and contused
which covered a quarter of her derrière,
with two black moustaches. At least her poor abused
skin there, thank heaven, was taut and spare
like a well-tuned drumskin;
because if it had been a little more slack
I don't believe we'd have ever got it back.

It seemed to me, meanwhile, that the two black 'taches
Were a little too symmetrical;
I rub and I rub and where I scratch
I can see that the black material
Comes off on my hands, cross-hatch-
ing my paws with grey greasy stuff.
I sniff and a bad smell comes to tax
my nose – table oil and candle wax.

Ah rascal! Rogue of a lamplighter!
Here is the trial, the evidence of the crime!
You can hoof around, play the foreigner,
counting beams to while away the time . . .
But if I catch you on my patch, you blighter,
you won't have to go to Rome to repent.
I have judged you, dirty layabout,
and when I come to judge you, you'd better watch out!

8

Dystopia

Jonathan Swift, *Gulliver's Travels*
(Harmondsworth: Penguin, 1985), pp. 256–60, 308–11

There is a strange fate common to many cardinal books: they do not fall into oblivion but they come to be expurgated to a greater or lesser degree, and are transmitted to posterity as books for children. Sometimes the process is acceptable, because a good book, being universal, is also a book for children; it is readable by all, even if different readers might discover in it different meanings. At other times the tampering is a falsification, or at best an exorcism: the devil is expunged from the book and nothing remains but a shell.

Such would be the case with Gulliver's Travels, *if one read only the familiar voyages to Lilliput and Brobdingnag: inspired relativistic and geometrical fairy tales, non-toxic, with a spiced aftertaste that can only be grasped by shrewd readers. But the discourse on the Immortals of Luggnagg, and the sojourn in the land of horses, will not be exorcised so easily.*

Gulliver lands at Luggnagg, learns that the Struldbruggs, that is to say, the Immortals, live here: he envies their destiny, and expounds to the notables of Luggnagg the exciting way of life he would adopt if fate had caused him to be born immortal. One of the notables replies:

That the system of living contrived by me was unreasonable and unjust, because it supposed a perpetuity of youth, health, and vigour, which no man could be so foolish to hope, however extravagant he might be in his wishes. That the question therefore was not whether a man would choose to be always in the prime of youth, attended with prosperity and health, but how he would pass a perpetual life under all the usual disadvantages which old age brings along with it. For although few men will avow their desires of being immortal upon such hard conditions, yet in the two kingdoms before-mentioned of Balnibarbi and Japan, he observed that every man desired to put off death for some time longer, let it approach ever so late, and he rarely heard of any man who died willingly, except he were incited by the extremity of grief or torture. And he appealed to me whether in those countries I had travelled, as well as my own, I had not observed the same general disposition.

After this preface he gave me a particular account of the Struldbruggs among them. He said they commonly acted like mortals, till about thirty years old, after which by degrees they grew melancholy and dejected, increasing in both till they came to fourscore. This he learned from their own confession; for otherwise there not being above two or three of that species born in an age, they were too few to form a general observation by. When they came to fourscore years, which is reckoned the extremity of living in this country, they had not only all the follies and infirmities of other old men, but many more which arose from the dreadful prospect of never dying. They were not only opinionative, peevish, covetous, morose, vain, talkative, but uncapable of friendship, and dead to all natural affection, which never descended below their grandchildren. Envy and impotent desires are their prevailing passions. But those objects against which their envy seems principally directed, are the vices of the younger sort, and the deaths of the old. By reflecting on the former, they find themselves cut off from all possibility of pleasure; and whenever they see a funeral, they lament and repine that others are gone to an harbour of rest, to which they themselves never can hope to arrive. They have no remembrance of anything but what they learned and observed in their youth and middle age, and even that is very imperfect. And for the truth or particulars of any fact, it is safer to depend on common traditions than upon their best recollections. The least miserable among them appear to be those who turn to dotage, and entirely lose their memories; these meet with more pity and assistance, because they want many bad qualities which abound in others.

If a Struldbrugg happen to marry one of his own kind, the marriage is dissolved of course by the courtesy of the kingdom, as soon as the younger of the two comes to be fourscore. For the law thinks it a reasonable indulgence, that those who are condemned without any fault of their own to a perpetual continuance in the world, should not have their misery doubled by the load of a wife.

As soon as they have completed the term of eighty years, they are looked on as dead in law; their heirs immediately succeed to their estates, only a small pittance is reserved for their support, and the poor ones are maintained at the public charge. After that period they are held incapable of any employment of trust or profit, they cannot purchase lands or take leases, neither are they allowed to be witnesses in any cause, either civil or criminal, not even for the decision of meres and bounds.

At ninety they lose their teeth and hair, they have at that age no distinction of taste, but eat and drink whatever they can get, without relish or appetite. The diseases they were subject to, still continue without increasing or diminishing. In talking they forget the common appellation of things, and the names of persons, even of those who are their nearest friends and relations. For the same reason they never can amuse themselves with reading, because their memory will not serve to carry them from the beginning of a sentence to the end; and by this defect they are deprived of the only entertainment whereof they might otherwise be capable.

The language of this country being always upon the flux, the Struldbruggs of one age do not understand those of another, neither are they able after two hundred years to hold any conversation (farther than by a few general words) with their neighbours the mortals, and thus they lie under the disadvantage of living like foreigners in their own country.

This was the account given me of the Struldbruggs, as near as I can remember. I afterwards saw five or six of different ages, the youngest not above two hundred years old, who were brought to me at several times by some of my friends; but although they were told that I was a great traveller, and had seen all the world, they had not the least curiosity to ask me a question; only desired I would give them *slumskudask*, or a token of remembrance, which is a modest way of begging, to avoid the law that strictly forbids it, because they are provided for by the public, although indeed with a very scanty allowance.

They are despised and hated by all sorts of people; when one of them is born, it is reckoned ominous, and their birth is recorded very particularly; so that you may know their age by consulting the registry, which however hath not been kept above a thousand years past, or at least hath been destroyed by time or public disturbances. But the usual way of computing how old they are, is, by asking them what kings or great persons they can remember, and then consulting history, for infallibly the last Prince in their mind did not begin his reign after they were fourscore years old.

They were the most mortifying sight I ever beheld, and the women more horrible than the men. Besides the usual deformities in extreme old age, they acquired an additional ghastliness in proportion to their number of years, which is not to be described, and among half a dozen I soon distinguished which was the eldest, although there were not above a century or two between them.

The reader will easily believe, that from what I had heard and seen, my keen appetite for perpetuity of life was much abated. I grew heartily ashamed of the pleasing visions I had formed, and thought no tyrant could invent a death into which I would not run with pleasure from such a life. The King heard of all that had passed between me and my friends upon this occasion, and rallied me very pleasantly, wishing I would send a couple of Struldbruggs to my own country, to arm our people against the fear of death; but this it seems is forbidden by the fundamental laws of the kingdom, or else I should have been well content with the trouble and expense of transporting them.

The country of the Houyhnhnms is a particular example of the myth of the World Turned Upside Down. The Houyhnhnms are horses: that is what they call themselves in their language, nasal and guttural, that 'resembles very much High Dutch or German, but is more graceful and significant. The Emperor Charles 5th made almost the same observation when he said, that if he were to speak to his horse, it should be in High Dutch'. They are wise, good-natured and noble; they don't know theft, violence, or lying: on the contrary these terms are not in their language, and to refer to them requires circumlocutions. Their servants are the Yahoos: they are lazy, dirty, deceitful,

*vindictive, and they resemble humans in form, so that the noble horses are
astonished that Gulliver, to all appearances a Yahoo, should be a relatively
civilized creature. Overcoming his diffidence, one of the elder horses describes
the habits of their servants:*

[. . .] in some fields of his country there are certain *shining stones* of
several colours, whereof the Yahoos are violently fond, and when part of
these *stones* are fixed in the earth, as it sometimes happeneth, they will
dig with their claws for whole days to get them out, and carry them away,
and hide them by heaps in their kennels; but still looking round with
great caution, for fear their comrades should find out their treasure. My
master said, he could never discover the reason of this unnatural appetite,
or how these *stones* could be of any use to a Yahoo; but now he believed
it might proceed from the same principle of *avarice* which I had ascribed
to mankind; that he had once, by way of experiment, privately removed
a heap of these *stones* from the place where one of his Yahoos had buried
it: whereupon, the sordid animal, missing his treasure, by his loud
lamenting brought the whole herd to the place, there miserably howled,
then fell to biting and tearing the rest, began to pine away, would neither
eat, nor sleep, nor work, till he ordered a servant privately to convey the
stones into the same hole, and hide them as before; which when his
Yahoo had found, he presently recovered his spirits and good humour,
but took care to remove them to a better hiding-place, and hath ever
since been a very serviceable brute.

My master farther assured me, which I also observed myself, That in
the fields where these *shining stones* abound, the fiercest and most
frequent battles are fought, occasioned by perpetual inroads of the neighbouring Yahoos.

He said, it was common, when two Yahoos discovered such a *stone* in
a field, and were contending which of them should be the proprietor, a
third would take the advantage, and carry it away from them both; which
my master would needs contend to have some resemblance with our
suits at law; wherein I thought it for our credit not to undeceive him;
since the decision he mentioned was much more equitable than many
decrees among us: because the plaintiff and defendant there lost nothing

beside the *stone* they contended for, whereas our *courts of equity* would never have dismissed the cause while either of them had anything left.

My master, continuing his discourse, said, There was nothing that rendered the Yahoos more odious, than their undistinguished appetite to devour everything that came in their way, whether herbs, roots, berries, the corrupted flesh of animals, or all mingled together: and it was peculiar in their temper, that they were fonder of what they could get by rapine or stealth at a greater distance, than much better food provided for them at home. If their prey held out, they would eat till they were ready to burst, after which Nature had pointed out to them a certain *root* that gave them a general evacuation.

There was also another kind of *root* very *juicy*, but something rare and difficult to be found, which the Yahoos sought for with much eagerness, and would suck it with great delight; and it produced in them the same effects that wine hath upon us. It would make them sometimes hug, and sometimes tear one another; they would howl and grin, and chatter, and reel, and tumble, and then fall asleep in the mud.

I did indeed observe, that the Yahoos were the only animals in this country subject to any diseases; which, however, were much fewer than horses have among us, and contracted not by any ill-treatment they meet with, but by the nastiness and greediness of that sordid brute. Neither has their language any more than a general appellation for those maladies, which is borrowed from the name of the beast, and called *hnea-Yahoo*, or the *Yahoo's-evil*, and the cure prescribed is a mixture of *their own dung* and *urine* forcibly put down the Yahoo's throat. This I have since often known to have been taken with success, and do here freely recommend it to my countrymen, for the public good, as an admirable specific against all diseases produced by repletion.

As to learning, government, arts, manufactures, and the like, my master confessed he could find little or no resemblance between the Yahoos of that country and those in ours. For, he only meant to observe what parity there was in our natures. He had heard indeed some curious Houyhnhnms observe, that in most herds there was a sort of ruling Yahoo (as among us there is generally some leading or principal stag in a park), who was always more *deformed* in body, and *mischievous in disposition*, than any of the rest. That this *leader* had usually a favourite as *like himself* as he could get, whose employment was to *lick his master's feet and posteriors, and drive the female Yahoos to his kennel*; for which he was now and then rewarded with a piece of ass's flesh. This *favourite* is hated by the whole herd, and therefore to protect himself, keeps always *near the person of his leader*. He usually continues in office till a worse can be found; but the very moment he is discarded, his successor, at the head of all the Yahoos in that district, young and old, male and female, come in a body, and discharge their excrements upon him from head to foot. But how far this might be applicable to our *Courts* and *favourites*, and *Ministers of State*, my master said I could best determine.

I durst make no return to this malicious insinuation, which debased human understanding below the sagacity of a common *hound*, who hath judgement enough to distinguish and follow the cry of the *ablest dog in the pack*, without being ever mistaken.

My master told me, there were some qualities remarkable in the Yahoos, which he had not observed me to mention, or at least very slightly, in the accounts I had given him of human kind; he said, those animals, like other brutes, had their females in common; but in this they differed, that the she-Yahoo would admit the male while she was pregnant, and that the he's would quarrel and fight with the females as fiercely as with each other. Both which practices were such degrees of infamous brutality, that no other sensitive creature ever arrived at.

Another thing he wondered at in the Yahoos, was their strange disposition to nastiness and dirt, whereas there appears to be a natural love of cleanliness in all other animals. As to the two former accusations, I was glad to let them pass without any reply, because I had not a word to offer upon them in defence of my species, which otherwise I certainly had done from my own inclinations. But I could have easily vindicated human kind from the imputation of singularity upon the last article, if there had been any *swine* in that country (as unluckily for me there were not), which although it may be a *sweeter quadruped* than a Yahoo, cannot, I humbly conceive, in justice pretend to more cleanliness; and so his Honour himself must have owned, if he had seen their filthy way of feeding, and their custom of wallowing and sleeping in the mud.

My master likewise mentioned another quality which his servants had discovered in several Yahoos, and to him was wholly unaccountable. He said, a fancy would sometimes take a Yahoo to retire into a corner, to lie down and howl, and groan, and spurn away all that came near him, although he were young and fat, and wanted neither food nor water; nor did the servants imagine what could possibly ail him. And the only remedy they found was to set him to hard work, after which he would infallibly come to himself. To this I was silent out of partiality to my own kind; yet here I could plainly discover the true seeds of *spleen*, which only seizeth on the *lazy*, the *luxurious*, and the *rich*; who, if they were forced to undergo the *same regimen*, I would undertake for the cure.

9
A Testing Time

Joseph Conrad, *Youth*, from *Youth, and The End of the Tether*
(Harmondsworth: Penguin, 1975), pp. 30–39

Conrad, man of dry land, became a man of the sea through profound vocation;
a Polish aristocrat, he became English; a captain in the Merchant Marine, he
made himself a writer. It is a good example of how a man can remake himself.
He never chose the easy way, he always rowed against the current, and his
writing is like the man. He is never off duty, perhaps helped in this by the fact
of writing in a language not his own.

The long short story 'Youth' is for the most part autobiographical, but it is
not Conrad who speaks in the first person. His alter ego, Marlow, appears here
for the first time, and the narration is attributed to him. The reasons for this
split personality are profound; I believe that the main one is Conrad's modesty:
Marlow, although so like him, exempts him from the anguish of having to
say 'I'.

Marlow/Conrad is twenty years old, the third officer on the Judea *and*
brim-full of enthusiasm, although the voyage will have little to excite enthusi-
asm. The task to hand concerns a wretched cargo, 600 tons of coal to be
discharged at Bangkok, but over the Judea *hangs a malign destiny; after a*
series of incidents that have delayed the departure, in the Malay Sea the cargo
spontaneously catches fire, it spreads throughout the decrepit sailing boat, and
the crew are forced to abandon ship.

'The old man warned us in his gentle and inflexible way that it was part
of our duty to save for the underwriters as much as we could of the ship's
gear. Accordingly we went to work aft, while she blazed forward to give

us plenty of light. We lugged out a lot of rubbish. What didn't we save? An old barometer fixed with an absurd quantity of screws nearly cost me my life: a sudden rush of smoke came upon me, and I just got away in time. There were various stores, bolts of canvas, coils of rope; the poop looked like a marine bazaar, and the boats were lumbered to the gun-wales. One would have thought the old man wanted to take as much as he could of his first command with him. He was very, very quiet, but off his balance evidently. Would you believe it? He wanted to take a length of old stream-cable and a kedge-anchor with him in the long-boat. We said, "Ay, ay, sir," deferentially, and on the quiet let the things slip overboard. The heavy medicine-chest went that way, two bags of green coffee, tins of paint – fancy, paint! – a whole lot of things. Then I was ordered with two hands into the boats to make a stowage and get them ready against the time it would be proper for us to leave the ship.

'We put everything straight, stepped the long-boat's mast for our skipper, who was to take charge of her, and I was not sorry to sit down for a moment. My face felt raw, every limb ached as if broken, I was aware of all my ribs, and would have sworn to a twist in the backbone. The boats, fast astern, lay in a deep shadow, and all around I could see the circle of the sea lighted by the fire. A gigantic flame arose forward straight and clear. It flared fierce, with noises like the whirr of wings, with rumbles as of thunder. There were cracks, detonations, and from the cone of flame the sparks flew upwards, as man is born to trouble, to leaky ships, and to ships that burn.

'What bothered me was that the ship, lying broadside to the swell and to such wind as there was – a mere breath – the boats would not keep astern where they were safe, but persisted, in a pig-headed way boats have, in getting under the counter and then swinging alongside. They were knocking about dangerously and coming near the flame, while the ship rolled on them, and, of course, there was always the danger of the masts going over the side at any moment. I and my two boat-keepers kept them off as best we could, with oars and boat-hooks; but to be constantly at it became exasperating, since there was no reason why we should not leave at once. We could not see those on board, nor could we imagine what caused the delay. The boat-keepers were swearing feebly, and I had not only my share of the work but also had to keep at it two men who showed a constant inclination to lay themselves down and let things slide.

'At last I hailed, "On deck there," and someone looked over. "We're ready here," I said. The head disappeared, and very soon popped up again. "The captain says, All right, sir, and to keep the boats well clear of the ship."

'Half an hour passed. Suddenly there was a frightful racket, rattle, clanking of chain, hiss of water, and millions of sparks flew up into the shivering column of smoke that stood leaning slightly above the ship. The cat-heads had burned away, and the two red-hot anchors had gone to the bottom, tearing out after them two hundred fathom of red-hot chain. The ship trembled, the mass of flame swayed as if ready to collapse, and the fore top-gallant-mast fell. It darted down like an arrow of fire, shot under, and instantly leaping up within an oar's-length of the boats, floated quietly, very black on the luminous sea. I hailed the deck again. After some time a man in an unexpectedly cheerful but also muffled tone, as though he had been trying to speak with his mouth shut, informed me, "Coming directly, sir," and vanished. For a long time I heard nothing but the whirr and roar of the fire. There were also whistling sounds. The boats jumped, tugged at the painters, ran at each other playfully, knocked their sides together, or, do what we would, swung in a bunch against the ship's side. I couldn't stand it any longer, and swarming up a rope, clambered aboard over the stern.

'It was as bright as day. Coming up like this, the sheet of fire facing me was a terrifying sight, and the heat seemed hardly bearable at first. On a settee cushion dragged out of the cabin Captain Beard, his legs drawn up and one arm under his head, slept with the light playing on him. Do you know what the rest were busy about? They were sitting on deck right aft, round an open case, eating bread and cheese and drinking bottled stout.

'On the background of flames twisting in fierce tongues above their heads they seemed at home like salamanders, and looked like a band of desperate pirates. The fire sparkled in the whites of their eyes, gleamed on patches of white skin seen through the torn shirts. Each had the marks

65

as of a battle about him – bandaged heads, tied-up arms, a strip of dirty rag round a knee – and each man had a bottle between his legs and a chunk of cheese in his hand. Mahon got up. With his handsome and disreputable head, his hooked profile, his long white beard, and with an uncorked bottle in his hand, he resembled one of those reckless sea-robbers of old making merry amidst violence and disaster. "The last meal on board," he explained solemnly. "We had nothing to eat all day, and it was no use leaving all this." He flourished the bottle and indicated the sleeping skipper. "He said he couldn't swallow anything, so I got him to lie down," he went on; and as I stared, "I don't know whether you are aware, young fellow, the man had no sleep to speak of for days – and there will be dam' little sleep in the boats." "There will be no boats by-and-by if you fool about much longer," I said, indignantly. I walked up to the skipper and shook him by the shoulder. At last he opened his eyes, but did not move. "Time to leave her, sir," I said quietly.

'He got up painfully, looked at the flames, at the sea sparkling round the ship, and black, black as ink farther away; he looked at the stars shining dim through a thin veil of smoke in a sky black, black as Erebus.

' "Youngest first," he said.

'And the ordinary seaman, wiping his mouth with the back of his hand, got up, clambered over the taffrail, and vanished. Others followed. One, on the point of going over, stopped short to drain his bottle, and with a great swing of his arm flung it at the fire. "Take this!" he cried.

'The skipper lingered disconsolately, and we left him to commune for a while with his first command. Then I went up again and brought him away at last. It was time. The ironwork on the poop was hot to the touch.

'Then the painter of the long-boat was cut, and the three boats, tied together, drifted clear of the ship. It was just sixteen hours after the explosion when we abandoned her. Mahon had charge of the second boat, and I had the smallest – the 14-foot thing. The long-boat would have taken the lot of us; but the skipper said we must save as much property as we could – for the underwriters – and so I got my first command. I had two men with me, a bag of biscuits, a few tins of meat, and a beaker of water. I was ordered to keep close to the long-boat, that in case of bad weather we might be taken into her.

'And do you know what I thought? I thought I would part company as soon as I could. I wanted to have my first command all to myself. I wasn't going to sail in a squadron if there were a chance of independent cruising. I would make land by myself. I would beat the other boats. Youth! All youth! The silly, charming, beautiful youth.

'But we did not make a start at once. We must see the last of the ship. And so the boats drifted about that night, heaving and setting on the swell. The men dozed, waked, sighted, groaned. I looked at the burning ship.

'Between the darkness of earth and heaven she was burning fiercely upon a disc of purple sea shot by the blood-red play of gleams; upon a disc of water glittering and sinister. A high, clear flame, an immense and lonely flame, ascended from the ocean, and from its summit the black smoke poured continuously at the sky. She burned furiously; mournful and imposing like a funeral pile kindled in the night, surrounded by the sea, watched over by the stars. A magnificent death had come like a grace, like a gift, like a reward to that old ship at the end of her laborious days. The surrender of her weary ghost to the keeping of stars and sea was stirring like the sight of a glorious triumph. The masts fell just before daybreak, and for a moment there was a burst and turmoil of sparks that seemed to fill with flying fire the night patient and watchful, the vast night lying silent upon the sea. At daylight she was only a charred shell, floating still under a cloud of smoke and bearing a glowing mass of coal within.

'Then the oars were got out, and the boats forming in a line moved round her remains as if in procession – the long-boat leading. As we pulled across her stern a slim dart of fire shot out viciously at us, and suddenly she went down, head first, in a great hiss of steam. The unconsumed stern was the last to sink; but the paint had gone, had cracked, had peeled off, and there were no letters, there was no word, no stubborn device that was like her soul, to flash at the rising sun her creed and her name.

'We made our way north. A breeze sprang up, and about noon all the boats came together for the last time. I had no mast or sail in mine, but I made a mast out of a spare oar and hoisted a boat-awning for a sail, with a boat-hook for a yard. She was certainly over-masted, but I had the satisfaction of knowing that with the wind aft I could beat the other two. I had to wait for them. Then we all had a look at the captain's chart, and, after a sociable meal of hard bread and water, got our last instructions. These were simple: steer north, and keep together as much as possible. "Be careful with that jury-rig, Marlow," said the captain; and Mahon, as I sailed proudly past his boat, wrinkled his curved nose and hailed, "You will sail that ship of yours under water, if you don't look out, young fellow." He was a malicious old man – and may the deep sea where he sleeps now rock him gently, rock him tenderly to the end of time!

'Before sunset a thick rain-squall passed over the two boats, which were far astern, and that was the last I saw of them for a time. Next day I sat steering my cockle-shell – my first command – with nothing but water and sky around me. I did sight in the afternoon the upper sails of a ship far away, but said nothing, and my men did not notice her. You see I was afraid she might be homeward bound, and I had no mind to turn back from the portals of the East. I was steering for Java – another blessed name – like Bangkok, you know. I steered many days.

'I need not tell you what it is to be knocking about in an open boat. I remember nights and days of calm, when we pulled, we pulled, and the boat seemed to stand still, as if bewitched within the circle of the sea horizon. I remember the heat, the deluge of rain-squalls that kept us baling for dear life (but filled our water-cask), and I remember sixteen hours on end with a mouth dry as a cinder and a steering-oar over the stern to keep my first command head on to a breaking sea. I did not know how good a man I was till then. I remember the drawn faces, the dejected figures of my two men, and I remember my youth and the feeling that will never come back any more – the feeling that I could last for ever, outlast the sea, the earth, and all men; the deceitful feeling that lures us on to joys, to perils, to love, to vain effort – to death; the triumphant conviction of strength, the heat of life in the handful of dust, the glow in the heart that with every year grows dim, grows cold, grows small, and expires – and expires, too soon, too soon – before life itself.

'And this is how I see the East. I have seen its secret places and have looked into its very soul; but now I see it always from a small boat, a high outline of mountains, blue and afar in the morning; like faint mist at noon; a jagged wall of purple at sunset. I have the feel of the oar in my hand, the vision of a scorching blue sea in my eyes. And I see a bay, a wide bay, smooth as glass and polished like ice, shimmering in the dark. A red light burns far off upon the gloom of the land, and the night is soft and warm. We drag at the oars with aching arms, and suddenly a puff of wind, a puff faint and tepid and laden with strange odours of blossoms, of aromatic wood, comes out of the still night – the first sigh of the East on my face. That I can never forget. It was impalpable and enslaving, like a charm, like a whispered promise of mysterious delight.

'We had been pulling this finishing spell for eleven hours. Two pulled, and he whose turn it was to rest sat at the tiller. We had made out the red light in that bay and steered for it, guessing it must mark some small coasting port. We passed two vessels, outlandish and high-sterned, sleeping at anchor, and, approaching the light, now very dim, ran the boat's nose against the end of a jutting wharf. We were blind with fatigue. My men dropped the oars and fell off the thwarts as if dead. I made fast to a pile. A current rippled softly. The scented obscurity of the shore was grouped into vast masses, a density of colossal clumps of vegetation, probably – mute and fantastic shapes. And at their foot the semicircle of a bench gleamed faintly, like an illusion. There was not a light, not a stir, not a sound. The mysterious East faced me, perfumed like a flower, silent like death, dark like a grave.

'And I sat weary beyond expression, exulting like a conqueror, sleepless and entranced as if before a profound, a fateful enigma.

'A splashing of oars, a measured dip reverberating on the level of water, intensified by the silence of the shore into loud claps, made me jump up. A boat, a European boat, was coming in. I invoked the name of the dead; I hailed: *Judea* ahoy! A thin shout answered.

'It was the captain. I had beaten the flagship by three hours, and I was glad to hear the old man's voice again, tremulous and tired. "Is it you, Marlow?" "Mind the end of that jetty, sir," I cried.

'He approached cautiously, and brought up with the deep-sea lead-line which he had saved – for the underwriters. I eased my painter and fell alongside. He sat, a broken figure at the stern, wet with dew, his hands clasped in his lap. His men were asleep already. "I had a terrible time of it," he murmured. "Mahon is behind – not very far." We conversed in whispers, in low whispers, as if afraid to wake up the land. Guns, thunder, earthquakes would not have awakened the men just then.

'Looking round as we talked, I saw away at sea a bright light travelling in the night. "There's a steamer passing the bay," I said. She was not passing, she was entering, and she even came close and anchored. "I wish," said the old man, "you would find out whether she is English. Perhaps they could give us a passage somewhere." He seemed nervously anxious. So by dint of punching and kicking I started one of my men into a state of somnambulism, and giving him an oar, took another and pulled towards the lights of the steamer.

'There was a murmur of voices in her, metallic hollow clangs of the engine-room, footsteps on the deck. Her ports shone, round like dilated eyes. Shapes moved about, and there was a shadowy man high up on the bridge. He heard my oars.

'And then, before I could open my lips, the East spoke to me, but it was in a Western voice. A torrent of words was poured into the enigmatical, the fateful silence; outlandish, angry words, mixed with words and even whole sentences of good English, less strange but even more surprising. The voice swore and cursed violently; it riddled the solemn peace of the bay by a volley of abuse. It began by calling me Pig, and from that went crescendo into unmentionable adjectives – in English. The man up there raged aloud in two languages, and with a sincerity in his fury that almost convinced me I had, in some way, sinned against the harmony of the universe. I could hardly see him, but began to think he would work himself into a fit.

'Suddenly he ceased, and I could hear him snorting and blowing like a porpoise. I said –

'"What steamer is this, pray?"

'"Eh? What's this? And who are you?"

'"Castaway crew of an English barque burnt at sea. We came here tonight. I am the second mate. The captain is in the long-boat, and wishes to know if you would give us a passage somewhere."

'"Oh, my goodness! I say . . . This is the *Celestial* from Singapore on her return trip. I'll arrange with your captain in the morning, . . . and, . . . I say, . . . did you hear me just now?"

' "I should think the whole bay heard you."

' "I thought you were a shore-boat. Now, look here – this infernal lazy scoundrel of a caretaker has gone to sleep again – curse him. The light is out, and I nearly ran foul of the end of this damned jetty. This is the third time he plays me this trick. Now, I ask you, can anybody stand this kind of thing? It's enough to drive a man out of his mind. I'll report him . . . I'll get the Assistant Resident to give him the sack, by . . . ! See – there's no light. It's out, isn't it? I take you to witness the light's out. There should be a light, you know. A red light on the –"

' "There was a light," I said, mildly.

' "But it's out, man! What's the use of talking like this? You can see for yourself it's out – don't you? If you had to take a valuable steamer along this Godforsaken coast you would want a light, too. I'll kick him from end to end of his miserable wharf. You'll see if I don't. I will –"

' "So I may tell my captain you'll take us?" I broke in.

' "Yes, I'll take you. Good night," he said, brusquely.

'I pulled back, made fast again to the jetty, and then went to sleep at last. I had faced the silence of the East. I had heard some of its language. But when I opened my eyes again the silence was as complete as though it had never been broken. I was lying in a flood of light, and the sky had never looked so far, so high, before. I opened my eyes and lay without moving.

'And then I saw the men of the East – they were looking at me. The whole length of the jetty was full of people. I saw brown, bronze, yellow faces, the black eyes, the glitter, the colour of an Eastern crowd. And all these beings stared without a murmur, without a sigh, without a move-ment. They stared down at the boats, at the sleeping men who at night had come to them from the sea. Nothing moved. The fronds of palms stood still against the sky. Not a branch stirred along the shore, and the brown roofs of hidden houses peeped through the green foliage, through the big leaves that hung shining and still like leaves forged of heavy metal. This was the East of the ancient navigators, so old, so mysterious, resplendent and sombre, living and unchanged, full of danger and

71

promise. And these were the men. I sat up suddenly. A wave of movement passed through the crowd from end to end, passed along the heads, swayed the bodies, ran along the jetty like a ripple on the water, like a breath of wind on a field – and all was still again. I see it now – the wide sweep of the bay, the glittering sands, the wealth of green infinite and varied, the sea blue like the sea of a dream, the crowd of attentive faces, the blaze of vivid colour – the water reflecting it all, the curve of the shore, the jetty, the high-sterned outlandish craft floating still, and the three boats with the tired men from the West sleeping, unconscious of the land and the people and of the violence of sunshine. They slept thrown across the thwarts, curled on bottom-boards, in the careless attitudes of death. The head of the old skipper, leaning back in the stern of the long-boat, had fallen on his breast, and he looked as though he would never wake. Farther out old Mahon's face was upturned to the sky, with the long white beard spread out on his breast, as though he had been shot where he sat at the tiller; and a man, all in a heap in the bows of the boat, slept with both arms embracing the stem-head and with his cheek laid on the gunwale. The East looked at them without a sound.

'I have known its fascination since; I have seen the mysterious shores, the still water, the lands of brown nations, where a stealthy Nemesis lies in wait, pursues, overtakes so many of the conquering race, who are proud of their wisdom, of their knowledge, of their strength. But for me all the East is contained in that vision of my youth. It is all in that moment when I opened my young eyes on it. I came upon it from a tussle with the sea – and I was young – and I saw it looking at me. And this is all that is left of it! Only a moment; a moment of strength, of romance, of glamour – of youth! . . . A flick of sunshine upon a strange shore, the time to remember, the time for a sigh, and – good-bye! – Night – Good-bye . . . !'

He drank.

'Ah! The good old time – the good old time. Youth and the sea. Glamour and the sea! The good, strong sea, the salt, bitter sea, that could whisper to you and roar at you and knock your breath out of you.'

He drank again.

'By all that's wonderful it is the sea, I believe, the sea itself – or is it youth alone? Who can tell? But you here – you all had something out of life: money, love – whatever one gets on shore – and, tell me, wasn't that the best time, that time when we were young at sea; young and had nothing, on the sea that gives nothing, except hard knocks – and sometimes a chance to feel your strength – that only – what you all regret?'

And we all nodded at him: the man of finance, the man of accounts, the man of law, we all nodded at him over the polished table that like a still sheet of brown water reflected our faces, lined, wrinkled; our faces marked by toil, by deceptions, by success, by love; our weary eyes looking still, looking always, looking anxiously for something out of life, that while it is expected is already gone – has passed unseen, in a sigh, in a flash – together with the youth, with the strength, with the romance of illusions.

10

The Words of the Father

Ludwig Gattermann,* 'On the Prevention of Accidents',
Laboratory Methods of Organic Chemistry, 24th edition,
translated by W. McCartney (London: Macmillan, 1937), pp. 88–9

*The inclusion in my favourite reading of these three pages of my old textbook
of organic chemistry is not intended as a provocation. In thirty years in the
profession I have consulted them hundreds of times; I have learnt them almost
by heart, I have never found them at fault, and no doubt they have discreetly
kept me, my colleagues, and the tasks entrusted to us, well clear of trouble. But
in including them here I am not simply making an act of gratitude and homage.
In them, something shines through that is more noble than straightforward
technical information: it is the authority of one who teaches things because
he knows them, and knows them through having lived them; a sober but firm
call to responsibility that I first heard at the age of twenty-two, after sixteen
years of study and innumerable books read. The words of the father, then, that
awake you from childhood, and which declare you to be an adult* sub
conditione.

ON THE PREVENTION OF ACCIDENTS

*Whoever sets about preparative work carelessly and thoughtlessly may
easily come to harm. But even the careful are not secure against all danger.
The serious accidents which, alas, again and again occur in chemical
laboratories make it imperative that every worker in the laboratory should
fully and seriously consider his duty towards his fellows.*

It is most important to protect the eyes. Strong *goggles* with stout glass must be worn in all *vacuum* and *pressure* work, and hence when distilling in a vacuum, evacuating a new desiccator for the first time, or working with sealed tubes, pressure bottles, or autoclaves. Goggles must also be worn when carrying out *fusions with alkali* and during all operations in which *caustic* or *inflammable* substances may spurt, and therefore, in particular, during all work with *metallic potassium* and *sodium*.

Many a serious accident has occurred in laboratories as a result of working with metallic sodium. When handling it, therefore, every precaution must be taken, and no residues should be thrown into sinks or waste buckets. It should never be allowed to lie exposed, but should be immediately returned to the stock bottle or destroyed with 15 to 20 times its weight of alcohol. The use of the boiling water bath or of the steam bath is to be avoided when carrying out a reaction with metallic sodium or potassium. An oil or sand bath should always be used, even when distilling dried ether from sodium wire. Students should pay special attention to the soundness of apparatus when working with sodium and potassium, and always bear in mind the consequences which may, in certain circumstances, result from the use of a leaky condenser or of a cracked flask. **Protective goggles should invariably be worn.**

Work with *explosive substances* should *never* be done *without wearing goggles*, and the behaviour in the flame of unknown substances should always first be tested with small amounts on a metallic spatula after the preparation itself has been put in a place of safety.

In order to guard the eyes against unforseeable explosions, which can never be absolutely excluded, every worker in the laboratory should wear plain glasses, while not dispensing with goggles in the cases mentioned.

Care must invariably be taken when working with *ether* and other *volatile, readily inflammable liquids* that *no flame is burning in the neighbourhood*. If a *fire* occurs, *everything which may ignite must immediately be removed*. The fire should then be extinguished with moist *towels* or by *pouring on carbon tetrachloride*, but not water. The best extinguisher is a small portable CO_2 cylinder, which should be kept in every

75

laboratory.[1] A larger fire may be tackled by pouring on sand, but here also a large carbon dioxide cylinder is usually preferable.

Parts *injured with acids or caustic alkalis* should first be washed thoroughly with *water* and then with *bicarbonate solution* or *dilute acetic acid* respectively. *Slight burns* should be washed with *alcohol* and then covered with *linseed oil* or an *ointment*.

Cotton wool, bandages, and *plaster* must always be at hand. When *serious accidents* occur the nearest *doctor* should at once be called.

When a *caustic* or irritant *organic* substance attacks the skin, washing with water is usually without effect. Immediate removal by washing with *copious amounts* of a suitable solvent such as alcohol or benzene is the procedure indicated. It must be borne in mind that the organic solvent itself facilitates the penetration of the harmful substance into the skin and therefore the formation of concentrated solutions on the skin must be avoided.

Especial care is required when working with the following much used substances: *hydrocyanic acid, phosgene, dimethyl sulphate*, the lower *acid chlorides, chlorine, bromine, nitric oxide* and *nitrogen peroxide, carbon monoxide, sodium*, and *potassium*. Large scale operations with these should be carried out in a special room; in any case always in a *good fume chamber*.

Undiluted halogen compounds of the aliphatic series, such as *ethyl bromide, chloroform, bromoform*, and the like, should not be brought into contact with *metallic sodium* or *potassium*; thus they must not be dried with these metals since very violent explosions may occur as a result of detonation (Staudinger).

---

[1] These small cylinders are very useful, but it is necessary to hold them wrapped in felt or other thick cloth; otherwise, when they are used to extinguish an outbreak of fire, the rapid expansion of the gas causes a cooling so intense that it is impossible to hold it in the hands. [Note by Primo Levi.]

11

Better to Write of Laughter Than Tears

François Rabelais, *Gargantua and Pantagruel*, translated by
Burton Raffel (New York: W. W. Norton, 1990), Chapters 6, 21, 32

Born of the cultivated leisure of François Rabelais, monk, doctor, philologist, naturalist, humanist and traveller, Gargantua and Pantagruel *runs riot through every register for twenty years and a thousand pages, half robust popular comic epic, half packed with the moral energy of a great Renaissance intellectual.*

We find in it inspired scurrility, ribald or stupid, rubbing shoulders with quotations, authentic or cheekily fabricated, from Latin, Greek, Arabic; Aristotelian logic-chopping which releases a thunderous laugh, or sophistry vouched for by the honesty of a man pure of heart.

The giants of his dynasty are mounds of flesh, grotesque eaters and drinkers, elephantine carnival buffoons, and at the same time, paradoxically, they are enlightened princes and nimble philosophers; you cannot expect from Rabelais the geometrical conscientiousness and verisimilitude of Swift.

His world and his narrative style are incoherent, capricious, multicoloured, full of surprises; and this is precisely why the world of Rabelais is beautiful and full of joy, not for tomorrow but for today, since to everyone are disclosed the renowned joys of virtue and knowledge, but also the gluttonous joys, equally a divine gift, of vertiginously laden tables, of 'theological' drinking bouts, tireless debaucheries. To love human beings means to love them as they are, body and soul, warts and all. In this entire work it would be hard to find a single melancholy page, and yet Rabelais knew human misery well enough; he keeps quiet about it because, a good doctor even when he is writing, he doesn't accept it, he wants to cure it:

It is better to write of laughter than tears
For to laugh is the right of man.

CHAPTER SIX: HOW GARGANTUA WAS BORN IN AN EXTREMELY ODD WAY

While they were chattering away on the subject of drinking, Gargamelle began to feel sick in her lower parts. So Grandgousier rose from his seat on the grass and courteously tried to cheer her up, expecting that her labor had begun. He told her that she was lying on good grass under willow trees and that, before very long, there'd be someone new lying next to her. She ought to be encouraged by the imminent arrival of her little baby. It was certainly true that the pain would make her feel bad, but it would all be over very soon, and the happiness that always followed a birth would completely wipe away all the discomfort. Nothing would be left but a memory.

'I'll prove it to you,' he said. 'God – our Savior Himself – declares in the Gospel according to Saint John, chapter sixteen, "A woman in labor is sad, yes, but once she has her child she remembers nothing of all her pain."'

'Ha!' she said. 'It's easy enough for you to talk – you and all other men. By God, I'll do everything I can, since it's what you want. But I wish to God you'd cut it off!'

'What?' said Grandgousier.

'Oh,' she said, 'you're a fine one, you are! You know exactly what I mean.'

'My tool?' said he. 'Holy cow! If that's what you want, tell them to bring me a knife.'

'Ha!' she said. 'God forbid. May He forgive me! I didn't really mean it, so don't do it just for me. But I'll have plenty on my hands, today, without God's good help, and it's all because of that tool of yours, which makes you feel so good.'

'Be brave, be brave!' said he. 'Don't worry about anything. I'll just get myself something to drink. Remember: when you've got all your oxen

78

harnessed to the plow, and they're hauling away at it, just let the lead ox do the job. If you start to feel really bad, I won't be far off. Just cup your hands around your mouth and let out a good yell. I'll come right back.'

Not long after, she began to moan and cry and wail. And then midwives came from everywhere, to help her. Groping around underneath, they found some fleshy excrescences, which stank, and they were sure this was the baby. But in fact it was her asshole, which was falling off, because the right intestine (which people call the ass gut) had gone slack, from too much guzzling of tripe, as we have already explained.

Then one of them, a dirty old hag who was said to be a great doctor (she'd come from Buzançais, near Saint-Genou, sixty years earlier), made her a good stiff astringent – so ghastly that every sphincter in her body was locked up tight, snapped so fiercely shut that you couldn't have pulled them open with your teeth, which is pretty awful to think about. You couldn't have done it any better than the devil, listening to Saint Martin's mass and trying to get down on paper all the stupid chattering of a couple of stylish women: the parchment he was using was too short, so he tried to stretch it with his teeth (knocking himself silly in the process, his head banging up against a stone pillar).

This was not useful. It made her womb stretch loose at the top, instead of the bottom, which squeezed out the child, right into a hollow vein, by means of which he ascended through the diaphragm up to her shoulders, where that vein is divided in two. Taking the left-hand route, he finally came out the ear on that same side.

As soon as he was born, instead of crying, like other children, 'Wa! Wa! Wa!,' he shouted in a loud voice, 'Drink! Drink!' – as if inviting the whole world to join him – and he spoke so loud, and so clearly, that they heard him all over Toper and Tipple (where his words were naturally very well understood).

I'm not sure you're going to believe this strange birth. If you don't, I don't give a hoot – but any decent man, any sensible man, always believes what he's told and what he finds written down. Doesn't Solomon say, in Proverbs, 14, *Innocens credit omni verbo*, 'An innocent man believes every word'? And doesn't Saint Paul say, in I Corinthians, 13, *Charitas omnia credit*, 'Charity believes everything'? Why shouldn't you believe me?

79

Because, you say, there's no evidence. And I say to you that, for just this very reason, you must believe with perfect faith. Don't all our Orthodox argue that faith is precisely that: an argument for things which no one can prove?

And is there anything in this against the law? or our faith? or in defiance of reason – or Holy Scripture? Me, I find nothing written in the Holy Bible that says a word against it. And if God had wanted this to happen, can you possibly say it wouldn't have happened? Ha! But don't trouble your spirit with any such useless thoughts, because I tell you that for God nothing is impossible and, if He chose, from now on women would all have their babies coming out of their ears.

Wasn't Bacchus spawned by Jupiter's thigh?

And the giant Rocquetaillade, wasn't he born from his mother's heel?

And Croquemouche, wasn't he born out of his nurse's slippers?

And what about Minerva: wasn't she born out of Jupiter's head – and through his ear?

And Adonis, didn't he appear through the bark of a myrrh tree?

And Castor and Pollux, out from the shell of an egg laid and then hatched by Leda?

But you'd be even more flabbergasted and struck dumb if I took the trouble to lay out for you that whole chapter in Pliny, in which he speaks of strange, unnatural births. Anyway, I'm hardly the kind of established liar that he was. Read the seventh book of his *Natural History*, chapter three, and stop bothering me about this whole business.

CHAPTER TWENTY-ONE: HOW PANURGE FELL IN LOVE WITH A NOBLE PARISIAN LADY

Because of his success in this disputation against the Englishman, Panurge began to develop a certain reputation in Paris. This made his codpiece an even more valuable instrument, and he festooned it with bits of embroidery (in the Roman style). They sang his praises everywhere, even making up a song about him, which was sung by the little boys going to fetch mustard. And he became so welcome wherever women and girls were gathered, such a glamorous figure, that he began to think about tumbling one of the city's greatest ladies.

Indeed, not bothering with the long prologues and protestations poured forth by the usual whining, moody Lent lovers, who have no affection for flesh and blood, he said to her:

'Madame, the whole country would find it useful, and it would be a delight to you, an honor to your descendants and, for me, a necessity, for you to be bred to my blood: believe me, experience will show you how truthfully I speak.'

At these words the lady pushed him more than a hundred yards away, saying:

'You wicked idiot, what makes you think you have the right to talk to me like that? To whom do you think you're speaking? Go! Don't let me ever see you again – indeed, I'm tempted to have your arms and legs chopped off.'

'Now,' he said, 'it would be perfectly agreeable to lose my arms and legs, provided you and I could shake a mattress together, playing the beast with two backs, because' – and here he showed her his long codpiece – 'here's Master John Thomas, who's ready to sing you a merry tune, one you'll relish right through the marrow of your bones. He knows the game very well indeed: he knows just how to find all the little hidden places, all the bumps and itchy spots. When he's been sweeping up, you never need a feather duster.'

To which the lady answered:

'Go, you wicked man, go! If you say one more word to me, I'll call for help and have you beaten to a pulp.'

'Ho!' he said. 'You're not as nasty as you say you are – no, or I've been totally taken in by appearances. The earth will float up into the clouds, and the high heavens drop down into the abyss, and all of nature be turned upside down and inside out, before someone of such beauty, such elegance, possesses so much as a drop of bile or malice. It's truly said that you don't often find

A woman who's truly beautiful
Inclined to make herself dutiful

– but then, they say that about vulgar beauties. Yours is a beauty so excellent, so rare and unusual, so celestial, that I believe nature intended you as a model, letting us know what she could do when she wished to use all her power and all her knowledge. Everything about you is honey, is sugar, is heavenly manna.

'It's you to whom Paris should have given the golden apple, not Venus, no, or Juno, or Minerva, for Juno was never so magnificent, Minerva never so wise, or Venus so elegant, as you.

'O celestial gods and goddesses, how happy he will be, whoever you grant the grace of coupling with this woman, of kissing her, of rubbing his bacon against her. By God, it's got to be me, I see it perfectly well, because she already loves me. I see it, I know it, I was destined for this by all the fairies and elves. No more wasting time, push it, pull it, let's get to it!'

And he tried to take her in his arms, but she started toward the window, as if to call in her neighbors. So Panurge left at once, and as he went said to her:

'Wait right here, madame. Don't trouble yourself: I'll fetch them for you.'

And so he went off, not terribly concerned about the rebuff he'd experienced, and not particularly unhappy.

The next day he appeared at church right when she came to hear mass. As she entered the church, he sprinkled holy water on her and made her a profound bow, and then, as they were kneeling in prayer, he approached her familiarly and said:

'Madame, understand: I love you so much I can't piss or shit. I don't know what you think – but suppose I fall sick, whose fault will it be?'

'Go away,' she said, 'go away, I don't care! Leave me alone, let me say my prayers to God.'

'Ah,' he said, 'but think about *To Beaumont le Vicomte*.'

'I don't know it,' she said.

'Here's what it means,' he said. 'A *beau con le vit monte*, A prick climbs on a beautiful cunt. And pray to God that He grants me what your noble heart longs for. Here, let me have those prayer beads.'

'Take them,' she said, 'and leave me alone.'

And she tried to take off her rosary, which was fashioned of scented wood; the large beads were solid gold. But Panurge quickly pulled out one of his knives and neatly cut it for her, and started off to the pawn-shop, saying:

'Madame, may I offer you my knife?'

'No, no!' she said.

'But remember,' he said, 'it's always at your service, body and baggage, guts and bowels.'

But losing her rosary beads didn't make the lady very happy, for they were an important part of her appearance in church, and she thought to herself, 'This babbler is out of his mind; he must be a foreigner. I'll never get those beads back. What will I say to my husband? He'll be angry at me. But I'll tell him a thief cut them off while I was in church, and he'll surely believe me, seeing the end of the ribbon still tied to my belt.'

After dinner, Panurge went to see her, carrying hidden in his sleeve a fat purse, stuffed with tokens used in high-court business. And he began by saying:

'Who's more in love, me with you, or you with me?'

To which she answered:

'I certainly don't hate you, because as God commands I love the whole world.'

'But more specifically,' he said, 'don't you love me?'

'I've already told you,' she said, 'and over and over, that you're not to say such things to me! If you insist on speaking to me like this, I will show you, sir, that dishonorable words may be directed at some women, but not me. Leave – and give me back my rosary beads, in case my husband asks for them.'

'What?' he said. 'Your rosary beads, madame? Ah no, I can't do that, on my honor I can't. But I'd be delighted to give you others. Which would you prefer? Enameled gold, with large beads, or handsome love knots, or something truly enormous, with beads as fat as ingots? Or perhaps you'd prefer ebony wood, or big blue jacinth stones, or well-cut red garnets, and every tenth stone a gorgeous turquoise, or else maybe a fine topaz, or a shining sapphire, or maybe all in rubies with a fat diamond every tenth stone, something cut with twenty or thirty gleaming faces?

'No – no – that's not good enough. I know a beautiful necklace of fine emeralds, and every tenth stone marked with great round ambergris, and the clasp set with an oriental pearl as fat as an orange! It costs only twenty-five thousand gold pieces. I'd love to give you that; I can afford it without any trouble.'

And as he spoke he jiggled the court counters in his sleeve so they rang like gold pieces.

'Would you like a bolt of bright crimson velvet, striped with green, or some embroidered satin, or maybe crimson? What would you like – necklaces, gold things, things for your hair, rings? All you have to do is say yes. Even fifty thousand gold pieces doesn't bother me.'

He was making her fairly salivate, but she answered:

'No. Thank you, but I want nothing from you.'

'By God,' said he, 'I damned well want something from you, and it's something that won't cost you a cent, and once you've given it you'll still have it, every bit of it. Here' – and he showed her his long codpiece – 'here's my John Thomas, who wants a place to jump into.'

And then he tried to take her in his arms, but she began to scream, although not too loud. So Panurge dropped all pretense and said to her:

'You won't let me have even a little of it, eh? Shit to you! You don't deserve such a blessing, or such an honor. By God, I'll get the dogs to screw you.'

And then he got out of there as fast as he could, afraid of being beaten – for he was a terrible coward.

CHAPTER THIRTY-TWO: HOW PANTAGRUEL SHIELDED AN ENTIRE ARMY WITH HIS TONGUE, AND WHAT THE AUTHOR SAW IN HIS MOUTH

As Pantagruel and all his people entered the land of the Dipsodes, the inhabitants were delighted and immediately surrendered to him, bringing him of their own free will the keys to every city to which he journeyed – all except the Almyrods, who intended to resist him and told his heralds that they refused to surrender, except on good terms.

'What!' said Pantagruel. 'They want more than their hand in the pot and a cup in their fist? Let's go, so you can knock down their walls for me.'

So they got themselves ready, as if about to launch their attack.

But as they marched past a huge field, they were struck by a huge downpour, which began to knock their lines about and break up their formation. Seeing this, Pantagruel ordered the captains to assure them that this was nothing and he could see, past the clouds, that it was only a bit of dew. Whatever happened, however, they should maintain military discipline and he would provide them with cover. And when they had restored good marching order, Pantagruel stuck out his tongue, but just barely halfway, and shielded them as a mother hen protects her chicks.

Now I, who report these totally true tales to you, had hidden myself under the leaf of a burdock weed, which was at least as big as the Mantrible Bridge. But when I saw how well they had been shielded, I went to take cover alongside them, but I couldn't, since there were so many of them and (as they say) 'all things come to an end.' So I climbed up as best I could and walked along his tongue for a good six miles, until I got into his mouth.

But, O you gods and goddesses, what did I see there? May Jupiter blow me away with his three-pointed lightning if I tell you a lie. I walked along in there, as you might promenade around Saint Sophia's Cathedral in Constantinople, and I saw immense boulders, just like the mountains of Denmark (I think they were his teeth), and great meadows, and huge forests, with castles and large cities, no smaller than Lyons or Poitiers.

The first person I met was an old man planting cabbage. And quite astonished I asked him:

'My friend, what are you doing here?'

'I,' he said, 'am planting cabbage.'

'But why, and how?' I said.

'Oh ho, sir,' said he, 'we can't all walk around with our balls hanging down like mortars, and we can't all be rich. This is how I earn my living. They take this to the city you see over there, and sell them.'

'Jesus!' I said. 'Is this a whole new world in here?'

'Not at all,' he said, 'it isn't completely new, no. But I've heard that there is a new world outside of here, and that there's a sun and a moon out there, and all kinds of things going on. But this world is older.'

'Well, my friend,' I said, 'what's the name of that city where they sell your cabbage?'

'It's called Throattown,' he said, 'and the people are good Christians, and will be pleased to see you.'

So, in a word, I decided to go there.

Now, as I walked I found a fellow setting pigeon snares, and I asked him:

'My friend, where do these pigeons of yours come from?'

'Sir,' he said, 'they come from the other world.'

And then I realized that, when Pantagruel yawned, pigeons with fully extended wings flew right down his throat, thinking it was a great bird house.

Then I came to the city, which seemed extremely pleasant, well fortified, and nicely located, with a good climate. But at the gates the porters asked for my passport and my certificate of good health, which truly astonished me, so I said to them:

'Gentlemen, is there any danger of plague here?'

'Oh, sir,' they said, 'they're dying of it so rapidly, not very far from here, that the body wagon is always rattling through the streets.'

'Good God!' I said. 'And just where is this?'

So they informed me that it was in Larynx and Pharynx, which were two cities as big as Rouen and Nantes, rich and doing a fine business, and that the plague was due to a stinking, infectious odor recently flowing up to them from the abysses below. More than twenty-two hundred and seventy-six people had died of it in the last week. So I thought about this, and added up the days, and realized that this was a foul breath from Pantagruel's stomach, which had begun after he'd eaten so much garlic (at Anarch's wedding feast), as I've already explained.

Leaving there, I walked between the great boulders that were his teeth, and climbed up on one, and found it one of the loveliest places in the whole world, with fine tennis courts, handsome galleries, beautiful meadows, and many vineyards. And these delightful fields were dotted with more Italian-style summerhouses than I could count, so I stayed on there for four months and have never been happier.

Then I climbed down the back teeth, in order to get to his lips, but as I journeyed I was robbed by a band of highwaymen in the middle of a huge forest, somewhere in the neighborhood of his ears.

Then I found a little village on the slope (I forget its name), where I was happier than ever, and worked happily for my supper. Can you guess what I did? I slept: they hire day laborers to sleep, down there, and you can make five or six dollars a day. But those who snore really loud can make seven or even seven and a half. And I told the senators how I'd been robbed in the valley, and they told me that, truthfully, the people in that neighborhood were naturally bad, and thieves to boot, which made me realize that, just as we have the Right Side of the Alps and the Wrong Side of the Alps, so they have the Right Side of the Teeth and the Wrong Side of the Teeth, but it was better on the Right Side, and the air was better, too.

And I began to think how true it was that half the world has no idea how the other half lives, seeing that no one has ever written a thing about that world down there, although it's inhabited by more than twenty-five kingdoms, not to mention the deserts and a great bay. Indeed, I have written a fat book entitled *History of an Elegant Throat Land*, which is what I called that country, since they lived in the throat of my master Pantagruel.

Finally, I decided to go back, and going past his beard I dropped onto his shoulders, and from there I got down to the ground and fell right in front of him.

And seeing me, he asked:

'Where are you coming from, Alcofribas?'

And I answered him:

'From your throat, sir.'

'And how long have you been down there?' he said.

'Since you marched against the Almyrods,' I said.

'But that,' he said, 'is more than six months. How did you live? What did you drink?'

I answered:

'My lord, just as you did, and I took a tax of the freshest morsels that came down your throat.'

'Indeed,' he said. 'But where did you shit?'

'In your throat, sir,' I said.

'Ha, ha, but you're a fine fellow!' he said. 'Now, with God's help, we've conquered the entire land of the Dipsodes. And you shall have the castle of Salmagundi.'

'Many thanks, sir,' I said. 'You're far more generous than I deserve.'

12

A Different Way of Saying 'I'

Thomas Mann, *The Tales of Jacob*, translated by H. T. Lowe-Porter
(London: Martin Secker & Warburg, 1934), pp. 192–204

The Tales of Jacob *constitute the first volume of the cycle* Joseph and his
Brothers *by Thomas Mann. I believe that it is the greatest literary flowering of
the twentieth century. It feeds the reader, satisfies him, with a miraculous
prodigality that never flags through all its two thousand pages; it interweaves
poetry, wisdom and irony, in modulations that are always new. And yet, the
cycle is no more than the unfolding of chapters 25–50 of the Book of Genesis.*

*Jacob's 'practical joke' at Esau's expense is well known: once again it
represents the victory of the weak and shrewd over the strong and stupid, a
theme dear to the fairy tales of all times, in a sense the revenge of Remus and
Abel against their violent brothers; but here other deep and solemn themes
emerge. In truth, the author warns us: 'no one was deceived, not even Esau':
all the people in this episode (and in the entire book) live their event and at
the same time they* relive *it. They recognize in the present a mythical past:
everything that happens is a replica, a confirmation, and has already happened
an infinite number of times. The Flood appears in every mythology because
each people has recognized in one of their singular catastrophes an antecedent
catastrophe, far back in time, that in turn was repeated even further back, and
so on ad infinitum, right back to the birth of humanity. In this way, here Isaac
really dies, but also ritually performs his death; or rather the death of another
Isaac-Yitzchak; and Esau really is deceived while at the same time playing the
part of the dupe. The author reminds us that in this book 'we are talking of
people who did not know exactly who they were', and who have a different way
than ours of saying 'I'.*

[. . .] when the hour came, the brothers being almost thirty, when Yitzchak out of the darkness of his tent sent the slave who served him – a youth lacking in one ear, it having been cut off on account of his lightheadedness and manifold shortcomings, greatly to his amendment – to stand before Esau where he worked with the hands in the ploughed field, to fold his arms across his black chest, and announce: 'The master hath need of my lord,' Esau stood like one rooted to the ground, and his ruddy face paled under the sweat that covered it. He murmured the formula of compliance: 'Here am I.' But in his soul he thought 'Now is the time!' and that soul was full of pride and dread and solemn unrest of mind.

Then he left the sunny field and went in unto his father who lay in the half-light with two little damp pledgets on his eyes; made an obeisance and said: 'My lord hath summoned me.'

Isaac answered rather querulously:

'That is the voice of my son, Esau. Is it thou, Esau? I have called thee, for the hour is at hand. Come near to me, my eldest son, that I may be sure of thee.'

And Esau knelt in his goatskin apron beside the couch and raised up his eyes to the little pledgets as though he would bore through them into his father's eyes, while Isaac felt his shoulders and arms and breast, saying:

'Yea, these are thy fells and Esau's red fleece, I see them with my hands, which for good or evil have learned right well to fill the place of my declining eyes. Hearken now, my son, and open thine ears and receive the words of thy sightless father, for the hour is come. Behold, now I am old, I know not the day of my death and as my eyes have long since failed, so it may be that I shall soon fail utterly and disappear into the darkness so that my life is night and no more seen. Therefore, that I die not before I hand on the blessing and give the power from me and the inheritance, let it be now as it hath been: go hence, my son, and take thy weapons, thy quiver and bow, with which thou art mighty before the Lord, and go about in the plain and the field and take me venison. And make me savoury meat such as I love, cooked in sour milk by a bright fire and well seasoned and bring it to me that I may eat and be strengthened that I may bless thee before I die, with seeing hands. This is my will, now go.'

'It is already done,' murmured Esau perfunctorily, yet remained upon his knees and only bowed his head low so that the blind eyes stared over it into space.

'Art thou still there?' asked Isaac. 'A moment I thought thou wast already gone, and was not surprised, for the father is accustomed to have all performed quickly in love and fear according to his wish.'

'It is already done,' repeated Esau and went out. But after he had lifted the skin at the door of the tent he let it fall and came back, knelt again by the couch and spoke with breaking voice:

'My father!'

'What then!' asked Isaac, raising his brows above the pledgets. 'It is well,' he said then; 'go, my son, for the hour is come, that is great for thee and for us all. Go, hunt and cook, that I may bless thee.'

And Esau went out, with his head high, and stood before the tent, in the hour of his pride, and in a loud voice announced to all within hearing his impending honour. For events do not happen all at once, they happen point for point, they develop according to pattern, and it would be false to call a narrative entirely sad because the end is so. A tale with a lamentable close has yet its stages and times of honour, and it is right to regard these not from the point of view of the end, but rather in their own light, for while they are the present they have equal strength with the presentness of the conclusion. Thus Esau was proud in his hour and cried out with a ringing voice:

'Hear, ye people of the court, children of Abraham and who burn sacrifice to Ya, hear ye, too, ye who sacrifice to Baal, wives of Esau and your seed, the fruit of my loins! Esau's hour is come. The lord will bless his son to-day. Isaac sendeth me forth to the fields that with the bow I may find him savoury meat to strengthen him for my sake. Fall down!'

And while those at hand who heard him fell upon their faces, Esau saw a maid running so that her breasts danced up and down.

That was the maid who shortwindedly announced to Rebecca what Esau had said in his boasting. And again the maid, quite breathless from running, came to Jacob, who was tending the sheep in company with a crop-eared dog named Tam, and leaning sunk in thought, on a long staff with a crook at the top. She gasped with her forehead bent to the grass: 'The mistress!' Jacob looked at her and after a pause of some length answered very low: 'Here am I.' For in the pause he had thought in his soul: 'The hour is come!' And his heart was full of pride and awe.

He gave his staff to Tam to watch and went in to Rebecca, who was awaiting him impatiently.

Rebecca, the successor of Sarai, was a matron with gold earrings, stately and strong-boned, with large features that still possessed much of the beauty once so alluring to Abimelech of Gerar. The gaze of her black eyes was shrewd and steadfast beneath arched brows that were evenly accentuated with pencilling and showed between them the two perpendicular folds of an energetic character. Her nose was well formed and masculine, with a pronounced hook and distended nostrils. Her voice was deep and resonant, and there was a line of little black hairs on her upper lip. Her black and silver locks were parted in the middle and came down upon her forehead, veiled by the brown headcloth which hung far down her back but left uncovered the fine shape of her noble shoulders and arms – these were in colour an amber-brown and the years had had as yet no power to touch them. She wore an ungirdled garment of figured wool, reaching down to her ankles. Her small, veined hands had just now been busy at the loom set up in the middle of the floor, correcting the women who squatted there using their fingers and wooden pegs to urge the flaxen woof through the warp. But she had stopped their work and sent them away, and was waiting for her son inside her own tent – the mistress's tent, hung with skins and mats. She moved swiftly towards Jacob as he respectfully entered.

'Yekew, my son,' said she softly and low, and drew his upraised hands to her breast. 'The time has come. The master would bless thee.'

'Me would he bless?' asked Jacob, losing colour. 'Me, and not Esau?'

'Thee in him,' said she impatiently. 'It is not a time for quibbling. Speak not nor seek to reason, but do as it is commanded thee, that no wrong may happen and no error come to pass.'

'What is the command of my little mother from whom I have my life, as at the time when I was still within her?' Jacob asked.

'Hearken,' she said. 'He hath ordered him to slay and make him a savoury meat to strengthen him for the blessing. That canst thou do quicker and better than he. Go then to the flock, take two kids, kill them and bring them. Of the best parts I will make for the father a meal such that he will leave none for thee. Away!'

Jacob began to tremble, he did not cease to tremble unto the end. At times he had the greatest trouble to control the chattering of his teeth. He said:

'Merciful mother of men! As the word of a goddess is thy word to me, yet what thou sayest is more dangerous than can be told. Esau is hairy all over and thy child is smooth with but little exception. If now our lord lay hold upon me and feel my smoothness, how shall I stand before him? As though I would deceive him, surely, and I should have instead of his blessing his curse straightway upon my head.'

'Art again at thy hair-splitting?' she hectored him. 'Upon me be the curse. I will see to it. Away and fetch the kids. A mistake may happen.'

He ran. He hastened to the slope near the tents, where the goats were pastured, seized two of the young kids as they gambolled about their mother, and cut their throats, calling to the goatherd that they were for the mistress. He let their blood run out before the lord, flung them over his shoulder by the hind legs and went home, his heart thumping. The little heads hung down behind, with their small curling horns and cleft snouts, their eyes glazing – so early sacrificed, to so great an end. Rebecca stood waiting. She nodded.

'Quick,' said she. 'All is ready.'

There was a hearth built of stones under her roof, and a fire burnt under the brazen pot and all the gear was there for the cooking. His mother took the kids and began hastily to skin and cut them up. She moved about the blazing hearth, large and capable, fork in hand, stirred and seasoned, and during all this there was silence between the two. But while the dish was cooking Jacob saw how she took out of her clothes-press garments which lay there folded, shirt and smock: Esau's festal garments, which she kept for him, as Jacob remembered, going pale again. Then he saw her cut up into strips and pieces with the knife the skins of the kids, which were wet inside and sticky with blood, and he shuddered at

93

the sight. But Rebecca bade him take off the long smock with half-sleeves which was at that time his daily wear, and drew over his smooth and shivering arms the short shift and then the fine coat of blue and red wool, which left one shoulder bare. Then she said 'Come!' And while her lips moved in murmured words and the frown stood out on her brow she put on him the pieces of skin everywhere where he was bare and smooth, on neck and arms, on his shanks and on the backs of his hands and bound them fast with thread, although they were sticky and clung of themselves, most unpleasantly.

She murmured:

'I cover the child, I cover the youth, changed be the child, changed the youth, by the skin, by the fell.'

And again:

'I cover the child, I cozen the lord, the lord shall touch, the father shall eat, the brothers of the deep shall be made to serve thee.'

Then with her own hands she washed his feet, as she had done when he was small; took anointing oil that smelt of the fields and the fragrance of the fields, which was Esau's oil and anointed his head and his newly washen feet, and as she did so muttered through her clenched teeth:

'I anoint the child, I anoint the stone, the blind shall eat; at thy feet, at thy feet must fall the brethren of the deeps!'

Then she said: 'It is finished'; he stood up, clumsy and altered by his strange disguise, with his arms and legs stuck stiffly out, and his teeth a-chatter. Meanwhile she dished up the savoury meat, with wheaten bread and golden-clear oil to dip it in, and a jug of wine; gave the whole into his hands and said: 'Now go thy ways!'

And Jacob went, laden with the meal, awkward and straddling in his fear lest the hatefully sticky skins slip awry under the cords. His heart beat hard, his face was screwed up, and his eyes were on the ground. Many of the household saw him as he passed through the court, held up their hands and wagged their heads; they clucked with their tongues and kissed their finger-tips, and said: 'Lo, the master!' He came before his father's tent, put his mouth to the curtain and spoke:

'Here am I, my father. May thy servant lift his foot to enter unto thee?'

Out of the depths of the tent came Isaac's fretful voice:

'But who art thou? Art thou not a thief and the son of a thief, that thou comest before my tent and sayest it is I? For anyone can say I, but all depends upon who sayeth it.'

Jacob answered, and his teeth did not chatter, because he clenched them: 'It is thy son who hath said I, for I have hunted and killed for thee to eat.'

'Well and good,' answered Isaac then. 'Come thy ways in.'

Then Jacob entered into the twilight of the tent, at the back of which ran a covered clay ledge, and Yitzchak lay upon it, wrapped in his mantle and his head elevated upon a headrest with a bronze half-ring, and with the pledgets over his eyes. He asked again:

'Who art thou then?'

And Jacob answered, in a failing voice:

'I am Esau, the hairy, thy elder son, and I have done as thou hast commanded. Sit up then, my father, and strengthen thy soul, for here is the meat.'

But Isaac did not yet sit up. He asked:

'How, so soon hast thou found game and so quickly brought it within range of thy bow?'

'The Lord thy God, he hath given me good hunting,' answered Jacob, and his voice died away on some of the syllables. However, he had said 'thy' God, speaking for Esau, whose god was not the God of Isaac.

'But how is it then with me?' asked Isaac again. 'For thy voice is uncertain, Esau, my eldest son; yet it sounds to me like the voice of Jacob.'

Then Jacob knew not what to say for fear, and stood quaking. But Isaac spoke with mildness:

'Yet often are the voices of brothers alike, and words come with the same sounds out of their mouths. Come hither, that I may feel thee with my seeing hands, whether thou art Esau my eldest son or no.'

Jacob obeyed. He set down his burdens, came close and offered himself to be felt. And when he was near he saw that his father had bound the pledgets to his head with a cord that they should not fall off when he sat up, just as Rebecca had secured upon himself the hateful skins.

Isaac felt about a little in the air with his fingers spread out before he touched Jacob. Then the lean white hands found him out and felt him, over his neck and arms where no garment was, on the backs of his hands and down his legs, everywhere touching the skins of the kids.

'Yea,' said he, 'these are thy hairy limbs and Esau's red fleeces, I see them with my seeing hands and must be convinced. The voice is the voice of Jacob, but the hands are the hands of Esau. Art thou then my very son Esau?'

And he said: 'Thou seest and sayest it.'

'Then give me to eat,' said Isaac and he sat up, with his mantle hanging down over his knees. And Jacob took the dish and crouched down at his father's feet and held out the meat. But first Isaac bent over with his hands on Jacob's skin-covered hands and smelt of the dish.

'It is good,' he said. 'Thou hast prepared it well. It is in sour cream, as I have commanded, and there is in it cardamom and thyme and some-what of caraway.' And he named the names of other things that were therein which he discerned by his sense of smell. So he nodded and fell to and ate of the dish.

He ate it all, it took a long time.

'Hast thou bread likewise, Esau, my son?' he asked as he chewed.

'Wheaten cakes and oil, of a surety,' answered Jacob.

He broke off some of the bread, dipped it in the oil and brought it to his father's mouth. The old man chewed and took more meat, stroking his beard and nodding his satisfaction, while Jacob looked up in his face and watched him while he ate. It was very thin and transparent, this face, with fine hollows in the cheeks, and a sparse grey beard springing from them, a thin high nose with delicate nostrils, whose bridge was like the blade of a knife. Despite the pledgets on the eyes it looked so spiritual, so well-nigh holy, as to make the meal and the chewing appear unfitting. Jacob was almost ashamed to watch the old man while he ate – as though he must feel ashamed to be watched. But it may be that the pledgets protected him, at all events he chewed away very comfortably, his thin jaw moving up and down under the scanty beard, and as only the best parts of the kids were in the dish, he ate it all.

'Give me to drink,' he said then. And Jacob hastened to fetch the wine jug and hold it himself to the thirsty lips, Isaac's hands grasping it over his son's hairy ones. But as Jacob came thus close to his father the old man smelled the nard in his hair and the fragrance of the flowers of the fields in his garments; he turned away from the jug to say:

'Truly it is strangely deceiving, how my son's festal garments smell sweet, like the fields and the meadows in the spring of the year when the Lord hath sown them far and wide with blossoms for our delight.'

And with two thin finger-tips he lifted one pledget a very little and said:

'And thou art then verily Esau, my oldest son?'

Jacob laughed in desperation and asked in his turn:

'Who then else?'

'Then it is good,' spake Isaac and took a long draught, so that his Adam's apple went up and down under the beard. Then he commanded that water be poured over his hands. But when Jacob had done this and dried his hands, the father said:

'So let it be.'

And mightily strengthened by the food and drink, flushed of face, he laid his hands upon the trembling and crouching Jacob, to bless him with all his strength, and as his soul was strong from the meal he had taken, so were his words full of all the power and richness of the earth. Its fatness gave he him, and its voluptuousness like to a female's, and thereto the dew and the male water of the sky, gave him the fullness of the ploughland, tree and vine, and the rank fruitfulness of the flocks and a double shearing in each year. He laid upon him the covenant, and gave him to bear the promise and the inheritance of that which had been founded throughout time. His words were high-sounding and flowed like a stream. He gave him the victory in the battle of the hemispheres, the light and the dark, and victory over the dragon of the waste; he called him the beautiful moon and bringer of the equinox, with laughter and the renewal of the year. He used the fixed phrase which Rebecca had muttered: the primitive phrase which was so old that it was already a mystery; it did not precisely fit the case, for here the brothers were only two. But Isaac uttered it solemnly above his head: the children of his mother shall serve the bearer of the blessing, and all his brothers shall

97

fall down at his anointed feet. Then he cried out three times the name of God, and said: 'So be it and so may it come to pass!' and released Jacob out of his hands.

Jacob rushed away to his mother. But shortly afterwards Esau came home with a young wild goat which he had shot – and matters became both comic and tragic.

Jacob saw with his own eyes nothing of that which followed, nor had he any desire to, and kept himself hidden. But he knew all from hearsay, and remembered it as well as though he had been present.

Esau came back still in the same high mood, knowing nothing, of course, of what had happened in the meantime, for he had not reached that stage in the tale. Puffed up with pride and self-esteem, with his bow in his hairy fist and the buck over his shoulder, he marched in triumph, throwing out his legs, and beaming darkly in all directions to see if his splendour and preferment were being observed. Still at some distance he began to boast again, so loud and vaingloriously that it was both comic and painful for all who heard. And those who had seen Jacob go in unto the master in his skins and come out again all put their heads together, and likewise those who had not seen it. Only Esau's women and children drew not near, though he summoned them repeatedly to come and witness his greatness and his pride.

The household ran together and laughed to see him throw out his legs and made a circle round him to see and hear what he did. For he began to skin his buck, as he continued to boast; dressed and cut it up, made a fire with kindlings, hung a kettle over it and shouted out commands to the laughing watchers to bring him this and that of which he had need for the feast.

'Ha, ha,' he cried, and 'Ho, ho! Ye godly gapers! Fetch me the great cook's fork! And bring me sour milk of the sheep for he savours it best seethed in sheep's milk. And bring me salt from the salt mine, good-for-nothings and idlers: coriander and garlic, mint and mustard to tickle his palate, for I would cram him so that the strength breaks out at his pores. And bring me good *solet** bread to eat with the dish and oil pounded from olives, and strain the wine, ye sluggards and slumberers, so that no yeast come in the jug, or may the white ass trample you! Run

and fetch. For it is the feast of the feeding and the blessing of Isaac,
Esau's feast, the feast of the hero and son, whom the lord hath sent to
make him a meal, and whom he will bless within his tent in this hour!'

Thus he went on, with mouth and hand, with ha, ha! and ho, ho! and
bombast and braggadocio, with windy boasting of his father's preference
and the great day come to the red skin; so that the folk of the household
bent double and writhed with laughter and wept and held their sides.
He went off with his dish, holding it high before him like the tabernacle,
and throwing out his legs and prancing up to his father's tent; and
they shrieked aloud, clapping and stamping their feet – and then were
suddenly still. For Esau, at the door of the tent, was saying:

'Here am I, my father. Let my father arise and eat of his son's venison
that thy soul may bless me. Is it his will that I come in?'

Isaac's voice came forth:

'Who is it that sayest I and will come in to the blind man?'

'Esau, thy hairy-skin,' answered he, 'hath hunted and cooked for the
strengthening, as thou commandest.'

'Thou fool and robber!' the voice said. 'Why speakest thou falsehood
in my sight! For Esau, my eldest, he was here long since and gave me to
eat and drink, and I have blessed him.'

Then Esau was so startled that he almost let everything fall and he
gave such a jump that he spilled the sour cream sauce all over him. His
auditors roared with laughter. They wagged their heads feebly and wiped
the water out of their eyes and shook it off. But Esau rushed into the tent,
without more asking, and there came a silence, while those outside
covered their hands with their mouths and thrust their elbows into each
other's ribs. But presently came a roar from inside, a perfectly incredible
roar and Esau burst out again, no longer red, but purple in the face, with
uplifted arms. 'Curse it, curse it, curse it,' he shrieked, at the top of his
lungs – words we might use to-day on occasion of some trifling vexation.
But at that time, and from the lips of Esau the shaggy, it was a new cry,
full of the original meaning, for he himself had really been cursed,
instead of blessed, solemnly betrayed and made a mock of like no one
before him, in the eyes of the people. 'Curse it,' he shrieked. 'Betrayed,
betrayed, betrayed!' And he sat himself down on the ground and howled

with his tongue hanging out, his tears rolled down the size of hazel nuts, while the crowd stood round and laughed until they cried at this tremendous sell, the story of the hoaxing of Esau the red.

13

The Romance of Technology

Roger Vercel,* *Tug-Boat*, translated from *Remorques* by Warre Bradley Wells (London: Chatto & Windus, 1936), pp. 142–58, 263–73

Of Roger Vercel I know nothing, not even if he is alive or dead, but I should be happy if he were alive and well and still writing, because I like his writing, I should like to write like him, and to have recounted the stories he tells.

I feel an affinity with him also for a personal reason. At this point in the anthology there should be a cæsura, a discontinuity, which corresponds to my year in Auschwitz, in which, besides the hunger for food, I suffered a hunger for printed matter. Tug-Boat is the first book I held in my hands after this long fast, and I read the whole text in the frightening and decisive night in which the Germans hesitated between murder and flight, and chose flight. I referred to the book, without naming it, in the last pages of If This is a Man.

But this unusual book interests me also in itself, even today, independently of the manner of my first reading it. It deals with a topical theme, but one strangely little treated of: man's adventure in the world of technology. Perhaps the man of today considers adventure, the Conradian testing, superfluous? If so it would be an unhappy omen. But this book makes us see that adventure is still with us and not only at the ends of the Earth; that a man can show courage and ingenuity even in peaceful enterprises; that the relationship between man and machine is not necessarily one of alienation, but, in fact, can enhance and consolidate the old rapport between man and nature. The plot of the book is linear: it describes the work of the Cyclone, *a high-sea rescue tug, and its captain Renaud. In the first passage here the* Cyclone *is drifting towards a reef, the tow-rope is wrapped round the propeller, jamming it. In the second, the boat is responding to the SOS of an English ship that has caught fire.*

The investigation of paternity is always an uncertain business, but I should not be surprised if my character Libertino Faussone in The Wrench *harboured a gene transplanted from Captain Renaud.*

He went right down into the depths of the pit, by way of almost perpendicular steel ladders, whose handrails were greasy from the oily palms which passed along them.

He found the chief engineer, Lauran, a fat, red fellow in blue overalls, standing beside the pressure-gauges and the three dynamos which worked the pumps. Under his eyes he had the whole strong scaffolding of the engines, the cylinders, the shining connecting-rods, the enormous red exhaust-pipe. All he was doing was moving a gleaming steel shuttle first one way, and then the other, slowly: the shuttle which admitted the steam. Two other engineers leant against the wall, watching him.

His action – the sole action which could still save the ship and thirty lives – struck Renaud as utterly absurd. Lauran might have been a child playing motor-cars with chairs turned upside down and manipulating a steering-wheel made out of cardboard; for nothing stirred in all the powerful engines. In that deep pit, full of tireless steel arms, of masses of machinery whose whole purpose was to revolve in furious movement, the one thing that moved was this futile little lever. Nevertheless, at every half-turn, as he sent the steam first forwards and then backwards, the chief engineer was launching all the strength of eighteen hundred horse-power against his motionless pistons.

'When it happened,' he remarked, 'I thought everything had gone smash. But look – not even a nut started! I knew these engines were good stuff; but I'd never have believed they'd stand a shock like that.'

Renaud interrupted him.

'If you can't clear that hawser, old man,' he said, 'we're for it!'

The chief engineer nodded.

'I thought we might be,' he replied, with a catch of his breath. 'Just where are we?'

'Barely nine miles off the Basse Froide,' said Renaud, 'and the current is carrying us there at nine knots.'

'That gives us about an hour,' Lauran reckoned. 'Look,' he went on, 'it doesn't budge an inch. The shaft is strangled. There may be a hundred yards of "spring" round it . . . And yet look at the pressure I've got. It's enough to blow the boilers out!'

As he spoke, he kept on monotonously moving his arm: forward . . . back . . . forward . . . back.

He waited for a little when he got to the end of the run, with the admission wide open, in order to let the steam exert its pressure. But nothing responded – nothing but the hissing of the jets of steam which escaped from every joint, as though the place were a Turkish bath.

'Well,' Renaud wound up, 'do the best you can'; and he went away.

The men who stood aside to let him pass along the galleries asked him no questions, and barely looked at him. Nor did they talk among themselves. It was a tacit rule of honour on board the *Cyclone* never to be taken aback by anything that happened at sea. The whole crew were men who specialized in disaster. They knew that every time they put to sea, from the moment they left till the moment they got back, they were fighting for their own lives as much as for other people's lives; but they never said anything about it.

Yet Renaud, as he watched them setting off to work on the hawser, holding their crow-bars and their hatchets firmly in their hands, felt that they were trying to clear a ship which was doomed to destruction.

'But not a word out of them!' he said to himself. 'They're fine fellows . . .'

The accident had set the chief engineer marvelling by revealing to him the resistance of his engines. It set the captain marvelling by revealing to him the quality of his crew.

He went back on to the bridge.

'Nothing to do but wait,' he said to Tanguy.

The mate shrugged his shoulders, as though waiting or anything else were all the same to him.

Nothing to do but wait . . . Renaud knew very well that it was the one thing in the world to which he could not resign himself. His screw jammed, like a child's top by a tangle of string!

So he must drift ashore – he who had saved so many ships from drifting ashore! He must go to the bottom instead of them – he who had always been top-dog!

Above all, he could do nothing for his ship. He, the captain, had handed over his power of initiative to somebody else – to the man who, down there beneath his feet, was repeating his mechanical movement: forward . . . back . . . forward . . . back . . . A movement monotonous, absurd, irritating. Renaud had left the engine-room abruptly because he could not stand the sight of it any more.

He walked up and down the bridge, amid his useless instruments of command.

From the bridge he could catch sight of the lines of breakers. When the *Cyclone* rose with the swell, they showed like a white smear against the bilious grey of the sea. Renaud's keen eyes made out black dots. They were the teeth of that gigantic saw of rock.

'We're going straight on to the east of Ar-Men,' he said to himself. 'The lighthouse-keepers will see us, if it clears a bit. They'll be able to say what happened . . .'

He recalled the lighthouse, standing on its narrow base amid tortuous eddies, sometimes surrounded by a casing of waves, a cylindrical sheaf of waves which rose as high as the light. He had seen it quite close, one day when he accompanied the official engineer on a trip of inspection. In no weather could any ship, any boat land there. Men and supplies were transferred to the lighthouse in a breeches-buoy by means of pass-ropes.

Renaud's reflections shifted from Ar-Men and slid a little to the right. The *Cyclone* would split herself open on the eastern reefs, on Huron or Cornoc Argo . . . Before that, he would have cast his two anchors; but they would drag. Then he would have got the boats away; but they would crush the men against the side and be caught by the irresistible current . . .

The Greek ship's syren started mooing again. She was further ahead, and she could better see the reefs on to which she was running.

Positively, for the last ten minutes Renaud had forgotten all about her. He shrugged his shoulders at the sound of her syren.

'Oh, go on talking!' he exclaimed. 'What do you expect me to do about it?'

Then he caught sight of Gouédic at the top of the bridge-companion.

'The transmitter is mended, Captain,' the wireless operator reported.

'Good,' said Renaud. 'And those fellows ahead – what have they got to say?'

'We didn't catch all of it, because I was doing the repairs, and Le Gall was patching up the Greeks and the woman.'

'Oh yes, of course . . . And how is she?'

'She's got a broken arm, I think, and her shoulder's cut open. That's one reason why we couldn't catch everything they were saying. She was making such a row.'

Renaud shook his head.

'So she's come to life again, has she?' he said. 'She's picked a bad moment. She might as well have stayed dead, for all the time she's got left. Well, anyhow . . .'

He reflected that he would get her away in the first boat, as a bounden duty, and that would let him wash his hands of her.

'Well,' he went on, 'what have they got to say?'

'They're calling for help . . . They say they're driving on shore.'

'Quite so,' said Renaud. 'That's no news. After all, if the island lifeboat hears them, she may pick up one or two of them . . . Just to keep the record straight, Gouédic, tell them that I've got engine trouble, and that I'll take them in tow again if I get clear of it. Tell them, too, that I'll let them know when to cast anchor . . . You needn't add that it won't be any use. They'll find that out soon enough for themselves! But, above all, get them, if you possibly can, to stop that blasted syren of theirs. It doesn't do any good, and it only annoys us. That's all.'

Not for a moment did it enter Renaud's head to send out an SOS on his own account.

But Gouédic had no sooner turned his back than Renaud was possessed by a sudden fit of fury against all this inert ironmongery, these frustrate, fatuous engines. Their innermost life was outside his range – he was a sailing-ship man. They owed obedience to somebody else . . .

On board a three-master, you could put up a fight, you could man-œuvre. You had a living ship under your feet, and she answered to the touch of her captain's hand. Even when you were rounding Cape Horn, you kept your canvas stretched.

For his part, Renaud had trained those damned fellows of his to shin up to his mast-heads like monkeys; and he had never had a ship stripped even in the worst of cyclones, even when he was struck by a hundred-miles-an-hour squall and his barometer shuddered. Anyhow, you needn't be afraid of any breakdown, so long as you had a shirt-tail left to hoist to a yard. Whereas, on board an accursed hulk like this . . .

Renaud was the kind of man who is stifled by inaction. Head lowered, he strode up and down the bridge, with his hands clasped behind his back, working his fingers and digging his nails into his palms.

Looking over the rail, he caught sight of a sailor standing in the bow with a big pair of pincers in his hands. He stood there motionless for a moment or two, staring at the breakers. By now they looked like black clods of earth in a field from which the snow was beginning to melt. Renaud leant right over the rail.

'What the hell are you doing there?' he bellowed. 'Do you think you're paid to look at the scenery, like a tourist? You'll see them well enough when you get into them . . . Meanwhile until I tell you to abandon ship, you'll get on with your job, see?'

The man made haste to get to work on the shrouds which he was supposed to be 'seizing.' Two other sailors near him turned round for a moment and looked at the captain. Then they went on lashing the treads of a companion which had been half torn away.

The *Cyclone* was within four miles of the reefs. To the west Renaud could see the island of Sein, flat as a threshold, a worn black slab, as low on the water as a water-logged raft: so low that its thousand inhabitants sometimes awakened all together at night with water up to their waists. The rocky island was so worn by the waves that it had acquired the smooth, elongated curves of a sand-bank, and looked on charts like some sinister shape made out of ectoplasm. It ran out into boiling land-locked bays. Only its houses rose a little above the level of the water.

Renaud had rounded Sein so often that he had become curious about it. One day he had made a point of paying a visit to it and having a look at its womenfolk, with their black head-dresses.

His wife, Yvonne, went with him. He took a photograph of her standing between the 'Gossipers,' those two great menhirs which face one another at the extreme tip of the Old World.

'She's going to be terribly upset,' he said to himself. But further than that he was incapable of thinking. He was engrossed by his danger, and he could find interest only in memories which might become associated with his approaching shipwreck.

This was why he remembered climbing up the Men-Briale lighthouse, and being very glad he had done so. As he walked round the light, he saw for the first time, in the quivering light of that July Sunday, the whole stretch of the Sein causeway, off which he had often fought his way in darkness, in spray, in mist. But he had never really seen it before, even when he went to the rescue of ships caught in its claws.

He could recall the picture in every detail. It was indeed a 'causeway': a regular street of spray, an ill-laid avenue, four miles wide and bristling with thousands of black cobbles. Within it was an incoherent interlacing of currents and eddies, a kind of swarming of water, made up of senseless twists and turns and changes of direction. Along each side of this road ran a row of geysers, columns of spray, tree-shaped, which kept on dying down and springing to life again.

Renaud had held a muster of the reefs, like a victor calling the roll of a beaten army: to the north-west, the Tête du Chat, Dentock, Moédock, Penbara, Nerroth; to the west, Gouelvanic, Forhok, Men Mankik, together with all the other scattered ones, bearing Celtic names with grim or grotesque meanings.

At his feet, the wreckers' island lay spread, with its protoplasmic shape, its cuttle-fish's tentacles.

'There are even more wrecks than reefs down there,' remarked the lighthouse-keeper.

Then he chuckled.

'Still,' he went on, 'you can't say that a single fellow was ever drowned in the "causeway" . . .'

Renaud looked at him inquiringly.

'No,' the lighthouse-keeper explained, 'they're not drowned. They're dashed to pieces. It's a good thing for them: it means a quicker end . . . There's always so much sea running that it splits their skulls against the rocks. It breaks all their bones, too. Anybody who is fished out looks like a rag-doll . . .'

These memories comforted Renaud. It was a kind of revenge on shipwreck to look beyond it – and not care a curse . . .

'I was a diver before I came here,' the lighthouse-keeper had gone on, 'so I know what happens down below there. Once I saw crabs and lobsters fighting for a fellow – and how they fought! The crabs were digging into the chap's chest. You should have seen them coming out from under his ribs and striking with their claws at the lobsters who wanted a bit of him . . . Well, after all, it's more flattering to feed a fine lobster than to feed worms. Don't you think so, Captain?'

Renaud thought so, too.

'Wherever there's any depth,' the lighthouse-keeper added, 'you always find the sunken ships standing up, quite straight on their keels. For that, you want a depth of twenty to thirty fathoms. Higher than that, the swell attacks everything, dismasts the ship and smashes the bridge and the funnels. But, over twenty fathoms down, you find the ship intact, as straight as though she were in dry dock.'

That piece of information gave Renaud an obscure sense of satisfaction now. Where the *Cyclone* was going aground, there would be enough depth for her to stand straight on the bottom and stay there . . .

A squall broke, drowning everything. When it cleared again to northward, the breakers made their appearance so close that Renaud got a shock, as though he awakened to find the threat of a nightmare still present. A furious foam raced along them from east to west and smothered them. There was something monstrously alive about this galloping avalanche, like giant manes tossing in the air. Sometimes the rocks shot up out of the spray as though they were misshapen machinery that spat thunderous explosions to an astonishing height.

The immobility of these rocks, beneath the deadly rush that swept them, seemed miraculous, almost meritorious. In this hour of disaster, when a man ceases to choose his own thoughts, an absurd idea possessed

Renaud for a moment or two: a kind of sympathy for these rocks that stood up to the sea and reappeared after every wave, like a ship strongly anchored.

Then he reflected – and this affected him more – that he was going aground like a fool, caught in a clash of land and water which had nothing to do with him. The sea was now no more than a downward road which he was following. It was not striking directly at him any longer. It was simply going to carry him along in its chaotic currents, break him, together with itself, all in a moment, and then, after the end of him, go on crashing eternally against the reef.

The rain once more hid the Greek ship from him. She was drifting north-east a little ahead of him, still shrieking, as mad women shriek at sunset . . . All Renaud could see was a short stretch of choppy sea: sea which had suddenly turned yellow, as though someone had dumped cartfuls of earth into it.

The spray stung his eyes, and walled him in a few yards away from the rail. Renaud resented this. He did not like being blindfolded before he was stuck up against the wall.

Seeking for something definite on which to rest, his eyes encountered Tanguy's broad back. The mate was slouching over the rail, quite at his ease. He looked like a retired mariner in some little port, watching the tide rise at evening. His extreme tranquillity displeased Renaud, even though he could see nothing ostentatious about it. He glanced at his watch.

'Another half-hour,' he said, 'and it will be all over.'

The mate was letting himself sway slightly with the roll, from one elbow to the other.

'Perhaps a little longer,' he corrected, 'because the end of the hawser is trailing, and that slows us down a bit. About three-quarters of an hour, I should say . . .'

All at once, Renaud remembered something about Tanguy which had intrigued him. It was not his way to leave anything in doubt, so long as it could be cleared up. So he asked:

'What put it into your head to grouse about wireless just now?'

Tanguy straightened himself up and thought this over.

'With wireless,' he replied, 'everybody knows just when you're coming back . . .'

'Oh, I see,' said Renaud. The mate, he thought, really had ideas all his own.

'So,' Tanguy went on to explain, 'when you get home, you needn't be afraid of any surprises . . . You're expected . . .'

Renaud realised what he meant; and he felt sorry for Tanguy. The mate was running on the reefs with something gnawing at his inside.

Little Madame Tanguy came before Renaud's eyes, brazen and beckoning. He remembered her dubious conversation, whose 't's' her eyes crossed so explicitly. For the first time since he started, the memory of Yvonne made him glow all over. He, at least, would leave somebody to regret him . . .

But he felt how very dangerous was that thought. Unless he were careful, everything that was held in suspense in him, driven back in him as though by a dam, might burst through and overwhelm him. So, to escape himself, he made haste to Tanguy's rescue.

'Your wife doesn't deserve that, Tanguy,' he said. 'You shouldn't say that, at a moment like this . . . You know very well that women who like their little joke aren't always the flightiest . . .'

The mate straightened himself up still more, straddled his legs, and took a firm grip on the rail with his big hands. He stared at the captain, ponderously.

'That's where I ought to be to-morrow morning,' he said, 'to make quite sure . . .'

He jerked his head towards the east: towards Brest, towards home.

In a flash, Renaud imagined Yvonne just as she heard the news. He tried to moisten his lips. His eyes strayed to the hawse-holes. For the first time in his life, he begged for a bit of hope.

'Do you think the anchors will hold?' he asked.

'Of course they won't!' replied Tanguy.

'Still,' retorted Renaud angrily, 'we can try'; and he grasped his whistle.

At this moment, they felt a shock under their feet: a rapid blow struck at the stern of the ship. They stared at one another, breathlessly. The shaking was repeated. It went on longer. The screw had made a quarter-turn.

An instant of interminable suspense ensued. Then the screw shook the ship again, striking like an axe handled at too short range and lacking a swing behind it.

Subconsciously, Renaud strode to the engine-room speaking-tube. But he simply stood in front of its brass mouthpiece, staring at it. He realised that he must not disturb the man who was tackling the job down below.

Cautiously the screw started again, beating slowly, like a pulse after a heart attack. Renaud thrust his lips into the mouthpiece.

'Bravo, Lauran!' he shouted. 'Got it clear?'

A foundered voice answered him. Renaud could tell that it came short from exhausting effort. It issued from a mouth wide open in search of breath.

'Yes,' replied Lauran. 'All right now. Bitch of a thing! The trouble I've had to cut it! . . .'

He had done nothing, for the past half-hour, but move a little lever back and forth; and he was as spent as though he had hacked and sawn at that monstrous rope and got it clear with his own hands.

At the stern, some of the crew hung over the rail, trying to catch a glimpse of bits of the hawser twisting in the water.

Behind Renaud, the helmsman put his helm hard over to bring the ship round. All he said was:

'Well, I thought my corns would never trouble me again!'

*   *   *

The *Cyclone* reached the ship on fire at dawn. She was the only ship in sight. She was more or less on an even keel, barely showing a slight list to starboard. The *Cyclone* had kept on calling her by wireless all night; but she had made no reply. A column of dense smoke was rising from her bow, straight up into the calm morning. More smoke strayed over her sides and drifted along her hull.

She was on fire inside her. It was that furtive fire which saps ships slowly, as though it were lit in an oven: a fire which goes down, whereas all other fires go up, and seeks for something to devour right down to the depths of the holds. From a distance, a ship on fire is simply a ship smoking all over, a huge spring of smoke. Her lines remain intact, and her superstructure still holds together. It is only when you get close to her that such a floating ruin reveals herself shattered, twisted, worn away by the flames.

This ship's stern seemed to be intact. Her crew were presumably assembled there; but the insistent calls of the *Cyclone*'s syren produced no sign of movement on board the big steamer.

'That's funny,' said Renaud.

He was repeating the word which Corfec had used the night before by way of registering the mysterious fear aroused in him by the drunken man who had turned up in the rain at the door of the Café de la Douane.

Renaud rounded the ship, which was dancing gently with the swell. Seen from below, the steamer seemed to be entirely surrounded by mist: a white mist which came out of her. Renaud assumed that the whole crew had been seized with panic and taken refuge under hatches in the mess-room, and that even the wireless-operator had found his room too hot for his liking and fled from it. Renaud could not believe that the ship was abandoned; for she was in no state to be abandoned, especially in such weather. He came back under her bow. Then he suddenly reached a decision.

'Get a boat away,' he ordered. 'We'll go and have a look at this.'

Once he was on the steamer's deck, with Tanguy and a couple of sailors, he found that the fire had done more damage than he had supposed from the *Cyclone*'s bridge. It had devoured the forecastle. Nothing was left of it but a rubble of swollen plates, projecting over a hole from which flames rose. Renaud could tell that the fire was already undermining the central superstructure, for smoke was floating under the skylights. Every door they opened revealed a foetid cloud of smoke, which started swaying, as though it were taken by surprise, and tried to get out. Underfoot they could hear the flames reaping their harvest conscientiously, the moaning of overheated steel, things crackling and bursting, and a sullen growling like that of a storm: the blast of the fire in the holds.

'Not many people about!' said Renaud, turning towards Tanguy on the deserted deck.

The mate was holding a thick red line, intended to haul in the hawser later on. This line ran out to the *Cyclone*'s stern, and Tanguy looked as though he had the tug on a leash. He raised his eyebrows slightly as Renaud looked at him.

'Queer ship!' he said.

Renaud strode rapidly towards the stern. Since this was a British ship, everything about her was spick and span. Renaud went down the companion to the mess-room.

On the table there was food on the plates, there were glasses unemptied; but napkins had been hastily thrown down on the seats or on the floor. Off Cape Horn, Renaud had once watched his sailing ship, with all her masts torn off her, running on the rocks like a mad bull; and he had not turned a hair. But, at the sight of these napkins, he felt his astonishment turn into dismay.

It could be neither the sea, which was calm, nor the fire, which was still some distance away, that had scared these men who had fled from the mess-room. They were British; and yet they had left that room in disorder. They had abandoned a ship which they might have saved: a ship which Renaud proposed to save. They had abandoned her without even taking the time to wireless: 'We're off!' What mysterious menace had stampeded them?

Still, Renaud hesitated only for a moment.

'We'll have a look at what she's got inside her,' he said.

At sea, anything he could not understand exasperated him. He would risk anything to be done with uncertainty.

Yet, when he was back on deck again, instinctively he looked for his tug. He could not see her; for the *Cyclone* was masked by the British ship's hull. All he could see was the steamer's bow, spouting like a crater in the cold light: that light from limbo which broods on the face of the waters before sunrise.

Renaud shook himself.

'Come on!' he said.

The four of them got down to the bottom of one of the holds. It was entirely floored with packing-cases of thin wood. Tanguy lifted one, and was astonished to find it so light. This strange ship seemed to be carrying wind. The mate threw the case down and kicked it open. A head slid out of the hole: a tiny china head with fair hair.

Renaud tore the top off and pulled away packing paper. It was a case full of dolls, dolls in new clothes, all asleep; for they had see-saw eyes, and they were lying on their backs.

The four men stared at them, astounded. Renaud picked one up. As soon as he stood it straight, it opened its eyes. He put it down on its face. It cried: a long, shrill little cry, like the mew of a new-born kitten.

The presence of these dolls; their sleep, all in a row; the cry of the one which they had disturbed, now lying across the others with her little arms stretched out – all this was so unexpected, in such a spot, at such a time, that the four men hesitated about doing anything or saying any-thing. They were as abashed as though they were in church. One of the sailors picked up the doll Renaud had dropped, and gently put it back among its sisters, on its back. Renaud, for his part, ran an estimating eye over the tall rows of cases, all exactly alike, nodding his head as he reckoned.

'There's enough in there,' he said, 'to make hundreds of kids happy.'

He thought of the fire. He thought of these cases burning like matches, these thousands of tresses going up in flames, these little heads bursting, with their eyes popping out. The idea upset him more than many a valuable cargo he had seen go to the bottom. He turned towards his three companions.

'If you've got any little girls,' he said, 'now's the time to help yourselves.'

Tanguy did not stir. One of the sailors put the lid on the packing-case again. The other stiffened as though he had been shot. Then he carefully turned away, and busied himself pretending to inspect a bolt. His little girl had died of meningitis in January; and Renaud had forgotten all about it . . .

The rest of them, all three of them, stood there round the packing-case, ill at ease; for sailors love dolls and know all about them. They make dolls. They bring dolls back from the ends of the earth.

'Let's get out of here,' said Renaud.

Back on deck once more, staring again at this abandoned ship on the surface of the green sea, like a huge bonfire left to smoulder for days in a field, he was tormented by this enigma which baffled logic and left his clear head as a captain at fault.

'If that's their cargo,' he growled, 'why the hell did they abandon ship? If it were oil, I could understand it . . .'

He turned to Tanguy.

'Get me a dozen men to link the hawser,' he ordered.

Tanguy took himself off to the bow and leant over the smoking rail. He whistled, then he shouted an order. In this weather, his voice carried far over the water.

A few minutes later, Kerlo and his party came on board. They hauled in a hundred and fifty feet of hawser, and Renaud got them to link it directly to the anchor-ring. In a calm sea like this, that would hold it all right.

Then, before they left the ship, they smashed the skylights and stove in all the hatches they could. Dense smoke burst out, and the holes gave off braced blasts of heat. They were giving air to the furnace; but not for long.

Once they were back on board the *Cyclone*, the boatswain had hoses with brass nozzles at the end of them screwed on to the pumps. Renaud himself aimed the stern gun. Suddenly the fourteen hoses and the two extinguishing guns, like artillery supporting rifle-fire, spat all together. Every hose could discharge a hundred and fifty tons of water an hour. Each of the two guns could discharge twice as much, at a range of ninety yards. All the electrical power generated by the dynamos was harnessed to these spouting geysers. The *Cyclone* turned into one huge fountain, a ship dressed with powerful jets of water which whistled as they crossed one another, converged on the bow of the ship on fire, and crashed upon her in a cataract.

This went on till noon. By then, the smoke was so far subdued that it no longer rose from the ship's bow. Renaud could take it that the holds were drowned. He knew that a ship's fire was not so easily put out. It was merely slumbering; it would come to life again. But he would be able to master it at leisure in the Brest roadstead. He was going to take this ship in there.

Never had a ship in distress followed him so obediently. The hawser was a short one, barely three hundred feet, and it did not labour. The steamer in tow came along with her bow well ahead, rolling even more slightly than the tug, thanks to her heavier tonnage.

From the *Cyclone*'s bridge Renaud stared at her. He felt vaguely uneasy. Her docility was almost disquieting.

Wisps of smoke still strayed about her portholes and lingered on her deck as though they could not get away from it, like puffs of cigarette-smoke blown into rough tweed. But she was not the first ship whose fire the *Cyclone* had got under control, and Renaud could read the signs of smoke. There was nothing to fear before he reached the roadstead.

The *Cyclone* was making eight knots easily. Renaud started thinking about the report which he would send to Paris the next day.

'Anyhow,' he said to himself, 'there's nobody on board this time to cut the hawser . . .'

At six o'clock in the evening, abreast of the Stiff, the *Cyclone* fell in with some lobster-fishermen. They took off their berets and waved them. They realised that the *Cyclone* had got hold of a fine prize, and the knowledge warmed the blood of the old wreckers which still flowed in their veins.

At seven o'clock, off the Trois-Pierres fixed light, the *Cyclone*'s crew suddenly heard an explosion on board the ship in tow, like that of a mine. A surge set up under the surface of the water flung the tug violently to starboard. Then they saw Kerlo rush for the hawser-hook, set it swinging with a furious blow from a sledge-hammer, and uncouple the hawser. Behind them, the big steamer sank like a stone.

When the water had closed over her, the *Cyclone*'s crew were left bewildered, with their eyes fixed on the sea, still swirling from the tremendous suction of the sunken ship. Then the eddies died away, and the swell resumed its regular course. Huge, dirty bubbles rose to the surface and broke where the ship had gone down, and at the same time a strange smell reached their nostrils. It was the smell you breathe in small circuses: the smell of acetylene gas.

The ship of dolls had had her holds full of carbide. The *Cyclone*'s pumps had generated great quantities of gas in them. A spark had done the rest.

Renaud circulated a wireless message to all the French and British coastal stations, informing them that a ship had sunk and constituted a danger to navigation. He stayed on the spot until it was pitch dark, for fear wreckage should come to the surface and endanger other ships.

During this monotonous sentry-go, he strode up and down the bridge with his hands clasped behind his back, gritting his teeth over his disappointment. He was immersed in one of those mute rages of his which his crew had learned to know and to fear.

He cruised over the spot for an hour, sweeping the sea with his searchlights. Then, his duty done, he sailed for port.

He had but one desire. It was to get home, to get away from his ship and his rotten job, to get away from all these men with long faces over the disastrous loss of their prize. He felt that his crew, deep down inside them, suspected that fate was against them – that fate was against him.

As soon as the *Cyclone* was moored at her station alongside the quay, Renaud hurried ashore into the darkness.

'Look after things,' he said to Tanguy. 'See you to-morrow.'

14

The Dark Well of the Human Spirit

Herman Melville, *Moby Dick* (Harmondsworth: Penguin, 1992), pp. 124–7

I hesitated to include Melville in this personal album: I was afraid that he would be out of place, not through any lack but through excess; in short, that he would not get through the door. In Moby Dick, there is everything that I look for in a book but also much more. There is human experience, the monsters, the real world reflected in a visionary world, the hunt seen as both the judgement on, and justification of man, the dark well of humanity. It is a fable, but, as Pavese says in the Introduction to his exemplary translation, 'the richness of a fable lies in the capacity it has to symbolize the greatest number of experiences'.

I prefer to pass over the pages, at the same time biblical and barbaric, in which the sacred terror of the hunt is portrayed, to note instead the portrait of a man 'in full fig', replete with modesty and presentiment.

The chief mate of the *Pequod* was Starbuck, a native of Nantucket, and a Quaker by descent. He was a long, earnest man, and though born on an icy coast, seemed well adapted to endure hot latitudes, his flesh being hard as twice-baked biscuit. Transported to the Indies, his live blood would not spoil like bottled ale. He must have been born in some time of general drought and famine, or upon one of those fast days for which his state is famous. Only some thirty arid summers had he seen; those summers had dried up all his physical superfluousness. But this, his thinness, so to speak, seemed no more the token of wasting anxieties and cares, than it seemed the indication of any bodily blight. It was merely the condensation of the man. He was by no means ill-looking; quite the contrary. His pure tight skin was an excellent fit; and closely wrapped up in it, and embalmed with inner health and strength, like a revivified Egyptian, this Starbuck seemed prepared to endure for long ages to come, and to endure always, as now; for be it Polar snow or torrid sun, like a patent chronometer, his interior vitality was warranted to do well in all climates. Looking into his eyes, you seemed to see there the yet lingering images of those thousand-fold perils he had calmly confronted through life. A staid, steadfast man, whose life for the most part was a telling pantomime of action, and not a tame chapter of words. Yet, for all his hardy sobriety and fortitude, there were certain qualities in him which at times affected, and in some cases seemed well nigh to overbalance all the rest. Uncommonly conscientious for a seaman, and endued with a deep natural reverence, the wild watery loneliness of his life did therefore strongly incline him to superstition; but to that sort of superstition, which in some organizations seems rather to spring, somehow, from intelligence than from ignorance. Outward portents and inward presentiments were his. And if at times these things bent the welded iron of his soul, much more did his far-away domestic memories of his young Cape wife and child, tend to bend him still more from the original ruggedness of his nature, and open him still further to those latent influences which, in some honest-hearted men, restrain the gush of dare-devil daring, so often evinced by others in the more perilous vicissitudes of the fishery. 'I will have no man in my boat,' said Starbuck, 'who is not afraid of a whale.' By this, he seemed to mean, not only that the most reliable and useful courage was that which arises from the fair estimation of the encountered peril, but that an utterly fearless man is a far more dangerous comrade than a coward.

'Aye, aye,' said Stubb, the second mate, 'Starbuck, there, is as careful a man as you'll find anywhere in this fishery.' But we shall ere long see what that word 'careful' precisely means when used by a man like Stubb, or almost any other whale hunter.

Starbuck was no crusader after perils; in him courage was not a sentiment; but a thing simply useful to him, and always at hand upon all mortally practical occasions. Besides, he thought, perhaps, that in this business of whaling, courage was one of the great staple outfits of the ship, like her beef and her bread, and not to be foolishly wasted. Wherefore he had no fancy for lowering for whales after sun-down; nor for persisting in fighting a fish that too much persisted in fighting him. For, thought Starbuck, I am here in this critical ocean to kill whales for my living, and not to be killed by them for theirs; and that hundreds of men had been so killed Starbuck well knew. What doom was his own father's? Where, in the bottomless deeps, could he find the torn limbs of his brother?

With memories like these in him, and, moreover, given to a certain superstitiousness, as has been said; the courage of this Starbuck which could, nevertheless, still flourish, must indeed have been extreme. But it was not in reasonable nature that a man so organized, and with such terrible experiences and remembrances as he had; it was not in nature that these things should fail in latently engendering an element in him, which, under suitable circumstances, would break out from its confinement, and burn all his courage up. And brave as he might be, it was that sort of bravery, chiefly visible in some intrepid men, which, while generally abiding firm in the conflict with seas, or winds, or whales, or any of the ordinary irrational horrors of the world, yet cannot withstand those more terrific, because more spiritual terrors, which sometimes menace you from the concentrating brow of an enraged and mighty man.

But were the coming narrative to reveal, in any instance, the complete abasement of poor Starbuck's fortitude, scarce might I have the heart to write it; for it is a thing most sorrowful, nay shocking, to expose the fall of valor in the soul. Men may seem detestable as joint stock-companies and nations; knaves, fools, and murderers there may be; men may have mean and meagre faces; but man, in the ideal, is so noble and so sparkling, such a grand and glowing creature, that over any ignominious blemish in him all his fellows should run to throw their costliest robes. That immaculate manliness we feel within ourselves, so far within us, that it remains intact though all the outer character seem gone; bleeds with keenest anguish at the undraped spectacle of a valor-ruined man. Nor can piety itself, at such a shameful sight, completely stifle her upbraidings against the permitting stars. But this august dignity I treat of, is not the dignity of kings and robes, but that abounding dignity which has no robed investiture. Thou shalt see it shining in the arm that wields a pick or drives a spike; that democratic dignity which, on all hands, radiates without end from God; Himself! The great God absolute! The centre and circumference of all democracy! His omnipresence, our divine equality!

If, then, to meanest mariners, and renegades and castaways, I shall hereafter ascribe high qualities, though dark; weave round them tragic graces; if even the most mournful, perchance the most abased, among them all, shall at times lift himself to the exalted mounts; if I shall touch that workman's arm with some ethereal light; if I shall spread a rainbow over his disastrous set of sun; then against all mortal critics bear me out in it, thou just Spirit of Equality, which hast spread one royal mantle of humanity over all my kind! Bear me out in it, thou great democratic God! who didst not refuse to the swart convict, Bunyan, the pale, poetic pearl; Thou who didst clothe with doubly hammered leaves of finest gold, the stumped and paupered arm of old Cervantes; Thou who didst pick up Andrew Jackson from the pebbles; who didst hurl him upon a war-horse; who didst thunder him higher than a throne! Thou who, in all Thy mighty, earthly marchings, ever cullest Thy selectest champions from the kingly commons; bear me out in it, O God!

15

Survivors in the Sahara

Antoine de Saint-Exupéry,* *Wind, Sand and Stars*, translated by
William Rees (Harmondsworth: Penguin, 1995), pp. 96–102

*A funeral oration is a necessary but sad affair: likewise rereading an author
who once told us something but who no longer speaks to us in the same voice,
or if he speaks the voice no longer has the same resonance. Is it his fault or
ours? On paper it is all there, everything necessary for the book to live;
Saint-Exupéry is a good man and an accomplished writer, he has fought,
acted, suffered; he has loved nature and people, he has lived the adventure of
flying with an open spirit, like a new way of reading the universe: he died in
silence, somewhere in the sky, defending his country and all of us, at the age
of forty-four: that is young for a writer but old for a pilot in wartime. And yet,
even in the episode presented here, where a virile endurance shows through,
and an intelligent strategy against the hallucinations of being trapped in the
desert, one has the impression that he is not on the button, of a displacement
between the thing lived and the words that recount them. The music is there,
but at times the voice is mannered, grating, with strident wrong notes.*

*The author and Prévot, pilots of the postal aircraft, have seen their aircraft
crash on the edge of the Sahara. They have nothing to eat or drink, their
distress signals have not been seen. They seek salvation on foot.*

Farewell, you whom I loved. It is not my fault if the human body cannot
last three days without drinking. I did not believe myself to be such a
prisoner of flowing springs, or suspect that independence is so brief. We
think man can walk straight ahead, that man is free . . . We cannot see
the rope that attaches him to the well, that binds him like an umbilical

cord to the womb of the earth. If he takes one step too many, he dies.

Apart from your suffering, I have no regrets. When all's said and done I've had the best of it. If I could go back, I would start it all again. I need to live. There is no human life in cities now.

Flying is not the point. The aeroplane is a means, not an end. It is not for the plane that we risk our lives. Nor is it for the sake of his plough that the farmer ploughs. But through the plane we can leave the cities and their accountants, and find a truth that farmers know.

We do a man's work and we have a man's worries. We are in contact with the wind, with the stars, with the night, with the sand, with the sea. We try to outwit the forces of nature. We wait for dawn as a gardener waits for spring. We wait for the next port of call as a promised land, and we seek our truth in the stars.

I shall not complain. For three days I have walked, I have been thirsty, I have followed tracks in the sand, I have pinned my hopes on the dew. I have striven to rejoin my kind, whose dwelling-place on the earth I had forgotten. And those are concerns of the living. I cannot but judge them more important than choosing which variety show to go to in the evening.

I can no longer understand those dense crowds on the suburban trains, those men who think they are men and yet who are reduced like ants, by a pressure they do not feel, to the use that is made of them. When they are free, on their absurd little Sundays, how do they fill their time?

Once, in Russia, I heard Mozart being played in a factory. I wrote about it, and received two hundred offensive letters. I have nothing against those who prefer saloon bar honky-tonk, but I do blame the bar-owner. I don't like to see men damaged.

I am happy in my profession. I feel myself to be a ploughman of the skies. In the suburban train, I feel death pangs very different from these! All things considered, this is luxury! . . .

I have no regrets. I've gambled and I've lost. It was all in a day's work. But at least I have breathed the wind of the sea.

That is an unforgettable nourishment for those who have once tasted it. True, comrades? True. It isn't a matter of living dangerously. Such a

pretentious phrase. Toreadors don't thrill me. Danger is not what I love.
I know what I love. It is life.

The sky seems about to lighten. I free one arm from the sand and run
my hand over a piece of parachute within my reach. It is dry. But let's
wait. Dew falls at dawn. But dawn lightens the sky, and there is no
moisture on our cloths. My thoughts become a little blurred, and I hear
myself saying: 'There is a dry heart here . . . dry heart . . . a dry heart that
can form no tears! . . .'

'Come on, Prévot! Our throats are still open: we must keep walking.'

VII

Now the west wind is blowing, the wind that dries up a man in nineteen
hours. My oesophagus is still not closed, but it is hard and painful, and I
can already sense something rasping in it. That cough I have heard
described will begin soon; I am expecting it. My tongue is a hindrance.
But the worst thing is that I can already see spots of shining light. When
they turn into flames, I will lie down.

We are walking rapidly, taking advantage of the early morning coolness. We know only too well that when the sun is at its zenith, as they
say, we will walk no further. At its zenith . . .

We have lost the right to sweat. Along with the right to pause. This
coolness is merely the coolness of 18 per cent humidity. This wind that
is blowing comes from the desert, and under its deceitful and tender
caress our blood is evaporating.

On the first day we ate a few grapes. Then, through three days, half an
orange and a fragment of cake. Even if we had food, how could we
swallow it without saliva? But I feel no hunger, only thirst, and in fact
now the effects of thirst rather than thirst itself. The hard throat, the
plaster tongue, the rasping and the foul taste in the mouth. These are
sensations I have never known before. Water would cure them, no doubt,
but nothing in my memory associates them with that remedy. Thirst is
becoming more and more a sickness, less and less a craving.

Images of springs and fruits already seem less heartbreaking. I am forgetting the radiance of the orange, as I seem to have forgotten my affections. Perhaps my memory is already empty.

We have sat down, but we must keep going. No more long stretches now. Every five hundred yards we collapse with fatigue, and lying down is bliss. But we must keep going.

The landscape is changing. The stones are more sparse, and we are walking on sand. There are dunes a mile ahead, with some patches of stunted vegetation. I prefer the sand to the steely armour. I prefer the golden desert. The Sahara. I seem to recognize it . . .

Now two hundred yards are enough to exhaust us.

'But we're going to make it to those bushes, if that's all we ever do.'

That is the final limit. A week later, when we come back over our tracks in a car to search for the Simoun, we will confirm that our last effort took us fifty miles. So I have already done about a hundred and twenty. How could I carry on?

Yesterday I was walking without hope. Today those words have lost their meaning. Today we are walking because we are walking. Like oxen ploughing, I imagine. Yesterday I dreamed of a paradise of orange groves. Today, for me, there is no paradise. I do not believe the orange groves exist.

There is nothing more within me but a heart squeezed totally dry. I shall fall, and I acknowledge no despair. No suffering, even. This I regret, for sorrow would be as sweet as water. It would bring pity, compassion for myself as from a friend. But I have no friend in the world now.

When they find me, with my eyes burnt out, they will imagine that I must have cried out and suffered greatly. But surges of emotion, regrets and sweet sufferings are all forms of wealth, and I have no more wealth. Pure young girls know sorrow as their first love fades into its evening, and they weep. Sorrow is linked to the vibrant rhythm of life. And I have no more sorrow . . .

I am the desert. I can form no more saliva, but neither can I form the tender images that would call forth moans of grief. The sun has dried up the well of tears within me.

And yet, what have I just seen? A breath of hope has passed over me like a breeze rippling the sea. What sign has just awakened my instinct before striking my conscious mind? Nothing has changed, and yet everything has changed. This sheet of sand, these mounds and these sparse patches of greenery are no longer a landscape, but a setting. The stage is still empty, but the scene is set. I look at Prévot. The same amazement has struck him, but he too has no grasp of what he is experiencing.

I swear to you that something is about to happen . . .

I swear to you that the desert has come alive. I swear to you that this absence and this silence are suddenly more filled with stirring life than a square packed with people . . .

We are saved, there are tracks in the sand! . . .

We had lost the trail of the human species, we were cut off from our tribe, we had found ourselves alone in the world, left behind by the universal movement of men, and here now we discover, marked in the sand, their miraculous footprints.

'Look, Prévot, here two men separated . . .'

'Here a camel knelt down . . .'

'And here . . .'

But we are not saved yet. We cannot simply wait. In a few hours we will be past help. Once the cough sets in, thirst's onslaught is too swift. And our throats . . .

Yet I believe in that caravan, as it sways along somewhere, in the desert.

So we walked on, and suddenly I heard a cock crow. Guillaumet told me: 'Towards the end, I heard cocks crowing in the Andes. I heard railway trains too . . .'

I remember his story the instant the cock crows here, and tell myself:

'My eyes were the first to deceive me. It must be an effect of thirst. My ears have held out longer . . .' But Prévot grips my arm:

'Did you hear it?'

'What?'

'The cock crowing!'

'So . . . then . . .'

Yes, of course, you fool, it's life . . .

I had one final hallucination: three dogs chasing each other. Prévot was looking, but he couldn't see them. But there are two of us, stretching out our arms towards the Bedouin. There are two of us dragging every ounce of breath from our lungs. Two of us, laughing with joy! . . .

But our voices won't carry thirty yards. Our vocal chords have dried up. We've been speaking to each other in whispers, without knowing it!

The Bedouin and his camel have just appeared from behind the dune, but now, now they are slowly beginning to move away. Perhaps this man is alone. A cruel demon has shown him to us only to withdraw him from our sight . . .

And how could we run now?

Another Arab appears in profile on the dune. We shout, but it is no more than a whisper. So we wave our arms, as if filling the sky with giant signals. But the Bedouin is still gazing to the right . . .

And now he begins a leisurely quarter-turn. At the instant when he faces us head-on, the miracle will be accomplished. The very instant when he looks in our direction will itself obliterate thirst, death and mirages. He has made his quarter-turn, and the world has already changed. Merely a movement of his upper body, merely a shift in his gaze will create life, and to me he looks like a god . . .

It is a miracle . . . He is walking towards us over the sand, like a god on the surface of the sea . . .

The Arab simply looked at us. He placed his hands firmly on our shoulders, and we obeyed him. We lay down upon the sand. There are no races here, nor any languages, nor any discord . . . There is this poor nomad who has placed his archangelic hands on our shoulders.

We waited, our foreheads on the sand. And now we are drinking, flat on our stomachs, heads in the bowl like calves. The Bedouin is alarmed, and keeps making us pause. But as soon as he lets us go our faces plunge back into the water.

Water!

Water, you have neither taste, nor colour, nor scent. You cannot be defined. You are savoured, but you remain unknown. You are not a necessity of life: you are life. You fill us with a joy that is not of the senses. You restore to us all powers we had surrendered. Through your grace, all the desiccated springs of our hearts flow forth once more.

Of all the riches in the world you are the greatest, and the most delicate, you who lie so pure in the womb of the earth. A man can die by a magnesian spring. He can die a yard from a salt lake. He can die in spite of a quart of dew with chemicals suspended in it. You can accept no mixing, bear no adulteration; you are a sensitive divinity . . .

But you spread within us an infinitely simple happiness.

Yet as for you, our saviour, Bedouin of Libya, you will be for ever effaced from my memory. I will never be able to remember your face. You are Man, and you appear to me with the face of all men together. You have never set eyes on us, yet you have recognized us. You are our beloved brother. And I in my turn will recognize you in all men.

Bathed in a light of nobility and generosity you appear before me, great Lord with the power to give water to drink. All my friends and all my enemies are walking towards me in your person, and I have no enemy left in all the world.

16

The Curious Merchant

Marco Polo, *The Travels*, translated by Ronald Latham (Harmondsworth: Penguin, 1958), pp. 89–90, 156–7, 178–80, 253–5

Marco Polo, a merchant from a noble Venetian family, managed to accomplish a remarkable feat. Not only, at the age of twenty-one, together with his father and an uncle, did he reach the court of Kublai Khan, the Mongol Emperor who had subjugated China, but he knew also how to win the favour of this most powerful man, who even entrusted him with administrative and diplomatic duties. On his return he gave an account of his travels, in which difficult tasks and dangers are highlighted with sober reserve, and the wonderful sights and sounds are described with the good sense of a merchant, attentive to frauds, prices and profits, and with the amused precision of a curious man. For many centuries, his reports, essentially truthful, were derided as wild tales or accepted merely as exotic fantasies.

[CONCERNING SALAMANDER*]

Another province on the edge of the desert towards the north-north-east is Ghinghintalas, sixteen days in extent, which is also subject to the Great Khan. It has cities and towns in plenty. The inhabitants consist of three groups, idolaters, Mahometans, and Nestorian Christians.

Towards the northern boundary of this province is a mountain with a rich vein of steel and *ondanique*.* In this same mountain occurs a vein from which is produced salamander. You must understand that this is not a beast as is commonly asserted; but its real nature is such as I will now describe. It is a well known fact that by nature no beast or other animal can live in fire, because every animal is composed of the four elements. For lack of any certain knowledge about salamander, men spoke of it, and still do, as a beast; but this is not true. I will now tell you the real facts. First, let me explain that I had a Turkish companion named Zurficar, a man of great intelligence, who spent three years in this province, in the service of the Great Khan, engaged in the extraction of this salamander and *ondanique* and steel and other products. For the Great Khan regularly appoints governors every three years to govern this province and supervise the salamander industry. My companion told me the true facts and I have also seen them for myself. When the stuff found in this vein of which you have heard has been dug out of the mountain and crumbled into bits, the particles cohere and form fibres like wool. Accordingly, when the stuff has been extracted, it is first dried, then pounded in a large copper mortar and then washed. The residue consists of this fibre of which I have spoken and worthless earth, which is separated from it. Then this wool-like fibre is carefully spun and made into cloths. When the cloths are first made, they are far from white. But they are thrown into the fire and left there for a while; and there they turn as white as snow. And whenever one of these cloths is soiled or discoloured, it is thrown into the fire and left there for a while, and it comes out as white as snow. The account I have given you of the salamander is the truth, and all the other accounts that are put about are lies and fables. Let me tell you finally that one of these cloths is now at Rome; it was sent to the Pope by the Great Khan as a valuable gift, and for this reason the sacred napkin of our lord Jesus Christ was wrapped in it.

Let us now leave this province and turn to others lying towards the east-north-east.

[COAL]

It is a fact that throughout the province of Cathay there is a sort of black stone, which is dug out of veins in the hillsides and burns like logs. These stones keep a fire going better than wood. I assure you that, if you put them on the fire in the evening and see that they are well alight, they will continue to burn all night, so that you will find them still glowing in the morning. They do not give off flames, except a little when they are first kindled, just as charcoal does, and once they have caught fire they give out great heat. And you must know that these stones are burnt throughout the province of Cathay. It is true that they also have plenty of firewood. But the population is so enormous and there are so many bath-houses and baths continually being heated, and that the wood could not possibly suffice, since there is no one who does not go to a bath-house at least three times a week and take a bath, and in winter every day, if he can manage it. And every man of rank or means has his own bathroom in his house, where he takes a bath. So it is clear that there could never be enough wood to maintain such a conflagration. So these stones, being very plentiful and very cheap, effect a great saving of wood.

[THE CROCODILE]

On leaving Yachi and continuing westwards for ten days, the traveller reaches the kingdom of Kara-jang, the capital of which is also called Kara-jang. The people are idolaters and subject to the Great Khan. The king is Hukaji, a son of the Great Khan. In this province gold dust is found in the rivers, and gold in bigger nuggets in the lakes and mountains. They have so much of it that they give a *saggio* of gold for six of silver. Here too the cowries of which I have spoken are used for money. They are not found in this province, but come here from India.

In this province live huge snakes and serpents* of such a size that no one could help being amazed even to hear of them. They are loathsome creatures to behold. Let me tell you just how big they are. You may take it for a fact that there are some of them ten paces in length that are as thick as a stout cask: for their girth runs to about ten palms. These are the biggest. They have two squat legs in front near the head, which have no feet but simply three claws, two small and one bigger, like the claws of a falcon or a lion. They have enormous heads and eyes so bulging that they are bigger than loaves. Their mouth is big enough to swallow a man at one gulp. Their teeth are huge. All in all, the monsters are of such inordinate bulk and ferocity that there is neither man nor beast but goes in fear of them. There are also smaller ones, not exceeding eight paces in length, or six or it may be five.

Let me tell you now how these monsters are trapped. You must know that by day they remain underground because of the great heat; at nightfall, they sally out to hunt and feed and seize whatever prey they can come by. They go down to drink at streams and lakes and springs. They are so bulky and heavy and of such a girth that when they pass through sand on their nightly search for food or drink they scoop out a furrow through the sand that looks as if a butt full of wine had been rolled that way. Now the hunters who set out to catch them lay traps at various places in the trails that show which way the snakes are accustomed to go down the banks into the water. These are made by embedding in the earth a stout wooden stake to which is fixed a sharp steel tip like a razor-blade or lance-head, projecting about a palm's breadth beyond the stake and slanting in the direction from which the serpents approach. This is covered with sand, so that nothing of the stake is visible. Traps of this sort are laid in great numbers. When the snake, or rather the serpent, comes down the trail to drink, he runs full-tilt into the steel, so that it pierces his chest and rips his belly right to the navel and he dies on the spot. The hunter knows that the serpent is dead by the cry of the birds, and then he ventures to approach his prey. Otherwise he dare not draw near.

When hunters have trapped a serpent by this means, they draw out the gall from the belly and sell it for a high price, for you must know that it makes a potent medicine. If a man is bitten by a mad dog, he is given a drop of it to drink – the weight of a halfpenny – and he is cured forthwith. And when a woman is in labour and cries aloud with the pangs of travail, she is given a drop of the serpent's gall and as soon as she has drunk it she is delivered of her child forthwith. Its third use is when someone is afflicted by any sort of growth: he puts a drop of this gall on it and is cured in a day or two. For these reasons the gall of this serpent is highly prized in these provinces. The flesh also commands a good price, because it is very good to eat and is esteemed as a delicacy.

Another thing about these serpents: they go to the dens where lions and bears and other beasts of prey have their cubs and gobble them up – parents as well as young – if they can get at them.

[THE RHINOCEROS]

They have wild elephants and plenty of unicorns, which are scarcely smaller than elephants. They have the hair of a buffalo and feet like an elephant's. They have a single large, black horn in the middle of the forehead. They do not attack with their horn, but only with their tongue and their knees; for their tongues are furnished with long, sharp spines, so that when they want to do any harm to anyone they first crush him by kneeling upon him and then lacerate him with their tongues. They have a head like a wild boar's and always carry it stooped towards the ground. They spend their time by preference wallowing in mud and slime. They are very ugly brutes to look at. They are not at all such as we describe them when we relate that they let themselves be captured by virgins, but clean contrary to our notions. There are a great many monkeys here of many different sorts. There are also the goshawks, black as crows, of great size and very apt at fowling.

I would have you know that those who profess to have brought pygmy men from the Indies are involved in great falsehood and deception. For I assure you that these so-called pygmies are manufactured in this island; and I will tell you how. The truth is that there is a sort of monkey here which is very tiny and has a face very like a man's. So men take some of these monkeys, and remove all their hair, with a kind of ointment. Then they attach some long hairs to the chin in place of a beard, threading them through holes in the skin so that when the skin shrivels the holes shrink and the hairs seem to have grown there naturally. The feet and hands and other limbs which are not in conformity with the human figure are stretched and strained and remoulded by hand to the likeness of a man. Then the bodies are dried and treated with camphor and other drugs, so that they appear to be human. This is all a piece of trickery, as you have heard. For nowhere in all the Indies or in wilder regions still was there ever seen any man so tiny as these seem to be.

[SUMATRA]

So much for Basman. The next kingdom, situated in the same island, is called Sumatra. In this kingdom I myself Marco Polo spent five months, waiting for weather that would permit us to continue our voyage. Here again the Pole Star is never visible nor yet the stars of the Plough, either much or little. The people are idolaters and savages. They have a wealthy and powerful king and also profess allegiance to the Great Khan.

This is how we spent our five months. We disembarked from our ships and for fear of these nasty and brutish folk who kill men for food we dug a big trench round our encampment, extending down to the shore of the harbour at either end. On the embankment of the trench we built five wooden towers or forts; and within these fortifications we lived for five months. There was no lack of timber. But the islanders used to trade with us for victuals and the like; for there was a compact between us.

The fish here are the best in the world. The people have no wheat, but live on rice. They have no wine, except such as I will describe to you. You must know that they have a sort of tree,* of which they lop off the branches. Then they set a good-sized pot beside the raw stump left on the tree, and in a day and a night it is filled. The wine thus produced is very good to drink and is a sovereign remedy for dropsy, consumption, and the spleen. The trees are like little date-palms and bear four branches; they need only to be lopped in order to produce this amount of excellent wine. And let me tell you something more. When wine ceases to ooze from the stumps, they pour water round the foot of the trees, as much as they judge to be needful, leading it through channels from the rivers. Then, when they have been watered for an hour, they begin to emit the fluid as before. There is a white wine and a bright red one. They have abundance of fine, large coconuts. They eat all sorts of flesh, clean and unclean.

Let us now leave here and pass on to a kingdom called Dagroian.

[MEN WITH TAILS]

Let me tell you next of the kingdom of Lambri, which also has a king of its own but professes allegiance to the Great Khan. The people are idolaters. The country produces abundance of brazil, besides camphor, and other precious spices in profusion. In cultivating brazil they first sow the seed; then, when small shoots have sprung up, they dig them up and replant them elsewhere; there they leave them for three years and then dig them up, roots and all. I may tell you that we brought some of this seed back to Venice and sowed it in the earth there; but nothing came up. This was due to the cold climate.

Now here is something really remarkable. I give you my word that in this kingdom there are men who have tails fully a palm in length. They are not at all hairy. This is true of most of the men – that is, of those who live outside in the mountains, not of those in the city. Their tails are as thick as a dog's. There are also many unicorns and a profusion of wild game, both beast and bird.

Lastly, let us turn to the kingdom of Fansur, which is also part of the island of which we have been speaking.

17

The Poet-Researcher

Lucretius, *On the Nature of the Universe*, translated by
Sir Ronald Melville (Oxford: Clarendon Press, 1997), pp. 47–9

*If I had read Lucretius in high school I would have been enchanted, but he is
not willingly read in school, officially because he is too difficult, actually
because there has always been a whiff of impiety about his verses. For this
reason, at the end of antiquity a cloak of silence was wrapped around him and
today almost nothing is known of this extraordinary man. Consciously or not,
for a long time he was regarded as dangerous, because he sought a purely
rational explanation of nature, had faith in the evidence of his own senses,
wanted to liberate man from suffering and fear, rebelled against all superstition,
and described earthly love in lucid poetry.*

*His extreme faith in the explicability of the universe is the same as that of
modern-day atomists. His materialism, and hence his mechanical reductionism,
is naïve and now makes us smile, but here and there appear astonishing
intuitions: why is olive oil viscous, diamond hard, and seawater salty?*

> With this in mind it is easy to explain
> Why the fire of lightning penetrates much further
> Than our fire does which springs from earthly torches.
> For you could say that the heavenly fire of lightning
> Is finer, being composed of smaller shapes
> And therefore passes through apertures impassable
> By our fire sprung from wood and lit by torch.
> Besides, light passes through a pane of horn,* but rain
> Is thrown off. Why? Because the atoms of light

Are smaller than those that make life-giving water.
And though we see wine pass quickly through a strainer,
Yet olive oil by contrast lags and lingers;
No doubt, either because its atoms are larger
Or they are more hooked and more closely interwoven,
And therefore cannot separate so quickly
And trickle through the holes each one by one.

   And here's another thing. Honey and milk
Rolled in the mouth have a delightful taste;
But bitter wormwood and harsh centaury
Quite screw the face up with their loathsome flavour.
So you can easily see that smooth round atoms
Make up things which give pleasure to our senses,
But, by contrast, things that seem harsh and bitter
Are more composed of atoms that are hooked,
Which therefore tear their way into our senses,
And entering break the surface of our bodies.

   There is conflict between those things that strike the senses
As good or bad, because their shapes are different.
The strident rasping of a screeching saw
You must not think consists of elements
As smooth as melodies musicians shape
Waking the tuneful lyre with nimble fingers.
Nor must you think that atoms of the same shape
Enter men's nostrils when foul corpses burn
As when Cilician saffron* o'er the stage
Is freshly cast, or when a near-by altar
Exhales the perfumes of Arabia.
And colours too, whose beauty feeds the eye,
Cannot be composed of atoms similar
To those that prick the pupil and force tears,
Or bring through ugliness disgust and loathing.
For everything that charms the senses must

Contain some smoothness in its primal atoms.
But by contrast things that are harsh and painful
Are found to have some roughness in their matter.
Some atoms are rightly thought to be neither smooth
Nor altogether hooked, with curving points,
But rather to have angles projecting slightly;
These tickle our senses without harming them.
Of such kind are wine-lees and piquant endive.
And fire with heat and frost with cold have teeth
That bite our senses in quite different ways,
As touch in each case indicates to us.
For touch (by all the holy powers of heaven!),
Touch is the body's sense, whether from outside
A thing slips in, or something inside hurts us,
Or pleasure comes when something issues forth
In procreative acts of Venus, or when some blow
Upsets the body's atoms and we feel
Disordered by their ferment – and for proof
Hit yourself anywhere with your own hand!
So atoms must have widely different shapes
Since they can cause such varying sensations.

   Again, things that seem hard and dense must be
Composed much more of atoms hooked together
Held tight deep down by branch-like particles.
First in this class and in the leading rank
Stand diamonds, well used to scorn all blows.
Next come stout flints and the hard strength of iron
And bronze that fights and shrieks when bolts are shot.
But liquids in their fluid composition
Must consist more of atoms smooth and round.
You can pour poppy seeds as easily as water,
The tiny spheres do not hold each other back,
And if you knock a heap of them they run

Downhill in the same way as water does.
And all those things you see that in an instant
Disperse, like smoke or clouds or flames, must be,
If not composed entirely of smooth round atoms,
At least not hampered by a close-knit texture,
So they can sting the body and pass through stones
Without adhering together. So you can see
That all things of this kind that prick the senses
Are made of atoms sharp but not enmeshed.
And some things too can be both fluid and bitter,
Like the salt sea. This should cause no surprise.
For, being fluid, it consists of smooth round atoms,
And rough ones are mixed with them, thus causing pain.
There is no need for them to be hooked together.
You must know that they are round as well as rough
And so can roll and also hurt the senses.
It can be shown that Neptune's bitter brine
Comes from a mixture of atoms, rough with smooth.
There is a way to separate them. You can see
How the sweet water, when the same is filtered
Through many layers of earth, runs separately
Into a pit and loses all its saltness.
The atoms of nauseous salt are left on top.
Since being rough they adhere more to the earth.

18

The Jew on Horseback

Isaac Babel,* 'Crossing the Zbruz' and 'Salt', *Collected Stories* (Harmondsworth: Penguin, 1994), pp. 91–3, 163–7

I hope the reader will forgive me if I drag him from the half-lit study of a solitary poet to the roar and slaughter of a bitter war. I know of nothing more boring than an orderly reading curriculum, and believe instead in the unlikely juxtapositions. What do Lucretius and Isaac Babel have in common? There is something: the mysterious Epicurean poet killed by a love philtre and the Jewish-Cossack 'with autumn in his soul', shot by Stalin in 1941, would immediately have found common ground in compassion for the man who is overwhelmed by violence.

We are in the Russo-Polish War of 1920, and the cruelty of these two stories leaves us dumb. To what degree is it legitimate to exploit violence in literature? That there is a limit is certain; as soon as you cross it you fall into mortal sins, aestheticism, sadism, prostitution for the cannibalistic consumption of a certain public. Babel is close to that limit but he doesn't cross it. He is saved by his compassion, which is modest and swathed in irony.

CROSSING THE ZBRUCZ

Nachdiv 6* has reported that Novograd-Volynsk was taken at dawn today. The staff has moved out of Krapivno, and our transport is strung like a noisy rearguard along the high road, along the unfading high road that goes from Brest to Warsaw and was built on the bones of muzhiks by Nicholas I.

Fields of purple poppies flower around us, the noonday wind is playing in the yellowing rye, the virginal buckwheat rises on the horizon like the wall of a distant monastery. The quiet Volyn is curving. The Volyn is withdrawing from us into a pearly mist of birch groves, it is creeping away into flowery knolls and entangling itself with enfeebled arms in thickets of hops. An orange sun is rolling across the sky like a severed head, a gentle radiance glows in the ravines of the thunderclouds and the standards of the sunset float above our heads. The odour of yesterday's blood and of slain horses drips into the evening coolness. The Zbrucz, now turned black, roars and pulls tight the foamy knots of the rapids. The bridges have been destroyed, and we ford the river on horseback. A majestic moon lies on the waves. The horses sink into the water up to their backs, the sonorous currents ooze between hundreds of horses' legs. Someone sinks, and resonantly defames the Mother of God. The river is littered with the black rectangles of carts, it is filled with a rumbling, whistling and singing that clamour above the serpents of the moon and the shining chasms.

Late at night we arrive in Novograd. In the billet that has been assigned to me I find a pregnant woman and two red-haired Jews with thin necks: a third is already asleep, covered up to the top of his head and pressed against the wall. In the room that has been allotted to me I find ransacked wardrobes, on the floor scraps of women's fur coats, pieces of human excrement and broken shards of the sacred vessels used by the Jews once a year, at Passover.

'Clear up,' I say to the woman. 'What a dirty life you live, landlords . . .'

The two Jews get up from their chairs. They hop about on felt soles, clearing the detritus off the floor, they hop about in silence, monkey-like, like Japanese in a circus; their necks swell and revolve. They spread a torn feather mattress for me, and I lie down facing the wall, alongside the third, sleeping, Jew. A timid destitution immediately closes over my place of rest.

All has been murdered by silence, and only the moon, clasping her round, shining, carefree head in blue hands, plays the vagrant under the window.

I stretch my numbed legs, I lie on the torn mattress and fall asleep. I dream of *nachdiv* 6. He is pursuing the *kombrig** on a heavy stallion, and puts two bullets in his eyes. The bullets penetrate the *kombrig*'s head, and both his eyes fall to the ground.

'Why did you turn the brigade about?' Sativsky – *nachdiv* 6 – cries to the wounded man, and at that point I wake up because the pregnant woman is fumbling with her fingers in my face.

'*Panie*,'* she says, 'you are shouting in your sleep, and you're throwing yourself about. I'm going to make your bed up in the other corner, because you're pushing my Papasha* . . .'

She raises thin legs and a round belly from the floor and removes the blanket from the man who has fallen asleep. An old man is lying there, on his back, dead. His gullet has been torn out, his face has been cleft in two, dark blue blood clings in his beard like pieces of lead.

'*Panie*,' the Jewess says, as she shakes up the feather mattress, 'the Poles were murdering him, and he begged them: "Kill me out in the backyard so that my daughter doesn't see me die." But they did what suited them. He died in this room, thinking about me. And now tell me,' the woman said suddenly with terrible force, 'tell me where else in all the world you would find a father like my father . . .'

Novograd-Volynsk, July 1920

SALT

DEAR COMRADE EDITOR

I want to write to you about unconscious women who are harmful to us. The men hope and trust that, while you were travelling around the citizens' fronts, as you have made note, you did not miss the hardened station of Fastov, which is situated at the other end of the world, in a certain land, at an unknown distance; I have, of course, been there, and drunk home-brewed beer, wetting my whiskers but not my mouth.* Concerning this above-mentioned station there are many things to write, but as we say in our simple way – you can't clear up the Lord's dirt for him. So I shall write to you only about what my eyes have seen with their own hands.

It was a quiet, glorious night seven days ago when our honoured cavalry train stopped there, loaded with fighting men. We were all burning to promote the common cause and had Berdichev as our destination. Only thing was, we noticed that our train wouldn't pull out, not for nobody's business, our Gavrilka* wouldn't turn, and the men began to get worried, talking among themselves – what was the stop here for? And right enough, the stop turned out to be enormous for the common cause on occasion of the fact that the black-market traders, those vicious enemies, among whom there was also a countless number of the female sex, were acting in an insolent manner with the railway authorities. Fearlessly they grabbed hold of the handrails, those wicked enemies, they scooted over the iron roofs, romping around and stirring up trouble, and in each and every hand you could see the not-unfamiliar salt, sacks of up to five *poods*.* But not for long did the capitalist triumph of the black-market traders last. The initiative of the soldiers, who clambered out of the wagon, gave the profaned authority of the railwaymen a chance to get some air in its belly. Only the females with their bags stayed around. Taking pity on them, the soldiers put some of the women in the goods vans, and some they didn't. In our wagon, belonging to the Second Platoon, there were two girls, as it turned out, and when the first bell went, an impressive-looking woman with a baby came over to us, saying:

'Let me on, kind Cossacks. All the war I've been suffering at stations with my babe-at-arms and now I want to see my husband, because of the railway there's no way I can get to him. Haven't I deserved it of you?'

'Now, woman,' I said to her, 'whatever the platoon agrees, that's what we'll do.' And, turning to the platoon, I verified to them that the impressive-looking woman was requesting a ride to the place of destination of her husband and she really did have a bairn with her and what were they going to agree – to let her on or not?

'Let her on,' the lads shouted, 'after she's had us she won't want her husband . . .'

'Well,' I said to the lads, politely enough. 'I bow to you, platoon, only it surprises me to hear such stallion talk from you. Think of your own lives, platoon, and recall that you yourselves were babies in your mothers' arms once. It won't do to talk that way . . .'

And the Cossacks saying to one another what a persuasive fellow he was, Balmashov began to let the woman into the wagon, and she climbed in with gratitude. And each one of them, all a-boil with the truth of my words, found a seat for her, saying in eager rivalry:

'Sit down in the corner, woman, be nice to your little baby in the way that mothers are, nobody's going to touch you in the corner, and you will reach your husband untouched, as you desire, and we're relying on your conscience to raise some new recruits for us, 'cos the old ones are getting older and as you can see there's not much young blood about. We have seen a lot of trouble, woman, both among the active and the re-enlisted, hunger has squeezed us, cold has burned us. But you sit here, woman, and have no fear . . .'

And when the third bell* rang, the train moved off. And the glorious night spread itself over us like a marquee. And in that marquee there were stars like lanterns. And the men remembered the nights of Kuban and the green Kuban stars. And the thoughts flew by like birds. And the wheels went clackety-clack, clackety-clack . . .

After some time had passed, when the night was relieved at its post and the Red drummers had begun to beat the reveille on their Red drums, then the Cossacks came up to me, seeing that I was sitting there not sleeping and lonely as hell.

'Balmashov,' the Cossacks said to me, 'what are you doing sitting there all alone and not asleep?'

'Low do I bow to you, fighting men, and I ask your pardon, but allow me to have a couple of words with that citizeness . . .'

And trembling all over, I rose from my reclining bower, from which the sleep had fled like a wolf from a pack of evil hounds, I walked over to her and took the bairn from her arms and tore the swaddling off it and the rags and saw underneath the swaddling a good little *pood* of salt.

'Here's an interesting bairn, comrades, one that doesn't ask for a tit, doesn't pee on your skirt and doesn't wake up in the night . . .'

'Forgive me, kind Cossacks,' the woman says, butting into our conversation very cool-headed like. 'It was not I that deceived you – it was my trouble that deceived you.'

'Balmashov will forgive your trouble,' I reply to the woman. 'It's not much cost to Balmashov. For what Balmashov buys he sells again. But turn around, woman, and take a look at the Cossacks who have raised you up on high as a toiling mother of the Republic. Turn around and look at those two girls who are crying because we have made them suffer this night. Turn around and look at our wives in the wheatfields of the Kuban who are exhausting their womanly strength without husbands, and those others, who are also on their own, who from evil necessity are raping the girls that pass into their lives . . . But nobody has laid a finger on you, wretched woman, though they should have done. Turn around and look at Russia, overwhelmed by suffering . . .'

And she to me:

'I have been deprived of my salt. I'm not frightened of the truth. You don't care about Russia, you've just saving the Yids Lenin and Trotsky . . .'

'We're not talking about the Yids just now, you harmful citizeness. The Yids don't come into it. By the way, I will not speak for Lenin, but Trotsky is the desperate son of a Tambov governor and he joined the toiling class though he came from another class. Like men sentenced to hard labour they – Lenin and Trotsky – are leading us out on to the free road of life, while you, you vile woman, are more of a counter-revolutionary than the White general who threatens us with a sharp sabre, riding a horse that cost thousands . . . He can be seen, that general, from every road, and the toiler cherishes his dream of cutting his throat, while you, countless citizenry with your interesting little children that don't ask for bread and don't go running in the wind – you cannot be seen, you're like a flea, and you bite, bite, bite . . .'

And truly, I confess, I threw that woman off, down beside the rails, but she, being very coarse, just sat and waved her skirts, and then went her own little low-down way. And, when I saw that woman unharmed, with untold Russia all around her, and the peasants' fields without an ear of corn, and the violated girls, and the comrades many of whom go to the front but few come back, I wanted to jump down from the wagon and kill myself or kill her. But the Cossacks had pity on me and said:

'Give her one from your rifle.'

And taking my trusty rifle from the wall, I wiped that infamy from the face of the working land and the Republic.

And we, the fighting men of the Second Platoon, swear before you, dear comrade editor, and before you, dear comrades of the editorial office, that we will deal mercilessly with all traitors who haul us into a pit and want to turn back the tide and strew Russia with corpses and dead grass.

For all the fighting men of the Second Platoon –
Nikita Balmashov, Soldier of the Revolution.

19

An Irrepressible Quibbler

Sholem Aleichem,* *Tevye the Dairyman and the Railroad Stories,*
translated from the Yiddish with an Introduction by Hillel Halkin
(New York: Schocken Books, 1987), pp. 4–20 (with excisions indicated)

*Sholem Aleichem means in Hebrew: 'Peace be with you.' It isn't thus properly
speaking a name, but the curious and allusive pseudonym of Sholem Rabinov-
itch, a Ukrainian Jew born in 1859, who after having been a rabbi was an
unsuccessful merchant, but who, in covering his territory, was able to accumu-
late such a fund of human experiences that he became one of the most popular
Yiddish writers of his generation. His range is limited; eastern Judaism at the
turn of the century, in full transitional crisis, from its isolation in the country
to its urban, bourgeois integration, but in his microcosms the great modern
ferments are reflected (with their particular colours) – rationalism, socialism,
nationalism, naturalism, expressionism.* Tevye the Dairyman *is his master-
piece; here is the first chapter, slightly abridged.*

*We are in Tsarist Russia, at the beginning of the 1900s, in a world that
hasn't changed for centuries. Tevye belongs to this world; he suffers, but by
virtue of his long experience, he distrusts change. The only words on his lips
are those of resignation, his name (which is the Yiddish form of Toby) is that
of another of the just who accepts hardship, nevertheless he is not one of the
submissive. The instant sympathy that this pious man evinces, further into the
book, for the young revolutionary exiled in Siberia with his second daughter,
is a revelation, and amounts to a strain of genius in the author.*

*In his own way, Tevye senses the fracture that divides the world, he is himself
sadly divided: in so far as he is a Jew of the Diaspora his destiny is to be
wrenched in two. He is Russian in his enduring vitality and indifference to*

147

space and time; he is Jewish in his talmudic mania for quotation (but he quotes almost always haphazardly), and in his pronounced taste for distinctions ('between man and beast', 'between temple and wood'), which is a gentle parody of the Mosaic injunction of Killaim, against forbidden mixtures. Tevye is a simple man but he has a high and noble ideal of the life of man on earth; he is a priest because every Jew is a priest, but at the same time he wears his boots, drinks brandy, whips his poor horse, confined in the atavistic misery of the Russian countryside. He lives the contradictions in his own flesh, he does his utmost to resolve them, he seeks the just and the true with the intense courage of the patriarchs, and, like the characters of Thomas Mann, he recognizes himself in them, in a continuity that only the massacre was able to conquer.

The irrepressible quibbler, the sharp-witted sage ('God himself can't abide those who have no money. And why? Because if God loved the poor they wouldn't be poor any longer'), is no more. Tevye exists no longer: the gas of Auschwitz and Stalin's camps have destroyed him.

To get to the point, though . . . where were we? Oh, yes: in those days, with God's help, I was poor as a devil. No Jew should starve as I did! Not counting suppers, my wife and kids went hungry three times a day. I worked like a dog dragging logs by the wagonful from the forest to the train station for – I'm embarrassed even to tell you – half a ruble a day . . . and not even every day, either. You try feeding a house full of little mouths on that, to say nothing of a horse who's moved in with you and can't be put off with some verse from the Bible, because he expects to eat and no buts! So what does the good Lord do? I tell you, it's not for nothing that they say He's a *zon umefarneys lakoyl*, that He runs this world of His with more brains than you or I could [. . .] You don't know what I'm talking about? Why, I'm talking about myself, about the miracle God helped me to. Be patient and you'll hear all about it.

Vayehi hayoym, as the Bible says: one fine summer day in the middle of the night, I'm driving home through the forest after having dumped my load of logs. I feel like my head is in the ground, there's a black desert growing in my heart; it's all my poor horse can do to drag his feet along behind him. 'It serves you right, you schlimazel,'* I say to him, 'for belonging to someone like me! If you're going to insist on being Tevye's horse, it's time you knew what it tastes like to fast the whole length of a summer's day.' [. . .]

Well, one can't stop being a Jew in this world: it was time for the evening prayer. (Not that the evening was about to go anywhere, but a Jew prays when he must, not when he wants to.) Some fine prayer it turned out to be! Right in the middle of the *shimenesre*, the eighteen benedictions, a devil gets into my crazy horse and he decides to go for a pleasure jaunt. I had to run after the wagon and grab the reins while shouting 'God of Abraham, Isaac, and Jacob' at the top of my voice – and to make matters worse I'd really felt like praying for a change [. . .]

In a word, there I was running behind the wagon and singing the *shimenesre* like a cantor in a synagogue [. . .]

All of a sudden – whoaaa! My horse stopped short in his tracks. I rushed through what was left of the prayer, opened my eyes, and looked around me. Two weird figures, dressed for a masquerade, were approaching from the forest. 'Robbers!' I thought at first, then caught myself. Tevye, I said, what an idiot you are! Do you mean to tell me that after traveling through this forest by day and by night for so many years, today is the day for robbers? And bravely smacking my horse on the rear as though it were no affair of mine, I cried, 'Giddyap!'

'Hey, a fellow Jew!' one of the two terrors called out to me in a woman's voice, waving a scarf at me. 'Don't run away, mister. Wait a second. We won't do you any harm.'

It's a ghost for sure! I told myself. But a moment later I thought, what kind of monkey business is this, Tevye? Since when are you so afraid of ghouls and goblins? So I pulled up my horse and took a good look at the two. They really did look like women. One was older and had a silk kerchief on her head, while the other was young and wore a wig. Both were beet-red and sweating buckets.

'Well, well, well, good evening,' I said to them as loudly as I could to show that I wasn't a bit afraid. 'How can I be of service to you? If you're looking to buy something, I'm afraid I'm all out of stock, unless I can interest you in some fine hunger pangs, a week's supply of heartache, or a head full of scrambled brains. Anyone for some chilblains, assorted aches and pains, worries to turn your hair gray?'

'Calm down, calm down,' they said to me. 'Just listen to him run on! Say a good word to a Jew and you get a mouthful of bad ones in return. We don't want to buy anything. We only wanted to ask whether you happened to know the way to Boiberik.'

[. . .]

'The way to Boiberik?' I say. 'You're standing on it right now. This is the way to Boiberik whether you want to go to Boiberik or not.'

[. . .]

'Well,' they say, 'if it is the way to Boiberik, would you possibly happen to know by any chance just how long a way to Boiberik it is?'

'To Boiberik,' I say, 'it's not a long way at all. Only a few miles. About two or three. Maybe four. Unless it's five.'

'Five miles?' screamed both women at once, wringing their hands and all but bursting into tears. 'Do you have any idea what you're saying? *Only* five miles!'

'Well,' I said, 'what would you like me to do about it? If it were up to me, I'd make it a little shorter [. . .]'

'You're talking like a half-wit,' said one of the two women. 'I swear, you're off your trolley [. . .] We haven't the strength to take another step. Except for a cup of coffee with a butter roll for breakfast, we haven't had a bite of food all day – and you expect us to stand here listening to your stories?'

'That,' I said, 'is a different story [. . .] And you don't have to tell me what hunger tastes like; that's something I happen to know. Why, it's not at all unlikely that I haven't seen a cup of coffee and a butter roll for over a year . . .' [. . .]

'Do you know what, Reb Tevye?' the two women said to me. 'We've got a brilliant idea. As long as we're standing here chatting, why don't we hop into your wagon and give you a chance to take us back to Boiberik yourself? How about it?'

'I'm sorry,' I say, 'but you're spitting into the wind. You're going to Boiberik and I'm coming from Boiberik. How do you suppose I can go both ways at once?'

'That's easy,' they say. '[. . .] If you were a scholar, you'd have realized right away: you simply turn your wagon around and head back in the other direction ... Don't get so nervous, Reb Tevye. We should only have to suffer the rest of our lives as much as getting us home safely, God willing, will cost you.'

My God, I thought, they're talking Chinese; I can't make head or tail of it. And for the second time that evening I thought of ghosts, witches, things that go bump in the night. You dunce, I told myself, what are you standing there for like a tree stump? Jump back into your wagon, give the horse a crack of your whip, and get away while the getting is good! Well, don't ask me what got into me, but when I opened my mouth again I said, 'Hop aboard!'

They didn't have to be asked twice. I climbed in after them, gave my cap a tug, let the horse have the whip, and one, two, three – we're off! Did I say off? Off to no place fast! My horse is stuck to the ground, a cannon shot wouldn't budge him [. . .]

'Well, what are you waiting for?' the two women asked me.

'What am I waiting for?' I say. 'You can see for yourselves what I'm waiting for. My horse is happy where he is. He's not in a frisky mood.'

'Then use your whip,' they say to me. 'What do you think it's for?'

'Thank you for your advice,' I say to them. 'It's very kind of you to offer it. The problem is that my four-legged friend is not afraid of such things. He's as used to getting whipped as I'm used to getting gypped.' [. . .]

Well, why bore you? I let that poor horse have it. I whipped him as long as I whipped him hard, until finally he picked up his heels and we began to move through the woods [. . .]

'Why don't you go a little faster?' the two women asked, poking me from behind.

'What's the matter?' I said, 'are you in some sort of hurry? You should know that haste makes waste.' [. . .]

'Is it still a long way off?' one of them asked me.

'No longer off than we are from there,' I said. 'Up ahead there's an uphill and a downhill. After that there's another uphill and a downhill. After that comes the real uphill and the downhill, and after that it's straight as the crow flies to Boiberik . . .'

'The man's some kind of nut for sure!' whispered one of the women to the other.

'I told you he was bad news,' says the second.

'He's all we needed,' says the first.

[. . .]

[. . .] 'Excuse me,' I said to them, 'but where would you ladies like to be dumped?'

'Dumped!' they say. 'What kind of language is that? You can go dump yourself if you like!'

'Oh, that's just coachman's talk,' I say. 'In ordinary parlance we would say, "When we get to Boiberik safe and sound, with God's help, where do I drop *mesdames* off?"'

'If that's what it means,' they say, 'you can drop us off at the green dacha by the pond at the far end of the woods. Do you know where it is?'

'Do I know where it is?' I say. 'Why, I know my way around Boiberik the way you do around your own home! I wish I had a thousand rubles for every log I've carried there. Just last summer, in fact, I brought a couple of loads of wood to the very dacha you're talking about. There was a rich Jew from Yehupetz living there, a real millionaire. He must have been worth a hundred grand, if not twice that.'

'He's still living there,' said both women at once, whispering and laughing to each other.

'Well,' I said, 'seeing as the ride you've taken was no short haul, and as you may have some connection with him, would it be too much for me to request of you, if you don't mind my asking, to put in a good word for me with him? Maybe he's got an opening, a position of some sort [. . .] Well, bless my soul, will you look at what we have here: here's your pond and there's your green dacha!'

And with that I swung my wagon right through the gate and drove like nobody's business clear up to the porch of the house. Don't ask me to describe the excitement when the people there saw us pull up. What a racket! Happy days!

'Oy, Grandma!'

'Oy, Mama!'

'Oy, Auntie, Auntie!'

'Thank God they're back!'

'Mazel tov!'

'Good lord, where have you been?'

[. . .]

'[. . .] We lost our way in the woods and blundered about for miles. Suddenly, along comes a Jew. What, what kind of a Jew? A Jew, a schlimazel, with a wagon and a horse. Don't think we had an easy time with him either, but here we are!'

'[. . .] What an adventure, what an adventure. Thank God you're home safe!'

In no time lamps were brought out, the table was set, and there began to appear on it hot samovars flowing with tea, bowls of sugar, jars of jam, plates full of pastry and all kinds of baked goods, followed by the fanciest dishes: soup brimming with fat, roast meats, a whole goose, the best wines and salad greens. I stood a ways off and thought, so this, God bless them, is how these Yehupetz tycoons eat and drink [. . .] The crumbs that fell from that table alone would have been enough to feed my kids for a week, with enough left over for the Sabbath. Oh, my dear Lord, I thought: they say You're a long-suffering God, a good God, a great God; they say You're merciful and fair; perhaps You can explain to me, then, why it is that some folk have everything and others have nothing twice over? Why does one Jew get to eat butter rolls while another gets to eat dirt? A moment later, though, I said to myself, ach, what a fool you are, Tevye, I swear! Do you really think He needs your advice on how to run the world? If this is how things are, it's how they were meant to be; the proof of it is that if they were meant to be different, they would be. It may seem to you that they ought to have been meant to be different . . . but it's just for that you're a Jew in this world! A Jew must have confidence and faith. He must believe, first, that there is a God, and second, that if there is, and if it's all the same to Him, and if it isn't putting Him to too much trouble, He can make things a little better for the likes of you . . .

'Wait a minute,' I heard someone say. 'What happened to the coachman? Has the schlimazel left already?'

'God forbid!' I called out from where I was. 'Do you mean to suggest that I'd simply walk off without so much as saying good-bye? Good evening, it's a pleasure to meet you all! Enjoy your meal; I can't imagine why you shouldn't.'

'Come in out of the dark,' says one of them to me, 'and let's have a look at you. Perhaps you'd like a little brandy?'

'A little brandy?' I say. 'Who can refuse a little brandy? God may be God, but brandy is brandy. Cheers!' And I emptied the glass in one gulp. 'God should only help you to stay rich and happy,' I said [. . .]

'What name do you go by?' asked the man of the house, a fine-looking Jew with a skullcap. 'Where do you hail from? Where do you live now? What's your work? Do you have a wife? Children? How many?'

'How many children?' I say. 'Forgive me for boasting, but if each child of mine were worth a million rubles, as my Golde tries convincing me they are, I'd be richer than anyone in Yehupetz. The only trouble is that poor isn't rich and a mountain's no ditch. How does it say in the prayer book? *Hamavdil beyn koydesh lekhoyl* – some make hay while others toil. There are people who have money and I have daughters. And you know what they say about that [. . .] What's my work? For lack of any better suggestions, I break my back dragging logs [. . .] Really, there'd be no problem if it weren't for having to eat [. . .]'

'Bring the Jew something to eat!' ordered the man of the house, and right away the table was laid again with food I never dreamed existed: fish, and cold cuts, and roasts, and fowl, and more gizzards and chicken livers than you could count.

'What will you have?' I was asked. 'Come on, wash up and sit down.'

'A sick man is asked,' I answered, 'a healthy one is served. Still, thank you anyway . . . a little brandy, with pleasure . . . but to sit down and make a meal of it, when back home my wife and children, they should only be healthy and well . . . so you see, if you don't mind, I'll . . .

What can I tell you? They seemed to have gotten the hint [. . .]

'Here's a gift to take home to your wife and children,' they said. 'And now please tell us how much we owe you for your trouble.'

'To tell you the truth,' I said, 'who am I to tell you what you owe me? You pay me what you think it was worth. What's a few kopecks more or less between us? I'll still be the same Tevye when we're done.'

'No,' they say, 'we want you to tell us, Reb Tevye. You needn't be afraid. We won't chop your head off.'

Now what? I asked myself. I was really in a pretty pickle. It would be a crime to ask for one ruble when they might agree to two. On the other hand, if I asked for two they might think I was mad. *Two* rubles for one little wagon ride?

'Three rubles!' The words were out of my mouth before I could stop them. Everyone began to laugh so hard that I could have crawled into a hole in the ground.

'Please forgive me,' I said, 'if I've said the wrong thing. Even a horse, which has four legs, stumbles now and then, so why not a man with one tongue . . .'

[. . .]

'Stop laughing now, all of you!' ordered the man of the house. He pulled a large wallet from his pocket and out of it he fished – how much do you think? I swear you'll never guess – a ten-ruble note, all red as fire, as I hope to die! And do you know what else he says to me? 'This,' he says, 'is from me. Now children, let's see what each of you can dig out of your pockets.'

What can I possibly tell you? Five- and three- and one-ruble notes flew onto the table. I was shaking so hard that I thought I was going to faint.

[. . .]

'God reward you a hundred times over,' I said. 'May He bring you good luck and happiness for the rest of your lives.' [. . .]

[. . .] Away home we flew on top of the world, singing Yom Kippur songs as tipsily as you please. You wouldn't have recognized my nag; he ran like the wind without so much as a mention of the whip and looked like he'd been reupholstered. When we finally got home late at night, I joyously woke up my wife.

'Mazel tov, Golde,' I said to her. 'I've got good news.'

'A black mazel tov yourself,' she says to me. 'Tell me, my fine bread-winner, what's the happy occasion? Has my goldfingers been to a wedding or a circumcision?'

'To something better than a wedding and a circumcision combined,' I say. 'In a minute, my wife, I'm going to show you a treasure. But first go wake up the girls. Why shouldn't they also enjoy some Yehupetz cuisine . . .'

'[. . .] All I can say is, you're talking just like a madman, God help us!'

says my wife. When it comes to her tongue, she's a pretty average Jewish housewife.

'And you're talking just like a woman!' I answered. 'King Solomon wasn't joking when he said that out of a thousand females you won't find one with her head screwed on right. It's a lucky thing that polygamy has gone out of fashion.' And with that I went to the wagon and began unpacking all the dishes I'd been given and setting them out on the table. When that gang of mine saw those rolls and smelled that meat, they fell on it like a pack of wolves [. . .] I stood there with tears in my eyes, listening to their jaws work away like a plague of starving locusts.

'So tell me,' says my woman when she's done, 'who's been sharing their frugal repast with you, and since when do you have such good friends?'

'Don't worry, Golde,' I say [. . .] 'And now, Golde,' I said to her, pulling out my wad of bills, 'be a sport and guess how much I have here.'

You should have seen her turn pale as a ghost. She was so flabbergasted that she couldn't say a word.

'God be with you, Golde, my darling,' I said. 'You needn't look so frightened. Are you worried that I stole it somewhere? [. . .] This is kosher money, you sillyhead, earned fair and square by my own wits and hard work [. . .]'

In a word, I told her the whole story from beginning to end, the entire rigamarole. When I was through we counted all the money, then counted it again, then counted it once more to be sure. Whichever way we counted, it came to exactly thirty-seven rubles even.

My wife began to cry.

'What are you crying like a fool for?' I asked her.

'[. . .] What I wanted to ask you, though, Golde my dear, is what should we do with all the money?'

[. . .]

We thought. And the harder we thought, the dizzier we became planning one business venture after another. What didn't we deal in that night? First we bought a pair of horses and quickly sold them for a windfall; then with the profit we opened a grocery store in Boiberik, sold out all the stock, and opened a dry-goods store; after that we invested in some woodland, found a buyer for it, and came out a few more rubles ahead; next we bought up the tax concession for Anatevka, farmed it out again, and with the income started a bank . . .

[. . .]

To make a long story short, after quarreling and making up a few more times, we decided to buy, in addition to the beast I was to pick up in the morning, a milk cow that gave milk . . .

It might occur to you to ask why we decided to buy a cow when we could just as well have bought a horse. But why buy a horse, I ask you, when we could just as well have bought a cow? We live close to Boiberik, which is where all the rich Yehupetz Jews come to spend the summer in their dachas. And you know those Yehupetz Jews – nothing's too good for them. They expect to have everything served up on a silver platter: wood, meat, eggs, poultry, onions, pepper, parsley . . . so why shouldn't I be the man to walk into their parlor with cheese, cream, and butter? [. . .] You can make a fat living from them as long as they think they're getting the best – and believe me, fresh produce like mine they can't even get in Yehupetz. The two of us, my friend, should only have good luck in our lives for every time I've been stopped by the best sort of people, Gentiles even, who beg to be my customers. 'We've heard, Tevye,' they say to me, 'that you're an honest fellow, even if you are a rat-Jew . . .' I ask you, do you ever get such a compliment from Jews? My worst enemy should have to lie sick in bed for as long as it would take me to wait for one! No, our Jews like to keep their praises to themselves, which is more than I can say about their noses. The minute they see that I've bought another cow, or that I have a new cart, they begin to rack their brains: 'Where is it all coming from? Can our Tevye be passing out phony banknotes? Or perhaps he's making moonshine in some still?' Ha, ha, ha. All I can say is: keep wondering until your heads break, my friends, and enjoy it . . .

Believe it or not, you're practically the first person to have heard this story, the whole where, what, and when of it. And now you'll have to excuse me, because I've run on a little too long and there's a business to attend to. How does the Bible put it? *Koyl oyreyv lemineyhu*, it's a wise bird that feathers its own nest. So you'd better be off to your writing, and I to my milk cans and jugs . . .

There's just one request I have, Pani: please don't stick me in any of your books. And if that's too much to ask, do me a favor and at least leave my name out.

And oh yes, by the way: don't forget to take care and be well!

(1894, 1897)

20

Pity Hidden beneath Laughter

Giuseppe Gioacchino Belli,* *The Sonnets*, edited by Giorgio Vigolo
(Milan: Mondadori, 1952), No. 165, translated by Anthony Burgess,
in *Abba Abba* (London: Faber & Faber, 1977), Nos. 1217, 1627
and 1785 translated by Peter Forbes

*The poetic world of Giuseppe Gioacchino Belli has nothing grand about it.
Of humble origins, the author, with obsessive fidelity in all his enormous works,
almost never takes a speaking role, but transcribes, to the point of ventriloquism,
the voice of the ordinary Romans, and through this draws the reader into a
very precise vision of the world. In the sonnets included here, written during
the first decades of the nineteenth century, there is the Act of Creation, blended
with original sin in a startling conflation, baroque and tragic, the death of an
ass, broken by fatigue, the solitary senescence of Laetitia Bonaparte, the
desolation of the Roman countryside. Here are the three themes particular to
Belli: religion, sex and death. But from them in various combinations he
extracts an infinity of effects. There is no aspect of the human spirit that this
saturnine man, rebel to the point of subversion in his verses, reactionary
functionary in his life, has not portrayed.*

*Above all, the sonnet 'Dead' seems to me unforgettable. Reproducing a
theme dear to romantics and above all to Belli, 'pity, hidden beneath laughter,
for humble, humiliated and degraded creatures' (G. Vigolo). Also here we elicit
a strict moral lesson from a reversal of roles: here the man is cruel and stupid
'like the beasts', a mental stammerer, incoherent and fierce; the ass dies the
death of a martyr.*

THE CREATION OF THE WORLD

One day the bakers God & Son set to
And baked, to show their pasta-master's skill,
This loaf the world, though the odd imbecile
Swears it's a melon, and the thing just grew.
They made a sun, a moon, a green and blue
Atlas, chucked stars like money from a till,
Set birds high, beasts low, fishes lower still,
Planted their plants, then yawned: 'Aye, that'll do.'

No, wait. The old man baked two bits of bread
Called Folk – I quite forgot to mention it –
So he could shout: 'Don't bite that round ripe red
Pie-filling there.' Of course, the buggers bit.
Though mad at them, he turned on us instead
And said: 'Posterity, you're in the shit.'

No. 165

DEAD

Do you know who passed away this morning?
Repiscitto – he was my donkey.
Poor creature, he was such a willing flunkey
A queen could take his back without a warning.
We were just on the way back from the mill
With three two-hundred-kilo sacks of flour
And ten times already he'd hit the floor –
It was his bad leg that was making him ill –
I said to him: 'Please don't go and fall again'
But the cursed brute had no mind to please
So I hit him on the head with my stick, there and then.
He just came out with a kind of sneeze,

Splayed his legs and that was the end.
I'm truly sorry. Poor little beast!

No. 1217

MADAME LAETITIA

What does she do, the mother of the great
culler of kings with his homespun reaper?
she lives on soup, doesn't spend a groat,
says yes, no, spits, and stares in the mirror;
reclines on a couch, a groggy
slip of bleached and fragile bone.
There's more flesh in the ear of a moggy
than on this desiccated crone.
Her cheeks are the colour of a water-melon's skin,
her shinbones tap against her knee;
her waist's no thicker than a woollen skein,
each day there's a little less of her to see.
This is it, the amen-Jesus, the calling-in
of her final date with destiny.

No. 1627

THE DESERT

Rescue me, God, Christ and Madonna
From going to that farm again to buy cheese.
Before . . . how to say it? Before I choose
to get myself spayed by a butcher in Ritonna.
I walk ten miles, there's not a soul alive!
No people to jostle, just a stone instead!
Everywhere the silence hangs like lead,
However you howl there's no one to reply!
Wherever you turn it's countryside, shaven

As if you'd planed it down to stubble
Not the least trace of a haven!
The only thing on the whole trip that I encountered
(and that spelt trouble):
A cart with the body of its driver, murdered.

No. 1785

21

Why We are Not Happy

Bertrand Russell, 'Envy', *The Conquest of Happiness*
(London: Unwin Books, 1975), pp. 64–73

The very long working life of Bertrand Russell is a reflection of his famous zest, his legendary vitality. In The Conquest of Happiness *he enumerates, good humouredly but with his usual precision, the many absurd ways that we choose to render ourselves gratuitously unhappy, and the founts of happiness which are open to whoever is not too severely battered by fate. In this, as in many of his works, Russell intends to demonstrate that the eternal problems, not only of knowledge, but also of practical living, are amenable to our reason. He is a good companion: telling us that the human condition is miserable but that it is idle to mope around complaining, and that one ought to make every effort to improve it.*

ENVY

Next to worry probably one of the most potent causes of unhappiness is envy. Envy is, I should say, one of the most universal and deep-seated of human passions. It is very noticeable in children before they are a year old, and has to be treated with the most tender respect by every educator. The very slightest appearance of favouring one child at the expense of another is instantly observed and resented. Distributive justice, absolute, rigid, and unvarying, must be observed by anyone who has children to deal with. But children are only slightly more open in their expressions of envy, and of jealousy (which is a special form of envy), than are grown-up people. The emotion is just as prevalent among adults as among children. Take, for example, maid-servants: I remember when one of our maids, who was a married woman, became pregnant, and we said that she was not to be expected to lift heavy weights, the instant result was that none of the others would lift heavy weights, and any work of that sort that needed doing we had to do ourselves. Envy is the basis of democracy. Heraclitus asserts that the citizens of Ephesus ought all to be hanged because they said, 'there shall be none first among us'. The democratic movement in Greek States must have been almost wholly inspired by this passion. And the same is true of modern democracy. There is, it is true, an idealistic theory according to which democracy is the best form of government. I think myself that this theory is true. But there is no department of practical politics where idealistic theories are strong enough to cause great changes; when great changes occur, the theories which justify them are always a camouflage for passion. And the passion that has given driving force to democratic theories is undoubtedly the passion of envy. Read the memoirs of Madame Roland, who is frequently represented as a noble woman inspired by devotion to the people. You will find that what made her such a vehement democrat was the experience of being shown into the servants' hall when she had occasion to visit an aristocratic château.

Among average respectable women envy plays an extraordinarily large part. If you are sitting in the Underground and a well-dressed woman happens to walk along the car, watch the eyes of the other women. You will see that every one of them, with the possible exception of those who are better dressed, will watch the woman with malevolent glances, and will be struggling to draw inferences derogatory to her. The love of scandal is an expression of this general malevolence: any story against another woman is instantly believed, even on the flimsiest evidence. A lofty morality serves the same purpose: those who have a chance to sin against it are envied, and it is considered virtuous to punish them for their sins. This particular form of virtue is certainly its own reward.

Exactly the same thing, however, is to be observed among men, except that women regard all other women as their competitors, whereas men as a rule only have this feeling towards other men in the same profession.

Have you, reader, ever been so imprudent as to praise an artist to another artist? Have you ever praised a politician to another politician of the same party? Have you ever praised an Egyptologist to another Egyptologist? If you have, it is a hundred to one that you will have produced an explosion of jealousy. In the correspondence of Leibniz and Huyghens there are a number of letters lamenting the supposed fact that Newton had become insane. 'Is it not sad,' they write to each other, 'that the incomparable genius of Mr Newton should have become over-clouded by the loss of reason?' And these two eminent men, in one letter after another, wept crocodile tears with obvious relish. As a matter of fact, the event which they were hypocritically lamenting had not taken place, though a few examples of eccentric behaviour had given rise to the rumour.

Of all the characteristics of ordinary human nature envy is the most unfortunate; not only does the envious person wish to inflict misfortune and do so whenever he can with impunity, but he is also himself rendered unhappy by envy. Instead of deriving pleasure from what he has, he derives pain from what others have. If he can, he deprives others of their advantages, which to him is as desirable as it would be to secure the same advantages himself. If this passion is allowed to run riot it becomes fatal to all excellence, and even to the most useful exercise of exceptional skill. Why should a medical man go to see his patients in a car when the labourer has to walk to his work? Why should the scientific investigator be allowed to spend his time in a warm room when others have to face the inclemency of the elements? Why should a man who possesses some rare talent of great importance to the world be saved from the drudgery of his own housework? To such questions envy finds no answer. Fortunately, however, there is in human nature a compensating passion, namely that of admiration. Whoever wishes to increase human happiness must wish to increase admiration and to diminish envy.

What cure is there for envy? For the saint there is the cure of selflessness, though even in the case of saints envy of other saints is by no means impossible. I doubt whether St Simeon Stylites would have been wholly pleased if he had learnt of some other saint who had stood even longer on an even narrower pillar. But, leaving saints out of account, the only cure for envy in the case of ordinary men and women is happiness, and the difficulty is that envy is itself a terrible obstacle to happiness. I think envy is immensely promoted by misfortunes in childhood. The child who finds a brother or sister preferred before himself acquires the habit of envy, and when he goes out into the world looks for injustices of which he is the victim, perceives them at once if they occur, and imagines them if they do not. Such a man is inevitably unhappy, and becomes a nuisance to his friends, who cannot be always remembering to avoid imaginary slights. Having begun by believing that no one likes him, he at last by his behaviour makes his belief true. Another misfortune in childhood which has the same result is to have parents without much parental feeling. Without having an unduly favoured brother or sister, a child may perceive that the children in other families are more loved by their mother and father than he is. This will cause him to hate the other children and his own parents, and when he grows up he will feel himself an Ishmael. Some kinds of happiness are everyone's natural birthright, and to be deprived of them is almost inevitably to become warped and embittered.

But the envious man may say: 'What is the good of telling me that the cure for envy is happiness? I cannot find happiness while I continue to feel envy, and you tell me that I cannot cease to be envious until I find happiness.' But real life is never so logical as this. Merely to realise the causes of one's own envious feelings is to take a long step towards curing them. The habit of thinking in terms of comparisons is a fatal one. When anything pleasant occurs it should be enjoyed to the full, without stopping to think that it is not so pleasant as something else that may possibly be happening to someone else. 'Yes,' says the envious man, 'this is a sunny day, and it is springtime, and the birds are singing, and the flowers are in bloom, but I understand that the springtime in Sicily is a thousand times more beautiful, that the birds sing more exquisitely in the groves of Helicon, and that the rose of Sharon is more lovely than any in my garden.' And as he thinks these thoughts the sun is dimmed, and the birds' song becomes a meaningless twitter, and the flowers seem not worth a moment's regard. All the other joys of life he treats in the same way. 'Yes,' he will say to himself, 'the lady of my heart is lovely, I love her and she loves me, but how much more exquisite must have been the

Queen of Sheba! Ah, if I had but had Solomon's opportunities!' All such
comparisons are pointless and foolish; whether the Queen of Sheba or
our next-door neighbour be the cause of discontent, either is equally
futile. With the wise man, what he has does not cease to be enjoyable
because someone else has something else. Envy, in fact, is one form of a
vice, partly moral, partly intellectual, which consists in seeing things
never in themselves, but only in their relations. I am earning, let us say,
a salary sufficient for my needs. I should be content, but I hear that
someone else whom I believe to be in no way my superior is earning a
salary twice as great as mine. Instantly, if I am of an envious disposition,
the satisfactions to be derived from what I have grow dim, and I begin to
be eaten up with a sense of injustice. For all this the proper cure is
mental discipline, the habit of not thinking profitless thoughts. After all,
what is more enviable than happiness? And if I can cure myself of envy
I can acquire happiness and become enviable. The man who has double
my salary is doubtless tortured by the thought that someone else in turn
has twice as much as he has, and so it goes on. If you desire glory,
you may envy Napoleon. But Napoleon envied Caesar, Caesar envied
Alexander, and Alexander, I daresay, envied Hercules, who never existed.
You cannot, therefore, get away from envy by means of success alone,
for there will always be in history or legend some person even more
successful than you are. You can get away from envy by enjoying the
pleasures that come your way, by doing the work that you have to do,
and by avoiding comparisons with those whom you imagine, perhaps
quite falsely, to be more fortunate than yourself.

Unnecessary modesty has a great deal to do with envy. Modesty is
considered a virtue, but for my part I am very doubtful whether, in its
more extreme forms, it deserves to be so regarded. Modest people need
a great deal of reassuring, and often do not dare to attempt tasks which
they are quite capable of performing. Modest people believe themselves
to be outshone by those with whom they habitually associate. They are
therefore particularly prone to envy, and, through envy, to unhappiness
and ill will. For my part, I think there is much to be said for bringing up
a boy to think himself a fine fellow. I do not believe that any peacock
envies another peacock his tail, because every peacock is persuaded that

167

his own tail is the finest in the world. The consequence of this is that peacocks are peaceable birds. Imagine how unhappy the life of a peacock would be if he had been taught that it is wicked to have a good opinion of oneself. Whenever he saw another peacock spreading out his tail, he would say to himself: 'I must not imagine that my tail is better than that, for that would be conceited, but oh, how I wish it were! That odious bird is so convinced of his own magnificence! Shall I pull out some of his feathers? And then perhaps I need no longer fear comparison with him.' Or perhaps he would lay a trap for him, and prove that he was a wicked peacock who had been guilty of unpeacockly behaviour, and he would denounce him to the assembly of the leaders. Gradually he would establish the principle that peacocks with specially fine tails are almost always wicked, and that the wise ruler in the peacock kingdom would seek out the humble bird with only a few draggled tail feathers. Having got this principle accepted, he would get all the finest birds put to death, and in the end a really splendid tail will become only a dim memory of the past. Such is the victory of envy masquerading as morality. But where every peacock thinks himself more splendid than any of the others, there is no need for all this repression. Each peacock expects to win the first prize in the competition, and each, because he values his own peahen, believes that he has done so.

Envy is, of course, closely connected with competition. We do not envy a good fortune which we conceive as quite hopelessly out of our reach. In an age when the social hierarchy is fixed, the lowest classes do not envy the upper classes so long as the division between rich and poor is thought to be ordained by God. Beggars do not envy millionaires, though of course they will envy other beggars who are more successful. The instability of social status in the modern world, and the equalitarian doctrine of democracy and socialism, have greatly extended the range of envy. For the moment this is an evil, but it is an evil which must be endured in order to arrive at a more just social system. As soon as inequalities are thought about rationally they are seen to be unjust unless they rest upon some superiority of merit. And as soon as they are seen to be unjust, there is no remedy for the resulting envy except the removal of the injustice. Our age is therefore one in which envy plays a peculiarly large part. The poor envy the rich, the poorer nations envy the richer nations, women envy men, virtuous women envy those who, though not virtuous, remain unpunished. While it is true that envy is the chief motive force leading to justice as between different classes, different nations, and different sexes, it is at the same time true that the kind of justice to be expected as a result of envy is likely to be the worst possible kind, namely that which consists rather in diminishing the pleasures of the fortunate than in increasing those of the unfortunate. Passions which work havoc in private life work havoc in public life also. It is not to be supposed that out of something as evil as envy good results will flow. Those, therefore, who from idealistic reasons desire profound changes in our social system, and a great increase of social justice, must hope that other forces than envy will be instrumental in bringing the changes about.

All bad things are interconnected, and any one of them is liable to be the cause of any other; more particularly fatigue is a very frequent cause of envy. When a man feels inadequate to the work he has to do, he feels a general discontent which is exceedingly liable to take the form of envy towards those whose work is less exacting. One of the ways of diminishing envy, therefore, is to diminish fatigue. But by far the most important thing is to secure a life which is satisfying to instinct. Much envy that seems purely professional really has a sexual source. A man who is happy in his marriage and his children is not likely to feel much envy of other men because of their greater wealth or success, so long as he has enough to bring up his children in what he feels to be the right way. The essentials of human happiness are simple, so simple that sophisticated people cannot bring themselves to admit what it is they really lack. The women we spoke of earlier who look with envy on every well-dressed woman are, one may be sure, not happy in their instinctive life. Instinctive happiness is rare in the English-speaking world, especially among women. Civilisation in this respect appears to have gone astray. If there is to be less envy, means must be found for remedying this state of affairs, and if no such means are found our civilisation is in danger of going down to destruction in an orgy of hatred. In old days people only envied their neighbours, because they knew little about anyone else. Now through education and the Press they know much in an abstract way about large classes of mankind of whom no single individual is among their acquaintance. Through the movies they think they know how the rich live, through the newspapers they know much of the wickedness of foreign nations, through propaganda they know of the nefarious practices of all whose skin has a pigmentation different from their own. Yellows hate whites, whites hate blacks, and so on. All this hatred, you may say, is stirred up by propaganda, but this is a somewhat shallow explanation. Why is propaganda so much more successful when it stirs up hatred than when it tries to stir up friendly feeling? The reason is clearly that the human heart as modern civilisation has made it is more prone to hatred than to friendship. And it is prone to hatred because it is dissatisfied, because it feels deeply, perhaps even unconsciously, that it has somehow missed the meaning of life, that perhaps others, but not we ourselves, have secured the good things which nature offers man's enjoyment. The positive sum of pleasures in a modern man's life is undoubtedly greater than was to be found in more primitive communities, but the consciousness of what might be has increased even more. Whenever you happen to take your children to the Zoo you may observe in the eyes of the apes, when they are not performing gymnastic feats or cracking nuts, a strange strained sadness. One can almost imagine that they feel they ought to become men, but cannot discover the secret of how to do it. On the road of evolution they have lost their way; their cousins marched on and they were left behind. Something of the same strain and anguish seems to have entered the soul of civilised man. He knows there is something better than himself almost within his grasp, yet he does not know where to seek it or how to find it. In despair he rages against his fellow man, who is equally lost and equally unhappy. We have reached a stage in evolution which is not the final stage. We must pass through it quickly, for if we do not, most of us will perish by the way, and the others will be lost in a forest of doubt and fear. Envy therefore, evil as it is, and terrible as are its effects, is not wholly of the devil. It is in part the expression of an heroic pain, the pain of those who walk through the night blindly, perhaps to a better resting-place, perhaps only to death and destruction. To find the right road out of this despair civilised man must enlarge his heart as he has enlarged his mind. He must learn to transcend self, and in so doing to acquire the freedom of the Universe.

22

We are the Aliens

Fredric Brown,* 'Sentry', *Galaxy*, Vol. 7, No. 5-A (February 1954)

I am well aware that in these pages there are many examples of worlds turned upside down. I swear that this was not premeditated; it is a result I had not foreseen. Nevertheless, painters know well that in looking at a painting upside down one can see virtues and defects that were not at first observed. This story of exemplary concision, which we owe to Fredric Brown, one of the best-known and most prolific of American science-fiction writers, contains a stunning volte-face: the entire human race has become 'alien'. Besides the intellectual game, it also contains other more serious matter; the scars of the Second World War, the nightmare of the Third, the horror of death in battle, and I could continue if I didn't run the risk that the commentary would be longer than the text.

He was wet and muddy and hungry and cold and he was fifty thousand light-years from home.

A strange blue sun gave light and the gravity, twice what he was used to, made every movement difficult.

But in tens of thousands of years this part of war hadn't changed. The flyboys were fine with their sleek spaceships and their fancy weapons. When the chips are down, though, it was still the foot soldier, the infantry, that had to take the ground and hold it, foot by bloody foot. Like this damned planet of a star he'd never heard of until they'd landed him there. And now it was sacred ground because the aliens were there too. *The* Aliens, the only other intelligent race in the Galaxy ... cruel, hideous and repulsive monsters.

Contact had been made with them near the center of the Galaxy, after the slow, difficult colonization of a dozen thousand planets; and it had been war at sight; they'd shot without even trying to negotiate, or to make peace.

Now, planet by bitter planet, it was being fought out.

He was wet and muddy and hungry and cold, and the day was raw with a high wind that hurt his eyes. But the aliens were trying to infiltrate and every sentry post was vital.

He stayed alert, gun ready. Fifty thousand light-years from home, fighting on a strange world and wondering if he'd ever live to see home again.

And then he saw one of them crawling towards him. He drew a bead and fired. The alien made that strange horrible sound they all make, then lay still.

He shuddered at the sound and sight of the alien lying there. One ought to be able to get used to them after a while, but he'd never been able to. Such repulsive creatures they were, with only two arms and two legs, ghastly white skins and no scales.

23

The Measure of All Things

ASTM D 1382 – 55 T, *Annual Book of ASTM Standards*
(Philadelphia: American Society for Testing Materials, 1955)

In the 1700s, in his celebrated experiments on the infusorians,* Lazzaro Spallanzani measured time in credoes, that is to say as a unit of duration he used the time it takes to recite a Creed. Today we measure time based on the atomic emissions of the caesium clock, and an error of a second in a century seems intolerable. It is a necessary progression: the foundations of our civilization must be based on measurement and precise determination; in these subterranean regions, frequented only by specialists, there are those who measure the resistance to bending of raw spaghetti and the resistance to traction of the cooked variety, and who prescribe their respective maximum and minimum values.

What follows is not an invention: it is a 'specification', that is to say a method of quality control, conceived by the giant American Society for Testing Materials (ASTM). There are many ASTM methods (or other equivalents) to verify the suitability of any marketable object or material, from the simple button to armoured cars and from mayonnaise to enriched uranium. Barring an improbable return to the eighteenth century, the monstrous network of specifications is destined to grow, because each object named in a specification ought itself to be the subject of a specification.

Tentative Method of Test for

SUSCEPTIBILITY OF DRY ADHESIVE FILMS TO ATTACK BY ROACHES

ASTM Designation: D 1382 – 55 T

ISSUED, 1955.

This Tentative Method has been approved by the sponsoring committee and accepted by the Society in accordance with established procedures, for use pending adoption as standard. Suggestions for revisions should be addressed to the Society at 1916 Race St., Philadelphia 3, Pa.

SCOPE

1. This method is intended for use in determining to what extent adhesive-impregnated paper, compared with blanks, is damaged by American roaches.

Note. – This method, with appropriate changes in experimental detail, may be adapted for use with other vermin.

APPARATUS

2. (*a*) *Balance*, having a sensitivity of 1 mg.

(*b*) *Glass Beaker*, having a capacity of about 2000 ml, and coated heavily with petrolatum on a 2- to 3-in.-wide strip from the rim down, around the inner wall.

(*c*) *Bottle Cap*, about 1 in. in diameter, and filled with moist cotton.

(*d*) *Wooden Board* of white pine, about ½ in. thick, 3 in. long, and 3 in. wide, having two holes drilled with a No. 72 drill perpendicular to the board, and about 1½ in. from diagonally opposite corners.

(*e*) *Wire*. – Two pieces of rigid wire, about 4 in. long and 0.025 in. in diameter.

(*f*) *Box*. – One cardboard or wooden box, large enough to hold the beaker.

(*g*) *Filter Paper*. – Two square pieces of 2 by 2-in. coarse qualitative filter paper, having small holes near the edges of diagonally opposite corners.

PREPARATION OF TEST SPECIMENS

3. (*a*) *Adhesive*. – Freshly prepare,

according to directions provided by the manufacturer, about 200 g of the adhesive to be evaluated, and dilute to a dipping consistency with the diluent recommended by the manufacturer.

(b) *Impregnated Specimen.* – Dip one piece of the filter paper in the diluted adhesive and drain to remove the excess. Suspend the impregnated paper in a suitable manner and air-dry it for about 24 hr. Weigh the dried test specimen to the nearest milligram, and record the weight.

(c) *Blank.* – Weigh to the nearest milligram, and record the weight of the second undipped piece of filter paper, for use as a blank.

TEST ROACHES

4. Ten healthy American roaches (*periplaneta americana*),[1] 5 to 6 months old, and starved for 48 hr. Five shall be males and five females.

TEST CONDITION

5. The test shall be carried out at a relative humidity of 50 ± 2 per cent and at a temperature of 73.4 ± 2 F (23 ± 1.1 C), unless otherwise agreed upon by the manufacturer and the purchaser of the adhesive.

[1] Available from the Quivira Specialities Co., 420 W. 21 St., Topeka, Kans.

PROCEDURE

6. (a) Insert the two wires into the holes in the board. Attach the impregnated specimen to one wire and the blank to the other in vertical positions. Place the board in the beaker and the bottle cap next to the board. Place the roaches in the beaker, and cover the beaker with a box to provide darkness.

(b) Weigh to the nearest milligram and record the weight of the impregnated test specimen and the blank daily for the first four days, and then every second day for a total of 14 days (Note). If more than three roaches die during the test, discontinue and repeat.

Note. – Remoisten the cotton in the bottle cap from a pipet when necessary.

CALCULATION

7. Calculate the percentage of destruction of each specimen for every period as follows:

Destruction,
$$\text{per cent} = 100 - \left(\frac{A}{B} \times 100 \right)$$

where:
A = final weight of the specimen, and B = original weight of the specimen.

REPORT

8. The report shall include the following:

(1) Complete identification of the adhesive tested, including type, source, manufacturer's code number, method of preparation for use, and type and percentage of diluent used,

(2) Percentage of destruction of the adhesive-impregnated specimen and the blank specimen for each test period,

(3) Number of surviving roaches for every test period and for the total duration of the test, and

(4) Any other pertinent observations.

24

Urchin Death

Stefano D'Arrigo,* *Horcynus Orca* (Milan: Mondadori, 1975),
pp. 632–40, translated by Peter Forbes

You are constructing your own private decalogue (work in progress, but you have the illusion of having done it already). Your writing shall be concise, clear, composed; you will avoid whatever is willed and over-elaborated; you will know how to use each of your words, because you have used this and not another; you will love and imitate those that follow the same path.

Then you come across Horcynus Orca *and everything flies out of the window. It is a book of extremes, crude, visceral and Spanish, fleshing out a single gesture over ten pages; in places it has to be studied and decoded like an ancient text, yet I like it, I never tire of rereading it and each time it comes up fresh. I feel it to be internally coherent, a work of art and not artificial; it could not have been written otherwise. It makes me think of a certain tunnel that was excavated centuries ago, in the rock of the Susa Valley by a man working alone for ten years; or of a lens with aberrations but with enormous magnification.*

It attracts me above all because D'Arrigo, like Mann, Belli, Melville, Porta, Babel and Rabelais, has known how to invent a language, his own, inimitable: a versatile instrument, innovative and adapted to his scope.

We are in Naples, in the last days of the popular uprising of September 1943. A German armoured car has fallen into the hands of a group of armed children: playing to kill, the only game they know.

[. . .] When the tank arrived on the hillock, and just at the precise moment of equilibrium, the urchin, who already had the grenade between his hands, turned round, ripped out the pin with his teeth, and threw it under the belly of the huge animal. 'With that one I would sign up blindfold,' said an ex-army or ex-Italian-marine type, at the same time. The Tiger shattered on the hillock, then tumbled down towards a kind of ditch among the rubble, while here and there little flames flickered as if it were on the point of catching fire. Then the driver climbed down from his machine, and, seeing the urchins who had immediately encircled him, threw a supercilious glance that was eloquent of his astonishment, as if taken unawares, as if from the inside of his tank he had never once been able to see outside, not from the firing slit, nor from the periscope. 'These urchins in rags,' he said, addressing himself and looking around him from the depth of his amazement, 'these runts, you'd think that if you pinched their nose milk would still come out, these miserable urchins of skin and bone, minus a leg here, an arm there, half naked, almost entirely festooned with weapons which they drape across their backs, with sub-machine guns, rifles and haversacks with hand-grenades and rounds of ammunition around their shoulders or crosswise on their torsos, most of them with bandages dressing wounds in various parts of their bodies, these poor urchins have single-handedly put us *hors de combat*, us and our great Tiger. These hospital cases. And it is to them I must give myself up?'

But this was indeed the case: there was no escaping it: anyone else would have simply stuck their hands in the air and said: 'Here I am then, the wise always die by the hand of an idiot.' On the other hand, a German would never have known this expression, a German would never have allowed himself to die by the hand of an idiot, nor even simply to die. Instead, he stuck a crazed and cunning smile on his lips and, getting down from the tank, rather than raise his arms, he pulled from his sleeve this amazing card: a brazen handshake, putting out his right hand; but his own hand betrayed him: it was as if the nerves and bones had taken the form of the objects that his hand habitually grasped, the right hand he proffered wasn't tendered upturned, with an open palm, but, without in the least noticing it, he presented it twisted as if he were pointing a pistol, with the little finger, the ring, middle and index fingers held together, as if to suggest the barrel of a revolver, and the thumb held high, like a trigger, cocked to fire.

But he could try, he could always try, without hurrying, no one hurried here, there was absolutely no haste. He could try, attempt, in the middle of that circle, try, attempt, whatever ruse, or expedient or stratagem that occurred to him, any old ruse or low trick: only, he would never emerge alive from this circle. He could try, attempt, no one would stop him doing it, in fact this was the very reason they had wanted to take him alive, didn't he understand that? It was for this that they had wanted to lure him, still alive, into this ditch, among the debris, right in front of the famous sea of Santa Lucia, completely alone. It was for this, to be able to see what he would do, destined to die at any moment, to look at him and to be able to remember him alive, a German who already sensed the stench of death, and took his leave naturally, as a coward, throwing himself under the Neapolitan colours, under those tattered flags. For this, to be able to look at him and to remember him alive when he knew he was going to die in a few minutes. The Dead they had already seen during these days, but once dead even a German is no more than a corpse, and dead, already dead, it was not like that that they wanted to remember him, to remember him as a German, as a dead German. They wanted him like this, just a little before dying, still alive, alive enough to be devoured by their eyes, robbed of his power, when he was nothing any more, a vile wretch of no consequence, slowly devoured by their eyes, with a fierce, melancholy dilatoriness, engulfed and committed to memory, branded in memory for ever: because later, remembering him like this, vile and wretched, it would always bring back the warmth of smoking weapons which were growing cold in their hands. It was clear that for the urchins this German alone was worth more than all the Germans downed by rifle fire and this moment worth more than all the battles of recent days; it was enough to look at them to understand this, to look at them while they inspected the German tank-man who twisted and turned and, with an icy smile, with his hand held out, menacing, as he aimed it at a chest, when most of the urchins hardly came up to his waist, tried his luck now with one now with another; now, he ought to be arranging for prayers to be said for him, but to look at him it seemed, on the contrary, that the idea that he was going to die, sooner or later, hardly entered his mind. He must have relied upon his handshake, his German handshake, as if it were invested with a magic power, he must have thought that sooner or later at least one of the urchins would succumb to him, and the circle, the encirclement would break, a breach would open among the urchins, just to allow him to get away.

Meanwhile, however, he thought that he was offering a hand and he pointed a pistol, four fingers like the barrel of a firearm, the thumb raised like a trigger, and from his face one couldn't say to what extent he was oblivious, provocative, credulous, crazy or cunning. Perhaps that is why the urchins never let out of their sight for an instant the hand that projected from his torn sleeve, stained with dirty grease and blood, that is why they seemed to be attracted to it as the only part still alive and German, of a German who was as good as dead in their eyes. The urchins looked at him in a manner so disarming that everything they thought was reflected in their eyes. And what they thought was how privileged they felt to find themselves there, in a situation so rich, rare and fortunate, and how privileged they felt to have disarmed a living German and to have him there, alone, down on his luck, without arms or comrades, stark naked, while death took his measurements. Oughtn't they to celebrate such a privilege? Shouldn't they enjoy it in a leisurely way? In fact it was worth a smoke, even worth rolling one by hand, the cigarette, as if to say how much they wanted to celebrate this privilege, how they would like to take their time, with each and every ease.

The cigarettes were rolled by a forty-year-old bourgeois who had red eyes with sparse eyelashes, and wore spectacles with a bit of wire in place of one of the earpieces; he was dressed in deep mourning, with a very thick beard and he too had slung over his arm a haversack half full of hand-grenades. This Neapolitan had drawn from one of his pockets a little piece of tissue-paper, and rummaging in his trouser pockets and his jacket, bit by bit he had filled it with tobacco, had rolled it and then had lit the cigarette, taken a few drags, and had passed it to his neighbour so that he could circulate it. He had then taken another scrap of paper, and searching again in his pockets, he had rolled another cigarette, lit it and passed it to his neighbour at the other end of the circle. The urchins took the cigarette proffered by their neighbour, took a drag, and passed it on, gazing all the time intently through the smoke at the German, following the gestures that he made or thought he wanted to make, the gestures that repeated themselves, always the same, that he repeated each time moreover perfectly identically, like a puppet on a string, with that fixed smile, feigned, tigerish, which roamed around and which from time to time stopped in front of one of the urchins, tried again this gesture of offering his hand, but which only succeeded in embodying the loaded pistol that he was used to carrying.

The German didn't keep his eyes on his immediate surroundings right up to the end; twice he turned his eyes away from them to look elsewhere. The first time it was as if a bird, which he alone heard, was singing above their heads, so that he raised his eyes to seek it out, turning on his heel with his arms still held out and turning with his torso as if he were made of wood. But when he had totally turned round, from the sea towards the mountain, and his line of sight picked out the castle that could be seen on one of the heights of the town, it was as if he had followed the invisible bird up there, and the castle seen from below seemed to him enchanted, although it was only a military fortress called Castel Sant'Elmo.

This was a matter of seconds, no time at all, a blink of the eye, but there in the circle, we could have sworn, he hadn't been the only one to see something strange, like a sign that the German was cracking, a sign that the idea of his impending death was getting to him now and that he was getting used to this idea: because if he started to hear birdsong, and if he started to raise his eyes to the sky, in short, if a barbarian like him started to come out with poetry, whether you liked it or not, this meant that, despite his nerves of steel, the German was losing his self-possession, must mean that he felt his heart growing heavy. Certainly it could well be that some wound was behind this turn of the eyes, an invisible wound which now no longer bled, but which didn't mean that it was improving rather than getting worse.

The second time that the German took his eyes off the urchins was to look in front of himself, towards the jetty, over the heads of his encirclers, as if he discovered at this moment, scanning the line of sight which loomed between the piles of rubbish, although very narrow and zig-zagged, that one could see a sliver of sea. But the German, almost without stopping, passed beyond and deflected his gaze, and it was hard to know if he had had the time to see the two people who had appeared there on the quay, a young girl who might have been twelve or sixteen years old, dressed in a skirt made from a military blanket, a blouse with large green flowers, and cork shoes, and a tall brittle man, his neck bent like a question mark; the little girl gave him her hand and it wasn't long before you realized that the man was blind and that he must have been her father, as we shall soon see. The girl led her father to the end of the jetty and helped him to sit down with his legs dangling over, the father took from his pocket a line and the girl took it from his hands, detached the fish hook from the cork float, and fastened to it one of the worms taken from a box that the father drew from the other pocket of the bush shirt which served as his jacket. His daughter then swung the lead weight of the line to give it momentum, and cast it out to sea, about ten metres from the quay; at this moment she passed the line to her father, while exchanging a few words with him; her father tested the line with his index finger, and she turned round, casting an eye on the sea of debris behind them. When she saw this monument of sorts, like living statues that formed a circle around something or someone among the piles of rubbish, she opened her mouth as if to cry out, and at the same time moved a little to the side, the better to see, and then she spoke to her father: he passed her the end of the line and she attached it to a stone, helped her father to get up, took him by the hand and led him towards the debris. The noise that the blind man made in walking between the stones and the debris, as father and daughter came closer, instead of growing, diminished, and when they arrived by the shoulders of the urchins, you could hear only the steps of the girl. The only ones who turned their heads and looked at them were him, 'Ndrja,* and the other four or five exes from this or that, Royal Navy or Army, who framed the group, for as far as the urchins were concerned, it was as if no one had come.

The little girl, when she saw the tank, the German with his icy smile, his villainous hand, levelled like a pistol, and the armed urchins who never took their eyes off him, even for the time it takes to swat a flea, instantly had a clear picture of the scene: taking him by the hand and making him bend down, she spoke in her father's ear and in two words she told him what was happening. When she raised her little minnow face again, the face of one who, ever anxious at heart, is always fleeing in her soul, the little girl found the German, who, by the way, must have a barbarous courage, who watched her eyeball to eyeball and who held his head a little to one side, as if he sought an angle from which he would have been able to appreciate what deserved to be seen, and meanwhile, with that smile of his now a little tired and his arms held out, he seemed to say to her: can we shake hands, miss? Can we get to know each other? The little girl then, turning towards her father, all the while continuing to look at the German, for she was going to toss her words into his face, said in a loud voice; 'If you could only see him, Papa, how beautiful the bastard is . . .' Now it was the father who took the girl by the hand. They turned round to the jetty, the girl retrieved the line and discovered that a little fish had taken the bait, a sardine, perhaps, or an anchovy: she cried out and laughed at the little fish which thrashed at the end of the line and she tried to get it to jump into her father's hands, which finally met the line and taking the little fish in his left hand, with his right hand removed the hook. At this moment, they left the field of view, disappeared behind the mounds of rubbish and were not seen again.

In the moment that followed, one could hardly credit that this diversion had taken place, at least if you judged by the German who once more started to play the charlatan with his door-knocker face, and to offer to the crowd around him his terrible merchandise, unspeakable, that handshake that he could never get rid of, and if you judged by the urchins who, like statues, stayed as immobile as before. There were nevertheless those few words by way of a funeral elegy that the little girl with the terrified minnow eyes had addressed to the bastard in homage to his beautiful face, and those seemed true, they lingered, they must perhaps also have remained in the ears of the statuesque urchins and perhaps – why not? – persuaded them to put an end to this stupid and wicked farce, by finally and conclusively expelling, indeed forcibly removing, from the stage-set of the life of the world, this German and the farce that he had played with us too long. Because afterwards, for the German it was effectively as if the *Miserere* had been intoned for him, after this it was effectively as if the urchins, all of them or only the one who did the deed, were saying to themselves: look here, it seems as if we've all become statues, and while we're acting like statues, this bastard is profiting by offensively continuing to live before our eyes, although in our minds it is as if his death had already happened, only he doesn't know it yet, and is deluding himself, because since we have had him here and encircled him, he has been looking at us as if in his eyes we really were statues.

And from the way in which they looked at him, there was no doubt they seemed to be statues: statues in a circle, and there inside, encircled, this damn fool played his barbarous pantomime of the handshake and now he put forward a hand first to one then another, and each time he had the air of believing that the statue would come alive, he proffered then he deflected his arm, but he retrieved it just after, with the hand held out and the smile that accompanied it, a grimace of white lifeless lips, prominent like the scar of a wound.

They really regarded him like this: as if they were made of an immortal material, the indestructible matter of marble or bronze, and he of the common mortal stuff of men, flesh and bone, the dust that humans are made of. They looked at him like monumental statues that had been erected to their own glory, in honour of what they had accomplished. And no doubt, if they had had their way, they would have wanted it never to end, this monumental moment, never to come down from the pedestal whence they surveyed the last spasms of life of the German tank-man. In short, it was as if they were bewitched and what the little girl did, in entering unknowingly into the enchantment, was to say the right words, absolutely those that should have been said, and the spell was broken. In fact, after, immediately after, Death, which had been playing cold and cool with the German, at this moment became warm, warmer, hot.

Now it was the turn of Death to give him the handshake that he was longing for, from now on there was no one but her, Old German Mother Death,* who would be giving him a handshake; in this and the other world there was no one besides her, his boss, the great mistress of the German slaughter. She alone could do it, and so she shook it, clawed it to be precise, because as is notorious she grabs everything indiscriminately, and as a result it must give her a double pleasure, if and when she runs into him too, the German, her great tormenter by piece rate, her everlasting day labourer.

She was there, present: she was one of the faces in the circle, the faces of urchins and adolescents with large clear eyes with wrinkled lids, black velvet eyes of carnival or mourning, the cheeks and lips shadowed with the first down. To look at them, from one to the other, one had the impression of always seeing the same face, in fact it was the face of Death, and it was like a second face on the urchins, like one painted on the true face with soot during carnival, all teeth, dark-ringed eyes, grotesque stub nose, and if they painted it from memory as they had always known and seen it, the Death's Head Mask, it was as if they knew that to totally camouflage life, there was only its opposite, Death.

At this moment, the German with his stupid and devious hand outstretched, addressed himself precisely to someone, but if he had had an eye for faces as he certainly had for a gun-sight, he would have known better than to look at him: but in mitigation you could say that the pantomime that he played henceforth was head to head with Death, and it was to the Death's Head, in the guise of the urchin, that he offered his hand, twisting it madly as if in an aria of agony.

He put out his heavy hand, stained with blood, and he smiled at this urchin Death, smiled at it with tigerish teeth that no longer shone, their whiteness had dulled and put you in mind of a stuffed beast; he smiled and it was as if he had already started to die and, through the smile, to decompose.

The urchin blinked his eyelids and, his eyes screwed up, blinking, stared wide-eyed at the German, took a step out of the circle, and planted himself in front of him, there, put out his right arm which was bare to the shoulder, and seemed as if its hand were amputated, with the stump bandaged and still soaked in blood. He gave a tap on the shoulder and pushed the stump against the German as if to say: shake that. And, meanwhile, he fixed him with large black eyes which scrutinized him with an intense expression, as if preoccupied: one would have said that he fixed him with his real eyes, and at the same time with the eyes of the soul and which must have made him see the German by turns as a little less and a little more real than he was, now near, now far, now shrunken and now enlarged, so much an individual and so much less than one, a true zero, and so much more than an individual, a people, an army in itself.

As to whether or not the German was astonished, he alone knew, because he kept grinning with that grimace of a smile left hanging on his lips: save for one or two times – and at this point you couldn't tell any more if he were more mad than wicked – he sketched with his hand very nimble little darts of invitation towards the stump. The urchin kept staring at him intently, with knitted brow, pensive, and with eyelashes that, meanwhile, fluttered like the wings of a butterfly agitated by the light. And he stared at him even more closely, eyebrows raised, pensive, when from behind his back his left hand appeared with lightning speed, holding one of those German bayonets, narrow and tapered like a dagger, that he gripped so hard that it seemed that his fist, as in the paladins of the Opera, served him as the hilt, and, almost without moving, in a flash his hand appeared and struck, burying its whole length in his belly.

For a moment it looked as though it was he who was keeping the German upright, holding him by the hilt of his bayonet, then, little by little, he started to let him go, following his death with relish: and as the German fell to his knees, with that mad and accursed hand always held out, that stupid and cunning smile on his lips, he, although he had remained intent, the eyebrows raised, pensive, on his brow appeared furrow after furrow, as if a sudden catastrophic precocious ageing had befallen him, because perhaps that was the price that Death made him pay for having chosen him as her right arm.

25

TV According to Leonardo

Arthur C. Clarke, *Profiles of the Future: An Enquiry into the Limits of the Possible* (London: Gollancz, 1962), pp. 75–80

Astronomer, radar specialist in World War II, author of happy science-fiction romances, Arthur C. Clarke is a living refutation of the commonplace notion that to practise science and to cultivate the imagination are mutually exclusive tasks; his life and work show, on the contrary, that a modern scientist must have imagination, and that the imagination is vastly enriched if its owner has enjoyed a scientific education.

Profiles of the Future is a fertile book, clear and above all honest. The author himself paraphrases the argument thus:

It is impossible to predict the future, and all attempts to do so in any detail appear ludicrous within a few years. This book has a more realistic, yet at the same time more ambitious, aim. It does not try to describe the future, but to define the boundaries within which possible futures must lie.

The idea of instantaneous transport – 'teleportation' – is very old, and is embodied in many Eastern religions. There must be millions of people alive at this moment who believe that it has already been achieved, by Yogis and other adepts, through the exercise of sheer will-power. Anyone who has seen a good display of firewalking, as I have done, must admit that the mind has almost unbelievable powers over matter – but in this particular case I beg to be sceptical.

One of the best proofs that mental teleportation is *not* possible was given, somewhat ironically, in a novel which described a society based upon it. Alfred Bester's *The Stars My Destination* opened with the interesting idea that a man threatened by sudden death might unconsciously and involuntarily teleport himself to safety. The fact that there is no authentic record of this happening, despite the millions of opportunities provided every year for putting the matter to the test, seems an excellent argument that it is not possible.

So let us consider teleportation in terms of known and foreseeable science, not wholly unknown and hypothetical mental powers. The only approach to the problem seems to be through electronics; we have learned to send sounds and images round the world at the velocity of light, so why not solid objects – even men?

It is important to realise that the above sentence contains a fundamental mis-statement of fact, though I doubt if many people would spot it. We don't, by radio or TV or any other means, *send* sounds and images anywhere. They remain at their place of origin, and there, within a fraction of a second, they perish. What we do send is information – a description or plan which happens to be in the form of electrical waves – from which the original sights and sounds can be recreated.

In the case of sound, the problem is relatively simple and may now be regarded as solved, for with really good equipment it is impossible to distinguish the copy from the original. The task is simple (with due apologies to the several generations of scientists and audio engineers who have beaten out their brains over it) because sound is one-dimensional. That is to say, any sound – no matter how complex – can be represented as a quantity which at any instant has a *single* value.

It is, when one thinks about it, quite extraordinary that the massed resources of Wagner or Berlioz can be completely contained in a single wavering line etched on a disc of plastic. But this is true, if the line's excursions are sufficiently detailed. Since the human ear cannot perceive sounds of frequencies beyond 20,000 vibrations a second, this sets a limit to the amount of detail that a sound channel need carry – or its band-width, to use the technical term.

For vision, the situation is much more complicated, because we are now dealing with a two-dimensional pattern of light and shade. Whereas *at a single instant* a sound can possess just one level of loudness, a scene possesses thousands of variations in brilliance. All these have to be dealt with if we wish to transmit an image.

The television engineers solved the problem not by tackling it as a whole, but by carving it up into bits. In the TV camera a single scene is dissected into some quarter of a million picture elements, in much the same way that a photograph is screened by the block-maker for newspaper reproduction. What the camera does, in effect, is to carry out an incredibly rapid survey or sampling of the light values over the scene, and to report them to the receiving end of the equipment, which acts on the information and reproduces corresponding light values on the screen of the cathode-ray tube. At any given instant, a TV system is transmitting the image of a single point, but because a quarter of a million such images flash upon the screen in a fraction of a second we get the illusion of a complete picture. And because the whole process is repeated thirty times a second (twenty-five in countries with 50-cycle mains) the picture appears to be continuous and moving.

In a single second, therefore, an almost astronomical amount of information about light and shade has to be passed through a TV channel. Thirty times a quarter of a million means 7,500,000 separate signals a second; in practice a band-width of 4,000,000 cycles per second gives the adequate but hardly brilliant standard of definition provided by our domestic TV sets. If you think that is good, compare it for detail some day with a high-quality photograph of the same size as your screen.

Now let us do some technological day-dreaming, following in the footsteps of a great many science-fiction writers. (Perhaps starting with Conan Doyle; see one of his lesser-known Professor Challenger stories, *The Disintegration Machine*, published in the 1920s.) Imagine a super X-ray device that could scan a solid object, atom by atom, just as a TV camera scans a scene in the studio. It would produce a string of electrical impulses stating in effect: here is an atom of carbon; here a billionth of an inch further to the right is nothing; another billionth of an inch along is an atom of oxygen – and so on, until the entire object had been uniquely and explicitly described. Granted the possibility of such a device, it would not seem very much more difficult to reverse the process and build up, from the information transmitted, a duplicate of the original, identical with it in every way. We might call such a system a 'matter transmitter', but the term would be misleading. It would no more transmit matter than a TV station transmits light; it would transmit information from which a suitable supply of unorganised matter in the receiver could be arranged into the desired form. Yet the result could be, in effect, instantaneous transportation – or at least transportation at the speed of radio waves, which can circle the world in a seventh of a second.

The practical difficulties, however, are so gigantic that as soon as they are spelled out the whole idea seems absurd. One has only to compare the two entities involved; there is a universe of difference between a flat image of rather low definition, and a solid body with its infinite wealth and complexity of microscopic detail down to the very atom. Can any words or description span the gulf between the photograph of a man – and the man himself?

To indicate the nature of the problem, suppose you were asked to make an *exact* duplicate of New York City, down to every brick, pane of glass, kerbstone, doorknob, gas pipe, water main and piece of electric wiring. Especially the latter, for not only would the replica of the city have to be perfect in all its physical details, but its multitudinous power and telephone circuits would have to be carrying exactly the same currents as were those of the original at the moment of reproduction.

It would, obviously, take an army of architects and engineers to compile the necessary description of the city – to carry out the scanning process, if we revert to television parlance. And in that time the city would have changed so much that the job would have to be done over again; in fact, it could never be completed.

Yet a human being is not less than a million, and probably a million million, times more complex than such a simple artifact as New York City. (We will ignore for the moment the not-unimportant distinction that one object is a living, sentient creature, and the other is not.) We can assume, therefore, that the copying process would take correspondingly longer. If it took a year to scan New York – a highly optimistic assumption – then to carry out the same process for a single human being would probably require all the time that is available before the stars go out. And to pass the resultant information through any communications channel would probably take about as long.

We can see this merely by looking at the figures involved. There are, very roughly, 5×10^{27} atoms in a human body, as compared with the 250,000 picture elements in a TV image. It takes a TV channel a thirtieth of a second to handle these; simple arithmetic shows that a channel of the same capacity would take about 2×10^{13}, or 20,000,000,000,000,000 years, to transmit a 'matter image' from one spot to another. It would be quicker to walk.

Though the above analysis is childishly naïve (any communications engineer can think of ways of knocking five or six zeros from this figure), it does indicate the magnitude of the problem, and the impossibility of solving it with presently imaginable techniques. It does *not* prove that it can never be done, but merely that it is far beyond the scope of today's science. For us even to attempt it would be as if Leonardo da Vinci tried to build a purely mechanical (i.e. non-electric) television system.

This analogy is such a close one that it is worth developing it a little further. How *would* Leonardo have tackled the problem of sending a high-definition (250,000 picture elements) image from one point to another?

You will be surprised to find that he could have done it, though it would have been a pointless *tour-de-force*. This is how he might have proceeded:

A large lens would have projected the image to be transmitted into a darkened room, on to a white screen. (The camera obscura, which does just this, was quite familiar to Leonardo, who described it in his notebooks.)

Over the picture would be laid a rectangular grid or sieve, with five hundred wires to a side, so that the image was divided into 250,000 separate elements. Each wire would be numbered, so that a pair of three-figure co-ordinates, such as 123:456, would identify every point in the field.

It would then be necessary for some sharp-eyed individual to examine the picture element by element and say 'Yes' or 'No' according to whether or not that element was illuminated. (If you imagine yourself going over a newspaper block with a magnifying glass, you have a very good idea of the procedure.) If 'o' meant darkness and '1' light, the whole picture could be described, within these limits of definition, by a series of 7-figure numbers. '1:111:111' would mean that the element on the extreme top left was illuminated; 'o:500:500', that the last one on the bottom right was dark.

Now Leonardo has the problem of transmitting this series of a 250,000 seven-figure number to a distant point. That could be done in many ways – semaphores, flashing lights and so on. At the receiving end, the image could be synthesised by putting black dots in the appropriate places on a blank 500 × 500 grid, or by having a quarter of a million tiny shutters that could be opened and closed in front of a white sheet, or in a dozen other ways.

And how long would all this take? The bottle-neck would probably be the semaphore; Leonardo would be very lucky to send one digit a second, and he has 1,750,000 to cope with. So it would require about twenty days, not to mention a fantastic amount of effort and eyestrain, to transmit this single image.

Leonardo could cut down the time, at the cost of mechanical complication, by having a number of men working in parallel, but he would soon reach the point of diminishing returns. Twenty operators, all scanning the image and sending their information over separate semaphores, would certainly get in each others' way; even so, they could not complete the task in less than a day. *That it could ever be performed in a thirtieth of a second would have seemed to Leonardo, perhaps the most far-seeing man who ever lived, an absolute and unquestionable impossibility.* Yet five hundred years after his birth, thanks to electronics, it was happening in most of the homes in the civilised world.

It may well be that there are technologies as much beyond electronics as that surpasses the clumsy machinery of the Middle Ages; within the frameworks of such technologies, even the scanning, transmission and reconstruction of an object as complex as a human being may prove to be possible – and in a reasonably short period of time, say a matter of a few minutes. Yet even this does not mean that we will ever be able to send a living man, with his thoughts, memories and his unique feeling of identity, over the equivalent of a radio circuit. For a man is more than the sum of his atoms; he is at least that, plus all the unimaginably large number of energy states and special configurations in which those atoms happen to be at a given moment of time. Modern physics (especially Heisenberg's Uncertainty Principle) maintains that it is fundamentally impossible to measure all those states and configurations with absolute accuracy – that, in fact, the very conception is meaningless. Like a carbon copy, the duplicate would have to have some degree of blurring, from the nature of things. The blurring might be too small to matter (like the noise on a high quality tape-recording) or it might be so bad that the copy would be unrecognisable, like a newspaper block that has been screened too many times.

26

Before and after the Crime

T. S. Eliot, *Murder in the Cathedral*
(London: Faber & Faber, 1935), pp. 42–4, 75–6

Before being canonized, Thomas Becket was the twelfth-century Archbishop of Canterbury; having come into conflict with England's King Henry II he was stabbed by four hired assassins during a divine service. Such is the argument of the verse drama Murder in the Cathedral *by T. S. Eliot, the great English poet of the twentieth century.*

Between the two choruses presented in this extract the horrible deed occurs. The women of Canterbury bear witness to it: these are simple women, who are not particularly pious, already hardened by the severity of their lives, but the anticipation of what is about to happen is beyond their ken, and the death of a minister of God shocks them. They sense that something has happened that cannot be repaired, it is an 'instant eternity of evil and wrong'. To efface this moment, it would be necessary to wash the wind and sweep up the sky.

CHORUS: We have not been happy, my Lord, we have not been too
     happy.
    We are not ignorant women, we know what we must expect
     and not expect.
    We know of oppression and torture,
    We know of extortion and violence,
    Destitution, disease,
    The old without fire in winter,
    The child without milk in summer,
    Our labour taken away from us,

Our sins made heavier upon us.
We have seen the young man mutilated,
The torn girl trembling by the mill-stream.
And meanwhile we have gone on living,
Living and partly living,
Picking together the pieces,
Gathering faggots at nightfall,
Building a partial shelter,
For sleeping, and eating and drinking and laughter.

God gave us always some reason, some hope; but now a new
terror has soiled us, which none can avert, none can avoid,
flowing under our feet and over the sky;
Under doors and down chimneys, flowing in at the ear and
the mouth and the eye.
God is leaving us, God is leaving us, more pang, more pain
than birth or death.
Sweet and cloying through the dark air
Falls the stifling scent of despair;
The forms take shape in the dark air:
Puss-purr of leopard, footfall of padding bear,
Palm-pat of nodding ape, square hyaena waiting
For laughter, laughter, laughter. The Lords of Hell are here.
They curl round you, lie at your feet, swing and wing through
the dark air.
O Thomas Archbishop, save us, save us, save yourself that we
may be saved;
Destroy yourself and we are destroyed.

*   *   *

CHORUS: Clear the air! clean the sky! wash the wind! take stone from
stone and wash them.
The land is foul, the water is foul, our beasts and ourselves
defiled with blood.

A rain of blood has blinded my eyes. Where is England?
  where is Kent? where is Canterbury?
O far far far far in the past; and I wander in a land of barren
  boughs: if I break them, they bleed; I wander in a land of
  dry stones: if I touch them they bleed.
How how can I ever return, to the soft quiet seasons?
Night stay with us, stop sun, hold season, let the day not
  come, let the spring not come.
Can I look again at the day and its common things, and see
  them all smeared with blood, through a curtain of falling
  blood?
We did not wish anything to happen.
We understood the private catastrophe,
The personal loss, the general misery,
Living and partly living;
The terror by night that ends in daily action,
The terror by day that ends in sleep;
But the talk in the market-place, the hand on the broom,
The nighttime heaping of the ashes,
The fuel laid on the fire at daybreak,
These acts marked a limit to our suffering.
Every horror had its definition,
Every sorrow had a kind of end:
In life there is not time to grieve long.
But this, this is out of life, this is out of time,
An instant eternity of evil and wrong.
We are soiled by a filth that we cannot clean, united to
  supernatural vermin,
It is not we alone, it is not the house, it is not the city that is
  defiled,
But the world that is wholly foul.
Clear the air! clean the sky! wash the wind! take the stone
  from the stone, take the skin from the arm, take the muscle
  from the bone, and wash them. Wash the stone, wash the
  bone, wash the brain, wash the soul, wash them wash them!

27

Death Fugue

Paul Celan, 'Death Fugue', *Selected Poems of Paul Celan*,
translated with an Introduction by Michael Hamburger
(London: Anvil Press Poetry, 1988), pp. 61–3

*The idea of writing poetry 'for everyone' flirts with utopianism, but I feel distrust
for whoever is a poet for the few, or for himself alone. To write is to transmit;
what can you say if the message is coded and no one has the key? You can say
that to transmit this particular message, in this specific way, was necessary to
the author, but with the rider that it is also useless to the rest of the world.*

*I think that this is the case with Paul Celan, the Jewish-German poet, upon
whose shoulders fell burden after burden, grief after grief, culminating in his
suicide at the age of fifty in 1970. I have not succeeded in penetrating the sense
of many of his lyrics; the exception being this 'Death Fugue'. I read that Celan
repudiated the poem, not considering it among his most typical poetry; that
doesn't matter to me, I wear it inside me like a graft.*

> Black milk of daybreak we drink it at sundown
> we drink it at noon in the morning we drink it at night
> we drink and we drink it
> we dig a grave in the breezes there one lies unconfined
> A man lives in the house he plays with the serpents he writes
> he writes when dusk falls to Germany your golden hair
>   Margarete
> he writes it and steps out of doors and the stars are flashing he
>   whistles his pack out

he whistles his Jews out in earth has them dig for a grave
he commands us strike up for the dance

Black milk of daybreak we drink you at night
we drink in the morning at noon we drink you at sundown
we drink and we drink you
A man lives in the house he plays with the serpents he writes
he writes when dusk falls to Germany your golden hair
    Margarete
your ashen hair Shulamith we dig a grave in the breezes there
    one lies unconfined

He calls out jab deeper into the earth you lot you others sing now
    and play
he grabs at the iron in his belt he waves it his eyes are blue
jab deeper you lot with your spades you others play on for the
    dance

Black milk of daybreak we drink you at night
we drink you at noon in the morning we drink you at sundown
we drink and we drink you
a man lives in the house your golden hair Margarete
your ashen hair Shulamith he plays with the serpents

He calls out more sweetly play death death is a master from
    Germany
he calls out more darkly now stroke your strings then as smoke
    you will rise into air
then a grave you will have in the clouds there one lies
    unconfined

Black milk of daybreak we drink you at night
we drink you at noon death is a master from Germany
we drink you at sundown and in the morning we drink and we
    drink you
death is a master from Germany his eyes are blue
he strikes you with leaden bullets his aim is true

a man lives in the house your golden hair Margarete
he sets his pack on to us he grants us a grave in the air
he plays with the serpents and daydreams death is a master from
    Germany

your golden hair Margarete
your ashen hair Shulamith

28

Tönle the Winterer

Mario Rigoni Stern,* *Storia di Tönle* (Turin: Einaudi, 1978), pp. 74–80, translated by Peter Forbes

The fact that Mario Rigoni exists has something of the miraculous about it. Firstly, there is the miracle of his own survival: this man, so hostile to all forms of violence, was pitched by fate into all the wars of his epoch, and he emerged unscathed and uncorrupted from the French, Albanian and Russian fronts, and the Nazi camps. But what is also miraculous is that Rigoni should be what he is, that he has managed to retain his authenticity and dignity in an era of suicidal urbanization and confusion of values.

It is rare to find such an accord between the man who lives and the man who writes; it is rare to find pages so packed with matter. This Tönle is a stoic and a stubborn man. Shepherd, miner, dealer in prints, smuggler, self-styled socialist, he is a polyglot globetrotter, not by choice, but by destiny: if he could have chosen he would have stayed at home with his cherry tree over the roof of the house, a 'partial shelter' like that of the women of Canterbury. Tönle, 'ardent defender of a rustic civilization', clings to the rocks and the roots, and his roots are here, on the splendid high plateau of Asiago, ravaged by all the conflicts. We are at the beginning of the punitive Austrian expedition of 1916.

In the afternoon he saw a suspicious-looking patrol of soldiers coming out of the woods and he gathered from their bearing and their uniforms that they were Austrians; walking with care and bowed backs behind the paving stones of the little road, they advanced towards the village, which was now completely destroyed. It was May the 28th.

In the same way that before he had avoided the soldiers of the Royal

Italian Army, now, redoubling his caution, he tried to evade the soldiers of the Imperial and Royal Army of Austria-Hungary. The battles meanwhile had moved to the south of our village, where there was desperate resistance: for entire days and nights the cannons and mortars had unremittingly pounded the woody hillocks, and the machine-guns had shredded the woods.

Tönle watched and listened, always hidden in the thicket, cocking his ear for the least sound near by to avoid being surprised or having his sheep stolen. During these afternoons, squatting in some crevice like a wild animal, he sometimes thought of his dead wife, of his friend the lawyer, or of the time he had worked as a gardener in the castle at Prague. Strangely, he never happened to think of his three sons who had emigrated to America, of the other two who were in the Alpine regiment, of his grandchildren, his daughters and daughters-in-law who had fled to the plain on the second day of the bombardment.

It was the 9th of June when he decided one evening to return to sleep in his house; and having left his sheep with the dog by the rocky cliff at Kheldar, he came down with a rapid and decisive step towards the abandoned settlement.

The light of the battle, to which he was accustomed by now, seemed to light up first the path, then the house. Entering, he noticed immediately that the soldiers had also passed through here, but perhaps because of the poverty of the house itself and its furnishings, they had not caused serious damage. That hadn't though prevented them from leaving their mark by making filthy stains in the kitchen, scattering to the air the contents of every drawer, and burning a chair in the grate. But the two old prints, that of the bear hunt and that of the wolves attacking the sledge, were still in place, there where their son Petra had hung them, when he was still a boy, that first year of their flight. He pulled up a chair to the wall and unhooked them: underneath appeared a white patch of lime, which seemed like a hole in the blackened wall. He looked around, searching for a place to hide them and, in the end, decided to slide them under a beam in the cowshed.

Re-entering the kitchen, on the threshold, he stepped in some human excrement; straight away, his anger flared up in him, he swore, seized the crab-grass broom and swept the filth outside; he drew a bucket of water from the rainwater tank and threw it with force on the flagstones, then brushed away the water with the broom; he put the objects back in the right place. Eventually, he closed the door again and retired to his bedroom, always the same, that he dreamt about in the course of his wanderings, and that he had enjoyed for so many winters.

He took out his watch from his waistcoat pocket to rewind it and hung it by its ring on the usual nail near the head of the bed. But before hanging it up he held it in his hand to feel its weight and its throb, and even if in the half-light he couldn't quite read the time, he saw the movement of the hammer that the quarryman raised and lowered to the rhythm of the seconds and, through contact with his fingers, the words embossed around the dial and, on the bottom, also embossed, the reproduction of the interior of a mine with its pit-props, a lantern and two miners. This watch, he had bought many years before passing through Ulm and the words engraved on it were the slogans of socialist workers who had just started their fight for a reduction in working hours. The raised inscription said in German: 'We want eight hours for work, eight hours for study, eight hours for rest,' and further: 'for social concord, fraternity and unity.' Hefting the watch in the palm of his hand, he thought: 'As for the hours, in the mine, you did sixteen, or even more, and now in place of fraternity there is the war and the poor are killing each other . . .'

He hung up the watch on its nail, took off his boots, lay down on the bed and pulled an old bedcover over himself. Far away there were always the lights of fires, the flashes of the cannons and the incessant noise, sometimes loud, sometimes muted.

Towards morning, he heard steps approaching the house and loud blows on the door. He didn't move from his bed, thinking: 'Now, if I'd left the door wide open no one would have knocked; a closed door in the middle of all the others that are open must mean there is someone inside and that's the kind of thing soldiers understand.' The battering grew louder, the latch gave way and the door crashed against the wall. He heard someone walk into the kitchen, enter the cowshed, and he thought again: 'Let's hope he doesn't find the tobacco.' The soldier re-entered the kitchen and climbed the stairs.

The door of the bedroom opened, and half opening his eyes in the dark he saw a young man in uniform halt for a moment, immobile on the threshold: he was looking around to case the room when his eyes stopped by the bed where Tönle was pretending to sleep. Attracted by the tick-tock and gleam of the watch, hung up above the bedhead, he approached it quietly and stretched out his hand to take it. Tönle opened his eyes and in a low voice said in German:

'Don't touch it, oaf!'

The soldier was dumbfounded, and when he regained his composure, he shot out, tripping on the stairs. When the soldier left the yard, Tönle got up, put on his boots in haste and went down to the cowshed to collect the swags of pipe tobacco he had hidden under the straw in the darkest corner. But coming out he found an Austrian patrol in front of his door, commanded by an ensign who walked up to him and declared in Italian: 'You are a spy and I hereby pronounce you under arrest!'

Tönle spat the black tobacco saliva to earth, murmuring something that the officer didn't understand entirely, and that's why he asked him, again in Italian:

'But what are you saying? Come with us!'

'I have to put my sheep out to pasture,' replied the old man in German, 'and I don't have time to waste with the military.'

He turned as if to leave but, on a sign from the ensign, two soldiers barred his way and seized him by the arms. With a violent jerk he broke away but, no longer having the agility of former days, he was quickly retaken and held firmly.

'Old devil!' said the ensign in Viennese-accented German, 'we're going to settle with you. We're taking you to the command post and we shall hear then what you say. We'll have you shot!'

'You, Mister Ensign,' said the old man, mimicking the Viennese accent, which made the soldiers laugh, 'you're just a kid who understands nothing. I tell you again that I have to go and pasture my sheep.'

They surrounded him, making him walk in the direction of the house of Pûne; they lurched towards the Grabo, and reached Petareitle where in 1909 Matío Parlío had built his house far from anyone. Now the Austrians had placed the command post of one of their regiments there.

Behind the house, kitchens were in the course of construction and there was a coming and going of soldiers: some were excavating, some carried wood, still others water from the Prunele. In Nicola Scoa's stable they must have installed a first-aid post for other soldiers were lounging there sporting large bandages.

A great number of the curious soon assembled around the old man, chatting among themselves. A corporal approached, offered him a hot cup of coffee, and he took it without a word. He drank it slowly under the eyes of the assembled soldiers, emptied the cup and said:

'Thank you, Corporal.'

'You speak German, Grandad?' the latter asked him.

'Yes,' he replied, 'and before you did.' And he didn't want to add another word.

They escorted him inside the house, to the kitchen, where a major, leaning his hands on the edge of the table, was studying the maps spread out on it. The ensign who had captured him kept a respectful two steps away. Evidently, he already knew how matters stood.

'Now,' the major said suddenly, addressing him, 'you have your sheep to pasture. And where are they?'

'By the rocky cliff at Kheldar.'

'And how many of them are there?'

'Twenty-seven with the lambs.' But the old man said lambs in our old tongue so that the commandant didn't understand.

'With what?'

'With the virgin sheep,' he replied. That made the ensign smile and he put his hand to his mouth.

'Why didn't you leave with the others when we bombarded?'

'Because. Because here is my home, and because I am an old man.'

'Have you spoken with or met up with any Italian officers?'

'I haven't seen anybody.'

'And where did the Bersaglieri* go who were on Mount Mosciagh?'

'I don't know.'

'Why do you speak German so well?'

'Why, always why. I was a soldier in Bohemia and afterwards I worked in all the territories ruled by the Emperor Franz-Josef.'

'Who was your chief in Bohemia?'

'Major Fabini.'

'Perhaps you mean Field Marshal von Fabini. But that means you are a faithful subject,' said the major with a certain enthusiasm.

'No,' he replied. 'I am only a simple shepherd and an old proletarian socialist.'

'Then you are an Italian spy and for that you will stay here!'

'To hell with you and the Italians. Leave me to get on with my business.'

But the major had also lost his patience and signalled to the two soldiers who accompanied Tönle and who led him outside again, behind the house.

Half an hour later, the ensign reappeared with a corporal; they took him with them and followed him the length of the path to Platabech as far as the rocky cliff at Kheldar to verify the story of the sheep. And two hours later they returned with the sheep and the black dog.

29

Trying to Understand

Hermann Langbein,* *Menschen in Auschwitz* (Vienna: Europa Verlag, 1987), pp. 576–9, translated by Peter Forbes and P. D. Royce

The pages that follow are the concluding ones of a book that is dear to me, one that seems to me to be fundamental, and that I should have liked to have written myself: but I would have been incapable of it, because at Auschwitz my horizon was limited. This was not the case with Hermann Langbein, Austrian, political prisoner, and an exceptional figure in the Resistance: his experience of fighting in Spain was his entrée into the secret society of the resistance that existed inside the camp: his guile enabled him to rise to the eventual post of secretary to a high-ranking medical officer in the SS. His double role exposed him to a serious and constant danger, but allowed him to amass an endless number of factual reports and personal stories.

The title of the book, Humankind in Auschwitz, *is rich in significance: the author wrote it for a precise purpose, not to accuse or to move, but to facilitate understanding. He has brought to fruition an unpleasant task; for many years after the liberation he wasn't content only to consult memoirs and to interview the few survivors among the prisoners, but he carried the inquest as far as concerning himself with the perpetrators, forcing himself (and us) to understand the way men can be induced to assume certain 'duties'. The result is surprising; there are no demons, the assassins of millions of innocents are people like us. They don't have different blood to ours but, consciously or not, they have chosen a dangerous road, the road of submission and acquiescence from which there is no return.*

CONCLUSIONS AND WARNING

For a long time, German public opinion refused to pay heed to Auschwitz. Those among the survivors who continued to draw the public's attention to the events of Auschwitz could not overcome this barrier. Their repeated warnings merely confirmed them in their status (first conferred at Auschwitz) of social outcasts.

For a change to come about, it needed the rise of a new generation who began to rebel against this oppressively burdensome heritage that their fathers tacitly tried to impose on them. The Eichmann trial in Jerusalem as well as the major Auschwitz lawsuit in Frankfurt signalled a change, after which the public could no longer deny the truth about Auschwitz.

However, a sober and objective attitude to the phenomenon of Auschwitz is hardly possible so long as there are still living those who were induced to stifle all their natural instincts and deaden their conscience in order to commit mass murder for years on end with the equanimity of those who crush noxious insects and who, at best, complained about the unpleasant work they were forced to carry out in the interest of society at large. Since, however, the phenomenon of Auschwitz required people to take up positions, this was done, as a rule, by adhering to one or other of the factions that arose. Some tried to belittle the facts – typical here is the shameful discussion as to whether the number of victims had not been exaggerated; as if the enormity of the crime would somehow be diminished supposing a million less had been flung into the gas ovens. It is the same faction that assiduously sought to establish comparisons with crimes committed on a massive scale against other peoples, in order to deny the uniqueness of Auschwitz. Against this tendency, another party acknowledged guilt and framed confessions and accusations but often with a strangely abstract vocabulary which was hardly convincing. A commitment to a dispassionate analysis of human reactions in the extreme situation of Auschwitz is still lacking and yet there is no event in the recent past that more cries out to be analysed. Only a generation capable of looking at Auschwitz from a distance, as we view the events of the nineteenth century, could undertake this study.

This book is intended to facilitate the task of this generation. And if, over and above this help, the generation whose fathers had a personal relationship with Nazism can be stimulated to draw from it some lessons, so much the better.

I have always been aware that, as a former inmate of Auschwitz, in spite of all my attempts at objectivity in this study, I would still remain partial, which will not have escaped the reader. I hope, however, that my efforts towards objectivity will likewise not be overlooked. They could even seem exaggerated to some; as for instance when the behaviour of the detainees who could be induced to act against their fellow sufferers is less thoroughly described than the action of the prisoners who even as officials sometimes conducted themselves humanely; or when the motives that induced some of the SS to treat prisoners humanely are researched in detail, whilst the guards who carried out every death sentence receive less attention. However, this attitude is not merely the result of efforts made by one ensnared in the events of Auschwitz to attain objectivity. The attention of the observer is always more struck by the exceptions than by the rule. The analysis of the exceptions that occurred at Auschwitz can lead to important perceptions on human reactions in extreme situations. One may add here that the crimes committed at Auschwitz have already been amply documented. A recapitulation of the atrocities did not seem necessary.

Whoever becomes aware of the extent of the massacre perpetrated at Auschwitz is inclined to seek out the guilty. My study should serve as a warning; no one should arrive at a verdict lightly; innumerable are those who would have acted no differently from the majority of gaolers at Auschwitz had they been posted there. It may likewise be assumed that most of those who were guilty of belonging to the machinery of extermination, would never have thought of killing had they not been pitched into the atmosphere of Auschwitz.

These considerations are of limited interest to lawyers whose duty it is to establish the actual guilt of the individual. However, for those who became aware of the role often played by mere chance in the selection of the individuals who were to co-operate in mass murder, the criteria of the law will not suffice. It is by chance that a Baretzki or a Neubert had been posted to Auschwitz. Dr Wirths and Dr Mengele would not have been transferred there if they had remained fit for active service; it is through a chain of adventitious circumstances that people such as Hans Stark and Irma Grese came under the sway of the SS at a tender age. Once these facts are known it becomes obvious that it would be too facile to apportion guilt for the mass murders exclusively to those who actively committed them and to the handful who gave the orders. It was not as simple as that, namely that a few thousand people merely executing orders could build up, under the strictest secrecy, a system of extermination of which the people were completely unaware. Every serious analysis of the comportment of the murderers of Auschwitz leads one outside this restricted circle of individuals.

The responsibility of the system for the culpability of the individuals appears with the utmost clarity when one examines the actions of those who committed bloody crimes while wearing the striped apparel of the inmates. Who bears the responsibility for a morally deficient man: the habitual delinquent who was granted sweeping powers over his fellow men or the camp's authorities who rewarded him when he gave vent to his criminal instincts and put his privileges at risk if he conducted himself humanely? Here, a serious warning must be given not to reach a hasty judgement on the behaviour of those who, although not having been sent as criminals to the camp, could be induced by the authorities to act as henchmen. Only someone who was himself a capo, a block warden, a prison doctor, or any similar functionary, knows the pressure that had to be endured, and those who managed to resist it successfully – and, similarly, all blandishments offered with a view to joining the masters (that is, the killers) – may pronounce judgement. Many of those who did not abuse the power delegated to them by the authorities of the camp hesitate to make such a judgement, precisely because they have known the tensions involved.

The responsibility for the fact that Auschwitz was possible in the twentieth century and in a country proud of its civilized traditions rests entirely with Nazism and consequently with those who contributed to that regime gaining unlimited power. Only a totalitarian system that tried to suborn every single individual could have created, in a terrifyingly short time, the conditions for a well-organized, unconcealed programme of genocide – hardly ten years had elapsed since Hitler assumed the reins of government in Germany before it had become a daily routine to cram the gas chambers of Auschwitz full of human beings.

Only after democratic institutions had been made a matter for scorn and the infallibility of the Führer proclaimed, when all the voices of criticism had been stifled and a regime of terror installed, could the ambitions of the likes of Höss and Mengele be given free rein and so lead to such devastating results. Only then could an order from the infallible Führer or from the omniscient party succeed in extinguishing all normal sense of responsibility and so bring about the conditions for Auschwitz to become a reality.

Only a totalitarian system that holds humanity in contempt could cold-bloodedly include genocide in its political programme. Hitler never denied it, nor can anyone who voted for him have been in any doubt about it. Auschwitz meant the realization of the slogan proclaimed time and time again: 'Die, Jew!'

Anyone who has learnt how quickly a totalitarian system can gain overwhelming powers over its subjects can appreciate the merits of a democratic system, even if one is not prepared to overlook its obvious weaknesses. Certainly, democratically organized communities have also committed crimes, but many examples prove that in such a system the voice of conscience cannot entirely be suppressed when injustice is being committed – in a democracy an Auschwitz would be unthinkable. On the other hand, there are examples to suggest that every totalitarian system is inclined to develop tendencies which lead in the direction of Auschwitz.

For a long time to come, the German people will have to bear the burden of guilt for the deeds perpetrated in its name by the government in its extermination camps. There is no doubt that the perfect organization of the apparatus of destruction shows typical German traits. Certainly, the organizers of genocide were able to exploit the militaristic cult of authority and blind obedience, the prestige of uniform and the desire to clack heels exclaiming smartly 'Jawohl' which was more pervasive in the German people than in other, neighbouring populations.

One shouldn't assume, though, that other countries with a totalitarian system would not find ways and means to arrive at similar developments. The recent past has shown all too often how mistaken this assumption is. The essential nature of Auschwitz does not lie in its detailed organization, but in the principles it embodies: utter contempt for human beings, an automatic division into friends and foes, and complete submission to the will of a führer are the elements that one comes across in every totalitarian system. They have led to the construction of a mechanism of annihilation for which the name of Auschwitz serves only as a symbol.

A fantasy came into my head once in Auschwitz and remains fresh in my memory: we were sitting one day in our prisoners' office in the SS infirmary – we didn't have much to do and I clattered away in a desultory fashion on my typewriter while in the adjoining office, divided only by a thin timber partition, members of the SS quietly discussed problems of leave and family matters. At that point I imagined that no one would be able to distinguish between members of the SS and the prisoners – i.e. who is boss and who is destined to die – if we were all naked and not wearing uniform. The fantasy was false. We would have been able to distinguish them by the numbers tattooed on their arms, their shaved heads as opposed to neat haircuts, and by their state of nourishment, which was in most cases widely different between the two groups. But this is not what my fantasy was all about; it concerned the omnipotence or total helplessness that attended wearing a uniform which separated human beings in such a way that the mood of one who wore an SS uniform could mean the death of someone who was forced to wear prisoners' garb. This is an indication of the violence of the system, which turned every human being into a uniform-wearer with its dire consequences.

Nobody could have had a clearer view of this system than we who were in Auschwitz. The example of Dr Eduard Wirths, a medical officer of the SS, shows us how easy it is to become an instrument of Nazism: a little bit of opportunism, a certain taste for uniform, were enough to lead him on to a path from which it became more difficult, day by day, to return, and which ultimately led to Auschwitz. From this and other examples one can learn how dangerous it is to dedicate oneself to an organization, without proper scrutiny, and to identify oneself with it; and the consequences that may follow if one is lured into the belief that human beings can be judged on a global basis. The temptation to pass judgement is then very great. Let everyone guard himself against it.

The lesson of Auschwitz is as follows: the first step, namely the tolerance of a social structure that pursues a total domination of man, is the most dangerous. Should that type of regime set its mind on a plan to exterminate 'subhuman' people (and this is not necessarily a matter of the Jews and Gypsies) and one wears its uniform (which may be adorned with symbols other than the runes of the SS and the skull), one has become its tool.

I, like many others, dreamt at Auschwitz that humanity would draw the proper lesson from what there became reality, even though, until then, everyone would have judged it unimaginable and totally out of the question. Will humanity do so?

30

We are Alone

Kip S. Thorne,* 'The Search for Black Holes',
Scientific American (December 1974), pp. 32–5, 43

We are in the middle of the greatest of all cultural revolutions: one that is being carried through in silence by the astrophysicists. The layperson (and we are all laypeople, with the exception of about a thousand specialists in the world) can only accept the vastness of the new celestial bodies, suppress fresh shudders, keep quiet and reflect. From the interplanetary expeditions of the last ten years we have learnt more about the cosmos than we had deduced in all the preceding millennia; we have seen, among much else, that Moonmen, Venusians and Martians don't exist and have never existed.

We are alone. If we have interlocutors, they are so far away that, barring unforeseeable turns of events, we shall never talk to them; in spite of this, some years ago we sent them a pathetic message. Every year that passes leaves us more alone. Not only are we not the centre of the universe, but the universe is not made for human beings; it is hostile, violent, alien. In the sky there are no Elysian Fields, only matter and light, distorted, compressed, dilated, and rarefied to a degree that eludes our senses and our language. Every year that passes, while earthly matters grow ever more convoluted, the challenge of the cosmos grows keener and more bitter: the heavens are not simple, but neither are they impermeable to our minds – they are waiting to be deciphered. The misery of man has another face, one imprinted with nobility; maybe we exist by chance, perhaps we are the sole instance of intelligence in the universe, certainly, we are immeasurably small, weak and alone, but if the human mind has conceived Black Holes, and dares to speculate on what happened in the first moments of creation, why should it not know how to conquer fear, poverty and grief?

Of all the conceptions of the human mind from unicorns to gargoyles to the hydrogen bomb perhaps the most fantastic is the black hole: a hole in space with a definite edge over which anything can fall and nothing can escape; a hole with a gravitational field so strong that even light is caught and held in its grip; a hole that curves space and warps time. Like the unicorn and the gargoyle, the black hole seems much more at home in science fiction or in ancient myth than in the real universe. Nevertheless, the laws of modern physics virtually demand that black holes exist. In our galaxy alone there may be millions of them.

The search for black holes has become a major astronomical enterprise over the past decade. It has yielded dozens of candidates scattered over the sky. At first the task of proving conclusively that any one of them is truly a black hole seemed virtually impossible. In the past two years, however, an impressive amount of circumstantial evidence has been accumulated on one of the candidates: a source of strong X-ray emission in the constellation Cygnus designated Cygnus X-1. The evidence makes me and most other astronomers who have studied it about 90 percent certain that in the center of Cygnus X-1 there is indeed a black hole.

Before I describe the evidence that leads to this conclusion, let me lay some groundwork and indulge my theoretical proclivities by describing some of the predicted properties of black holes [see 'Black Holes,' by Roger Penrose; SCIENTIFIC AMERICAN, May, 1972]. Physicists educate themselves and their students by means of 'thought experiments' whose results are predicted by theory. I shall resort to such an experiment to convey the basic reasoning that underlies the concept of the black hole.

Imagine that at some distant time in the future the human species has migrated throughout the galaxy and is inhabiting millions of planets. Having no further need for the earth, men choose to convert it into a monument: They will squeeze it until it becomes a black hole. To do the squeezing they build a set of giant vises, and to store the necessary energy they fabricate a giant battery. They then scoop out a chunk of the earth and convert its mass into pure energy, the amount of energy obtained being given by Einstein's equation $E = mc^2$, in which E is the energy, m is the mass and c is the speed of light. This energy is stored in the battery. The vises are arrayed around the earth on all sides and, powered by the battery, they squeeze the earth down to a quarter of its original size.

To check their progress the project engineers fabricate from a chunk of the earth a tight-fitting spherical jacket strong enough to hold the planet in its compressed state. They slip the jacket over the earth and open the vises. Then they measure the escape velocity of a rocket placed on the earth, that is, the velocity the rocket must attain in order to be able to coast out of the earth's gravitational field. Before the earth was compressed the escape velocity was the same as it is today: 11 kilometers per second. The compression of the earth, however, brings the earth's surface four times closer to its center, thereby quadrupling the kinetic energy that the rocket must have in order to escape. The escape energy is proportional to the square of the escape velocity; therefore the escape velocity after this first compression has doubled to 22 kilometers per second.

Satisfied that some progress has been made, the engineers repeat the process, compressing the earth still further until its original circumference of 40,000 kilometers is only 10 kilometers. I give the measurement of circumference instead of diameter because in the presence of strong gravitational fields space is so highly curved that the object's diameter (d) is no longer related to its circumference (C) by the Euclidean formula $C = \pi d$; moreover, in the case of a black hole the diameter cannot be measured or calculated. This time the rocket needs an escape velocity of 708 kilometers per second in order to coast away from the earth.

After several more compression stages the earth has been reduced to a circumference of 5.58 centimeters. The escape velocity is now 300,000 kilometers per second – the speed of light. One last little squeeze, and the escape velocity exceeds the speed of light. Now light itself cannot escape from the earth's surface, nor can anything else. Communication between the earth and the rest of the universe is permanently ruptured. In this sense the earth is no longer part of the universe. It is gone, leaving behind it a hole in space with a circumference of 5.58 centimeters. Outside the horizon, or edge, of the hole the escape velocity is less than the speed of light, and exceedingly powerful rockets can still get away. Inside the horizon the escape velocity exceeds the speed of light and nothing can escape. The interior of the hole, like the earth that gave rise to it, is cut off from the rest of the universe.

Let us return to the present and use the thought experiment to aid in understanding what happens in a star. There is a key difference between the earth and a massive star. For the earth to become a black hole external forces must be applied; for a star to become a black hole the necessary forces are provided by the star's own internal gravity. When a star of, say, 10 times the mass of the sun has consumed nuclear fuel through its internal thermonuclear reactions for a period longer than a few tens of millions of years, its fuel supply runs out. With its fires quenched the star can no longer exert the enormous thermal pressures that normally counterbalance the inward pull of its gravity. Gravity wins the tug-of-war, and the star collapses.

Unless the star sheds most of its mass during the collapse, gravity crushes it all the way down to a black hole. If, however, the star can eject enough material to reduce its mass to about twice the mass of the sun or less, then it is saved: nonthermal pressures, such as the electron pressures that make it difficult to compress rock, build up and halt the collapse. The star becomes either a white dwarf about the size of the earth or a neutron star with a circumference of some 60 kilometers. (A neutron star is a star where matter is so dense that the electrons have been squeezed onto the protons, converting them into neutrons.) In either case, as with the earth, to convert the object into a black hole one must apply external forces – forces that do not exist in nature.

These predictions, which follow from the standard laws of physics, tell us that there is a critical mass for compact stars (stars with a circumference smaller than the earth's) of about two times the mass of the sun. Below the critical mass a compact star can be a white dwarf or a neutron star. Above the critical mass it can only be a black hole. The magnitude of the critical mass is a key link in the arguments that Cygnus X-1 is a black hole. Therefore one would like to know the critical mass precisely. Precision is not possible, however, because we do not know enough about the properties of matter at the 'supernuclear' densities of a white dwarf or a neutron star, that is, at densities above the density of the atomic nucleus: 2×10^{14} grams per cubic centimeter. Nevertheless, an upper limit on the critical mass is known: Remo Ruffini of Princeton University and others have shown that it cannot exceed three times the mass of the sun. In other words, no white dwarf or neutron star can have a mass greater than three times the mass of the sun.

From a physical and mathematical standpoint a black hole is a marvelously simple object, far simpler than the earth or a human being. When a physicist is analyzing a black hole, he need not face the complexities of matter, with its molecular, atomic and nuclear structure. The matter that collapsed in the making of the black hole has simply disappeared. It exerts no influence on the hole's surface or exterior. It makes no difference whether the collapsing matter was hydrogen, uranium or the antimatter equivalents of those elements. All the properties of the black hole are determined completely by Einstein's laws for the structure of empty space.

Exactly how simple black holes must be has been discovered by three physicists: Werner Israel of the University of Alberta and Brandon Carter and Stephen Hawking of the University of Cambridge. They have shown that when a black hole first forms, its horizon may have a grotesque shape and may be wildly vibrating. Within a fraction of a second, however, the horizon should settle down into a unique smooth shape. If the hole is not rotating, its shape will be absolutely spherical. Rotation, however, will flatten it at the poles just as rotation slightly flattens the earth. The amount of flattening and the precise shape of the flattened hole are determined completely by its mass and its angular momentum (speed of rotation). The mass and angular momentum not only determine the hole's shape; they also determine all the other properties of the hole. It is as though one could deduce every characteristic of a woman from her weight and hair color.

[. . .] Thus far I have described only normal black holes created by the collapse of normal stars ranging in mass from three to 60 times the mass of the sun. There are probably supermassive holes and possibly miniholes as well. Donald Lynden-Bell of the University of Cambridge has argued that the dense milieu of gas and stars that fuels grand-scale explosions in the nuclei of some galaxies must ultimately collapse to form a supermassive black hole. If this is true, a galaxy such as our own, which probably had explosions in its nucleus long ago, might possess a huge black hole in its nucleus today. That hole would be a 'tomb' from a more violent past. Such a black hole in our own galaxy might be as massive as 100 million times the mass of the sun and have a circumference as large as two billion kilometers. The hole would suck gas from the surrounding galactic nucleus, perhaps forming a gigantic accretion disk analogous to the disks proposed for the spectroscopic-binary systems. Lynden-Bell and Rees calculate that such a disk would emit strong radio and infrared radiation but not X rays. The nucleus of our galaxy does give evidence of several bright infrared and radio 'stars.' Unfortunately for theorists an accretion disk around a supermassive black hole is not the only possible explanation of the observed objects, and so far no one has invented a definitive test for the hypothesis.

Miniholes far less massive than the sun cannot be created in the universe as it exists today. Nature simply does not supply the necessary compressional forces. The necessary forces were present, however, in the first few moments after the creation of the universe in the 'big bang.' If the big bang were sufficiently chaotic, then, according to calculations made by Hawking, it should have produced a great number of miniholes. Hawking has shown that miniholes behave quite differently from normal-sized holes. Any hole less massive than 10^{16} grams (the mass of a small iceberg) should gradually destroy itself by an emission of light and particles according to certain laws of quantum mechanics. Those laws, which are not important for the larger black holes, considerably modify the properties of the smaller holes. The result is that all the primordial black holes less massive than 10^{15} grams should be gone by now. Those with a mass between 10^{15} grams and 10^{16} grams are now dying. In its final death throes such a dying black hole would not be black at all. It would be a fireball powerful enough to supply all the energy needs of the earth for several decades yet small enough to fit inside the nucleus of an atom.

Hawking's results are less than a year old, and so their implications have not yet been explored in detail. They may motivate a flood of proposals for searching for miniholes. He and Page are exploring one possibility: that the bursts of cosmic gamma rays that have been detected by instruments on artificial satellites of the Vela series came from explosions of miniholes.

The present list of ways and places that black holes might be found is far from complete. With so many possibilities a theorist such as the author cannot help being excited – until he talks with his more down-to-earth experimenter friends. Then he realizes what a difficult job the search really is. We cannot expect quick results, but the future does not seem unpromising.

Afterword:
The Four Paths of Primo Levi

BY ITALO CALVINO

Last year Giulio Bolatti had the idea of asking some Italian writers to compile a 'personal anthology': in the sense that the choices should reflect not their own writing but what they judge to be essential reading; it was thus a case of sketching, over a series of selections of their favourite authors, a literary landscape and a cultural ideal. A simple juxtaposition of texts can thus become an autobiography or self-portrait; in this type of selection, in which what counts is the unexpected and partial nature of the texts chosen and rejected, an anthology can also be conceived as an affirmation of values in opposition to more received values, as a declaration of intent or a manifesto.

Among the authors who responded to this invitation, the only one to date who has fulfilled his commitment is Primo Levi, whose contribution was awaited as a crucial test for this type of project, inasmuch as his scientific education blends with his literary sensibility (whether in his evocation of lived experience or in his imaginative work) and with a keen sense of the moral and social component of all experience. (We haven't forgotten that in *The Periodic Table*, where all the elements come together, Levi has already given us the book of his formative influences.)

The autobiographical dimension of his education is also to the fore here in the Preface and the title (*The Search for Roots*), but what prevails in the body of the book is the systematic element, the 'encyclopaedic'. The principal quality of Levi the anthologist consists in establishing relations between texts which could not be more heterogeneous.

To give a representative sample of this multiplicity, it will suffice to say that the Homeric episode of Ulysses and Polyphemus jostles with an extract from Darwin's *The Origin of Species* on the function of beauty in nature, and that a chapter from a venerable treatise on organic chemistry is linked to a text by Conrad on the wisdom founded on practical experience. This element of a personal and inhabited library is accentuated by the fact that selections from familiar reading in modern literature, from D'Arrigo's *Horcynus Orca* to the poems of Paul Celan, alternate with old books by obscure authors, read by chance but kept after due consideration.

THE TRANSIT OF AUSCHWITZ

The most important page of the book is the graphic placed at the beginning to suggest 'four possible routes through some of the authors in view'. The scheme has the form of an ellipse or spheroid and has at one pole the Book of Job, which opens the book: the drama of 'the Just oppressed by injustice' is the point from which the first questions emerge. (I would suggest that it is the very presence of the Book of Job as an introduction to this 'search for roots' that reminds us that the journey of Primo Levi passed through Auschwitz.)

The opposite pole of the ellipse or spheroid is no less charged with negativity: here are the 'Black Holes' (the article chosen here is from *Scientific American*) which remind us that 'In the sky there are no Elysian Fields, only matter and light, distorted, compressed, dilated, and rarefied to a degree that eludes our senses and our language.' Between these two poles, which represent a challenge to the powers of mankind (above all, to his spiritual resources) on the part of a universe which is more or less unconcerned with him, Levi traces four meridians, four lines of resistance to all forms of despair, four responses that define his stoicism.

On one side there is 'salvation through laughter' (the comic, Rabelais, Belli and Porta, irony towards others, but above all towards one's own misery, as in Sholem Aleichem; as well as the disenchanted moralists who entertain no illusions, such as Swift or Parini); on the other side there is 'salvation through knowledge', in other words science (from the physician-poet Lucretius to the visionary futurist Arthur C. Clarke, also taking in along the way an old book of popularization on the structure of molecules that directed Levi towards his vocation as a chemist).

At the centre of the scheme appear two lines, which, far from indicating any solution or salvation, underline the moral attitudes which can constitute the first premises. On one side, the knowledge that 'man suffers unjustly' (we can see an echo of the questions of Job as much in the Cossack atrocities narrated by Babel as in the choruses from *Murder in the Cathedral* by T. S. Eliot). On the other side, the knowledge of 'the stature of man', of his capacity to rise to challenges that exceed his powers. Here Conrad is the ideal point of reference, followed by all those writers who can contribute by composing a sober epic of action, be they as celebrated as Saint-Exupéry or obscure. (Likewise, among the lessons of resistance to evil Levi reserves a place of honour for the accounts of endurance in the mountains by Rigoni Stern.)

One notices that a little collection of natural history and geographic descriptions by Marco Polo is inserted into the 'Conradian' line because, in the accounts of the Venetian's voyage, 'difficult tasks and dangers are highlighted with sober reserve, and the wonderful sights and sounds are described with the good sense of a merchant, attentive to frauds, prices and profits, and with the amused precision of a curious man'. In reality, we see that 'salvation through knowledge' and 'the stature of man' merge into each other just as 'salvation through laughter' is underscored with the pathos of suffering: in short, between the four lines there exists a dense series of connections and transfusions, proof – if one were needed – of a coherence which excludes mere eclecticism.

In contemplating the map proposed by Primo Levi one can't help reflecting on the possibility of each of us designing our own map, organizing it less by literary preference than by following the foundations of experience: an encyclopaedia rather than an anthology [. . .]

Concerning this encyclopaedic tendency we should understand what we mean. In other times, the term 'encyclopaedic' supposed a confidence in a global system that embraced within a unique discourse all other aspects of knowledge. Today, on the contrary, there is no system that holds; in place of the circle to which the etymology of the vocable 'encyclopaedia' refers, there is nothing but a whirlwind of fragments and debris. The persistence of the encyclopaedic tendency corresponds to a need to reassemble, in an ever-precarious equilibrium, the heterogeneous and centrifugal acquisitions which constitute the entire treasure of our uncertain knowledge.

La Repubblica (11 June 1981)

Notes

Introduction

Ulysses: English translations of Homer usually use the Greek forms Odysseus and Cyclops (or Kyklops), etc., but Primo Levi and Italo Calvino (p. 221) use the Latin forms Ulysses and Polyphemus. I have retained the Italian usage in Levi's and Calvino's texts to avoid putting unlikely words in their mouths (note, however, that Levi uses Cyclops for the tribe of which Polyphemus is a member). The Greek forms are used in the extract (p. 22).

Preface

the Grigne: An Alpine region north of Milan.

1. *The Just Man Oppressed by Injustice*

neesings: A word coined by biblical translators to translate 'breaths through the nose'; Leviathan breathes fire.
habergeon: A coat of mail.

4. *To See Atoms*

Sir William Bragg (1862–1942). Bragg studied mathematics at Trinity College, Cambridge, and held professorships in physics at various universities, including

Leeds (1909–15) and University College London (1915–25). In 1913–14, working with his son, Lawrence, he founded the new science of X-ray Crystallography, a technique for determining the structure of large crystalline molecules by analysing the way in which they scatter X-rays. This technique was subsequently used to determine the structure of important biological molecules, including proteins and, most important of all, DNA.

5. The Pact with the Mammoths

Joseph-Henri Rosny aîné (1856–1940) (pseudonym of Joseph-Henri Boex). Rosny was a prolific Belgian author of science fiction and historical fantasy. Many of his books are still in print, and he is regarded as the second most important francophone science-fiction writer after Jules Verne. *The Quest for Fire* was adapted for a major feature film in 1981. *The Navigators of Infinity* (1925) coined the word 'astronaut'.

Arminius: German tribal leader (18 BC?–AD 19) who inflicted a major defeat on the Romans in AD 9.

Vercingetorix: Gallic tribal leader (d. 46 BC) who led an uprising against Julius Caesar in 52 BC.

6. The Hobbies

Giuseppe Parini (1729–99). Parini was born near Lake Como and then lived in Milan where he worked as a tutor to a wealthy family. He has been compared to Pope and his long poem *The Day*, begun in 1763 and still unfinished at his death, deals with fashionable frivolous life in a mordantly satirical manner.

rappee: A coarse kind of snuff.

Corso: Avenue.

Mongibello: Mount Etna.

Maia: Pupil of Mercury: God of gain and of play.

Of Argos and of Phrygia: Of Greece and Troy.

the two Atrides: Agamemnon and Menelaus, sons of Atreus.

Cumæan cave: The cave of the Sibyl, the oracle.

7. A Deadly Nip

Carlo Porta (1775–1821) wrote in Milanese dialect at a time when Milan was under the yoke of the French. His identification with the oppressed under-classes had a powerful political dimension. *Olter Desgrazzi de Giovannin Bongee (More Misfortunes of Giovannin Bongee)* was written in 1814. The name Giovannin Bongee is Milanese dialect; Giovannino Bongeri the modern Italian. The original *Desgrazzi* was written in 1812. In these poems Giovannin always addresses his complaints to an unknown 'Esteemed Sir'. Milan came under Habsburg rule after the Treaty of Vienna in 1815.

Viganò: Salvatore Viganò, composer and designer of the ballet *Prometheus*, which was staged at La Scala in 1813 to huge acclaim.

. . . this is the first time/you've been empty for a scuffle like this: This anticipates the next scene in the poem, in which Bongee leaves the house, meets the lamplighter again, has a scuffle with him and spends the night in gaol.

10. The Words of the Father

Ludwig Gattermann (1860–1920). Gattermann was one of the great German organic chemists of the heroic age of chemistry. His name lives on in reactions named after him: the Gattermann Synthesis (1907) and the Gattermann–Koch Reaction (1897), both processes for the synthesis of aldehyde derivatives of benzene.

12. A Different Way of Saying 'I'

solet: A bread made from semolina flour.

13. The Romance of Technology

Roger Vercel (1894–1957) was a prolific author whose most famous novel, *Capitaine Conan*, about his experiences on the Eastern Front in World War I, won the Prix Goncourt in 1934.

15. *Survivors in the Sahara*

Antoine de Saint-Exupéry (1900–44). Saint-Exupéry grew up in his family's château near Lyons and qualified as a pilot during his National Service. In 1926 he became a civil pilot flying the mail route to Africa. His first account of flying, *Southern Mail*, was published in 1929. The crash in the desert recorded in the extract printed here happened on 30 January 1935. He flew reconnaissance missions until the fall of France in 1940 and went into exile in America, returning to fly again after the Allied invasion of Europe. He was shot down in 1944.

16. *The Curious Merchant*

salamander: Asbestos.
ondanique: Indian steel, used especially in the manufacture of sabres.
serpents: Crocodiles.
a sort of tree: The Toddy palm (*Palma indica vinaria*).

17. *The Poet-Researcher*

a pane of horn: This is an allusion to Roman lanterns which had thin walls of horn through which light could pass.
Cilician saffron: The use of this crocus to perfume the stage is attested by the first theatre in the walls of Rome (AD 55–60).

18. *The Jew on Horseback*

Isaac Babel (1894–1940). Babel came from an assimilated Jewish family in Odessa. In 1920 he joined the Red Army during the war in Poland and his most famous stories (*Red Cavalry*, 1926) come from this period. He was executed on trumped-up charges of treason and espionage.
Nachdiv 6: Divisional commander. The '6' refers to the number of the division.
kombrig: Brigade commander.

'*Panie*': Sir (Polish).

Papasha: Daddy.

wetting my whiskers but not my mouth: Lines of a popular rhyme.

Gavrilka: Popular name for an engine-driver.

five poods: About 16 kilograms.

the third bell: In Russia a train's departure was marked with three rings of a bell at long intervals.

19. An Irrepressible Quibbler

Sholem Aleichem (1859–1916) (pseudonym of Sholem Rabinovitz). Aleichem was born in Pereyaslav, Russia. He worked as a tutor and a rabbi before becoming a writer. He began to write in Yiddish in 1883 and his writing documents the life of the poor Jewish communities in Russia. He left Russia in 1906 and eventually settled in America. The musical comedy *Fiddler on the Roof* (1964) was adapted from his stories.

schlimazel: One dogged by ill luck.

20. Pity Hidden beneath Laughter

Giuseppe Belli (1791–1863) is the popular poet of Rome. He wrote in the Roman dialect and was deeply influenced by Carlo Porta.

22. We are the Aliens

Fredric Brown (1906–72). Brown was educated at the University of Cincinnati night school and began writing in the detective pulp magazines of the 1930s. He became known for his science fiction with the publication of *Unknown and Weird Tales* (1941). He wrote many novels and short stories in both the thriller and science-fiction genres.

23. *The Measure of All Things*

infusorians: Microscopic plant-life found in water; Spallanzani showed that they
are living creatures.

24. *Urchin Death*

Stefano D'Arrigo (1919–92). The Sicilian writer Stefano D'Arrigo's magnum opus
Horcynus Orca (*Killer Whale*) was begun in 1950 and not published until 1975. It
begins with a narrative of a Sicilian marine returning home after the war but
develops into a Dantesque fantastic journey through memory and the depths of
the sea. D'Arrigo's only other book was a collection of poems: *Codice Siciliano*
(*The Sicilian Code*) (1957).
'Ndrja: 'Ndrja Cambrìa, the protagonist of the novel.
Old German Mother Death: Levi notes that Belli also used this phrase.

28. *Tönle the Winterer*

Mario Rigoni Stern was born in Asiago, an upland region between the Alps and
the Adriatic, in 1921. In 1999 he was awarded the Italian PEN Prize, a major
literary award, for *Sentieri sotto la neve* (*Paths beneath the Snow*).
Bersaglieri: Troops of an Italian rifle regiment.

29. *Trying to Understand*

Hermann Langbein (1912–95). Langbein was born in Vienna. In 1938 he fought
in the Spanish Civil War, was captured and interned in France for two years. He
was moved to Dachau in 1941 and was in Auschwitz from August 1942 to October
1944 where he was active in the resistance. His book *Against All Hope: Resistance
in the Nazi Concentration Camps* was published in English translation in 1994.

30. We are Alone

Kip S. Thorne (b. 1940) is Feynman Professor of Theoretical Physics at the California Institute of Technology. He is a leading authority on Black Holes.

Acknowledgements

The editor and publishers wish to thank those copyright holders who have given permission for their work to be included in this anthology:

Except from The Book of Job, from the Canongate Edition of *THE BIBLE*. Reprinted by permission of Canongate Books.

Excerpt from Book IV, 'New Coasts and Poseidon's Son' from Homer: *THE ODYSSEY*, translated by Robert Fitzgerald. Copyright © 1961, 1963 by Robert Fitzgerald. Copyright renewed 1989 by Benedict R. C. Fitzgerald, on behalf of the Fitzgerald children. Reprinted by permission of Farrar, Straus & Giroux, LLC.

Excerpt from Sir William Bragg's *CONCERNING THE NATURE OF THINGS: SIX LECTURES DELIVERED AT THE ROYAL INSTITUTION*, published by G. Bell & Sons, London, 1925. Reprinted by permission of the Royal Institution of Great Britain.

Excerpt from *LA GUERRE DU FEU* by Joseph-Henri Rosny aîné, published by Plon, Paris, 1911. Reprinted by permission of Plon, Paris.

Excerpt from *OLTER DESGRAZZI DE GIOVANNIN BONGEE* by Carlo Porta in *LE POESIE*, published by Feltrinelli, Milan, 1964. Reprinted by permission of the publisher.

Excerpt from *GARGANTUA AND PANTAGRUEL* by François Rabelais, translated by Burton Raffel. Copyright © 1990 by W. W. Norton & Company, Inc. (1990). Reprinted by permission of W. W. Norton & Company, Inc.

Excerpt from *THE TALES OF JACOB* in *JOSEPH AND HIS BROTHERS* by Thomas Mann, translated by H. T. Lowe-Porter, published by Martin Secker & Warburg, a division of Random House, Inc., 1923. Reprinted by permission of the publisher.

Excerpt from *WIND, SAND AND STARS* by Antoine de Saint-Exupéry, translated by

William Rees (Penguin Classics, 1995). Reprinted by permission of Penguin Books.

Excerpt from THE TRAVELS OF MARCO POLO, translated by Ronald Latham (Penguin Classics, 1958). Copyright © Ronald Latham, 1958. Reprinted by permission of Penguin Books.

Excerpt from ON THE NATURE OF THE UNIVERSE by Lucretius, translation by Sir Ronald Melville (OUP, 1997). Copyright © Sir Ronald Melville, 1997. Reprinted by permission of Oxford University Press.

Excerpt from TEVYE THE DAIRYMAN AND THE RAILROAD STORIES by Sholem Aleichem, translated by Hillel Halkin, © 1987 by Schocken Books. Reprinted by permission of Schocken Books, a division of Random House, Inc.

Guiseppe Belli's Sonnet No. 165, translated by Anthony Burgess in ABBA ABBA (Faber & Faber, 1977). Copyright renewed 2000 by Vintage, a division of Random House, Inc. Copyright © the Estate of Anthony Burgess, 2000.

Excerpt from THE CONQUEST OF HAPPINESS by Betrand Russell, 1975, published by Routledge (Unwin Hyman). Reprinted by permission of the publisher and The Bertrand Russell Peace Foundation.

Excerpt from 'Sentry' by Fredric Brown in GALAXY, Copyright © 1954 by Galaxy Publishing Corporation, copyright renewed 1982 by the Estate of Fredric Brown and reprinted by permission of the author's Estate and his agents, Scott Meredith Literary Agency, LP.

ASTM D 1382–55 T, American Society for Testing Materials, Philadelphia, 1955, reprinted with permission from ANNUAL BOOK Of ASTM STANDARDS, Copyright © American Society for Testing and Materials, 100 Barr Harbor Drive, West Conshohocken, PA 19428.

Excerpt from PROFILES OF THE FUTURE by Arthur C. Clarke, published by Gollancz, 1962. Reprinted by permission of David Higham Associates.

Excerpt from MURDER IN THE CATHEDRAL by T. S. Eliot, published by Faber & Faber, 1935. Reprinted by permission of Faber & Faber.

Excerpt from 'Death Fugue' from SELECTED POEMS OF PAUL CELAN, translated by Michael Hamburger. First published by Anvil Press Poetry 1988, Published in Penguin Books 1990, 1996. Reprinted by permission of Penguin Books.

Excerpt from Mario Rigoni Stern's STORY OF TÖNLE, Einaudi, Turin, 1978. Used with kind permission of Einaudi and Northwestern University Press.

Excerpt from MENSCHEN IN AUSCHWITZ by Hermann Langbein, Europa, Verlag, Vienna (1987). Reprinted by permission of the publisher.

Excerpt from Kip S. Thorne's 'The Search for Black Holes', published in